THE CHASE
AT
BRIGHTON COURT

THE CHASE AT BRIGHTON COURT

Amber Jakeman

Lorikeet Press

THE CHASE AT BRIGHTON COURT
First edition. October 31, 2025

Copyright © Amber Jakeman.
ISBN: 978-1-7637383-4-8
Written by Amber Jakeman.

Also by Amber Jakeman

***House of Jewels* series**
House of Diamonds
House of Hearts
House of Spades
House of Clubs
Full House

***Escape to the Coast* series**
Summer Beach
Midnight Beach
Sunset Beach

www.amberjakeman.com
www.lorikeetpress.com

For Annette and Brian

*Note to readers: As the Brighton Court series is set in the US,
I've adopted American English spelling and expressions where possible.
May all meanings be clear!*

Chapter 1

Lucy

TO DO:
Send flowers to Donna
Buy milk, bread etc
Find bedclothes/make bed
Find can opener

Moving is more than exhausting. Anyone who's done it can tell you it's about so much more than boxes. And leaving in a hurry makes it even harder.

It took me twenty years to create my "forever home" – and I have just two hours to leave it behind for good. More of that later.

Briefly back at my beloved old home, I am like a bird plucking bits of straw out of a hay bale – just enough to build my new life. It's like dismantling my soul, but hey. Who actually needs a custom built symmetrical entry staircase with stone supports to match the chimney? I don't even glance at my white rose gardens along the wide front fence and the perfectly curved pathway, my former pride and joy.

I've hired movers while Bart is in Barbados. I force the images of swaying palm trees and cocktails as far out of my mind as I can. He used to take me there; but now he'll be with the Minx, the traitor.

They're welcome to each other, I tell myself, as I load up the best of my remaining clothes, photos of Phoebe in silver frames, from bald baby dome to gap-toothed fairy, pink tween and rangy teen with attitude to beaming high school graduate, taken only a couple of years ago – plus kitchen necessities and a few items of furniture. There's not much space in my new place, but I don't need space. I need security. My own key. I can't wait to leave this showhouse – this house of betrayal.

My whole shabby chic furniture business is now bound for the ReUse charity. There was no way I could take it all back with me to my little rented apartment at Brighton Court, and I certainly can't afford to hire studio space.

The ReUse people are over the moon, and that's great. I'll do a media event to maximize their publicity, so when they auction my pieces they'll get a great return. Celebrity humiliation plus beautifully restored furniture should create a blockbuster fundraiser. It's great to think there's some kind of silver lining for heartbreak and divorce in your late forties. It has to be good for me, too, right? Better than living a lie. Why stay with Bart when he's in love with his Personal Assistant?

Besides, I'm done with suburbia, with its perfect lawns and tidy fences, the barking dogs and fresh air. That's what I tell myself. Thank goodness it's winter, and my beloved garden is hiding its treasures, the bare twigs blackened and bent against the bitter wind, roses all thorns against marauders – like my heart.

But this is no pity party. I'm determined to find the bright side. Life will be so much better without Bart. My future's an open book. Well, there's Phoebe, who doesn't return my calls and messages, but I can't solve everything at once. First, I'll get myself sorted out.

Dear Donna has sheltered me for almost a year and given me work in her relocation and unpacking business – her whole family is into every aspect of real estate – but it's time for my fresh start – at Brighton Court. I love my rental, so close to downtown. It's a brick apartment building from the late 1940s, a real mix of architecture styles. Solid. Full of character. There are even some trees and a bit of garden. Well, you wouldn't call that overgrown mess a garden, but wait till I get my hands on it.

Donna assures me it's a great neighborhood, west side of the river, just east of downtown, and she'd know. With her relocation business, she moves people in and out all over town. She says my area is "up and coming – cusp of uptown" even if some of the apartments at Brighton Court have seen better days. The curtains in the garden apartment are drawn and shabby – a bit sinister – and my apartment badly needs new paint, but there's a healthy mix of blinds and curtains in the windows of the other apartments, and I like that in a place – room for individuality.

I know for certain that the Brighton Court penthouse is sensational, because I recently took on the job of unpacking for the new owner of the penthouse. All those fixtures are brand spanking new. It even has one of those marble waterfall kitchen benches, recessed ceilings, lights under the bookshelves, a floating bathroom cabinet – the latest.

The purchaser's things fit perfectly – classy, timeless pieces in polished wood and pale leather, and expensive clothes. Men's clothes. Lots of books and original artworks. Must be someone professional, retired maybe. If someone with such good taste chose Brighton Court, surely it'll be great for me too. When I saw the "for rent" sign for one of the apartments below the penthouse while I was there, I had to inspect it. I'd already decided it was time to give Donna back her own space. The apartment for rent was in almost original condition, so a bit beat up, like me – but it had so much character I signed the lease on the spot.

Back at my old dream house, I pack all the makings for my lamps into boxes – all the fabrics and shades and bases and pompons and trims, and of course my beloved glue gun that makes everything so easy. Who knows? Maybe I'll offer to make lamps for all my new neighbors. That's an idea. My heart quickens at the thought of meeting everyone. I've always liked people.

The wiry guy with neck tattoos loads the final few boxes into the little truck without a hitch. We're almost done here. I force my eyes away from my show home, every last part of it decorated exactly as I'd wanted it – every picture hung in exactly the right place, each piece of furniture re-upholstered with love in the perfect fabric, every item selected and placed with so much care. For nothing. For a man who considered me dispensable, and a daughter who refuses to speak to me.

I can only focus on the future. One day soon, I'll buy my own place, more modest by necessity, but just as nice. Somewhere cosy, somewhere like Brighton Court, a place where my friends and Phoebe will always be welcome.

I'll patch things up with Phoebe – surely it's possible. I won't stop trying. Ever.

"Ready, Mrs Hardenburg?" says the stocky mover with the eyebrow ring.

"'Ms Beston' now, please," I say. "I guess I'll never be any more ready. Thank you so much. Couldn't have done it without you. Can I buy you pizza at the other end?"

"Sure, lady, Mrs Beston."

"Ms. Okay. Let's go!"

Back at Brighton Court, as the professional unpacker I've become, I make short work of my own belongings. I stash kitchen and bathroom essentials, hang clothes and line up my shoes. The bed's inviting, but the night is young.

I gaze with satisfaction out the old-fashioned bay window. The lavender velvet dusk lures me out into the cold. I grab my warm coat from my bentwood hatstand, and take a quick walk in my new neighborhood.

I love the run of boutiques just up the hill – a bakery and coffee shop, Jill's Frocks and Fancies – a must for daytime when it will be open – a bookshop, the realty company where I signed my lease, and the handy pizzeria.

On the opposite side, just before a picturesque church, shop windows glow. Chatter and laughter spill onto the street – an art exhibition is opening!

I'm hardly dressed in my best given all the unpacking, but viewing art is always fun, and artists need all the support they can get.

I'm welcomed at the door by a young woman with a tray of drinks, so I gladly take a long cool stem of bubbly.

Paintings of birds of all kinds stare out at me. They're striking; some, closeups of beaks and feathers, and others, huge – extraordinary clouds of birds above red barns, bright with movement. The detail's exquisite, but I'm not sure I could live with all of them.

If I had to choose, I'd buy the lone seagull, pure white, poised between a dark timber dock and shining slice of silver sea, its beak and feet bright orange, and its beady eye, gleaming, staring directly into mine. It's plucky. It's defiant – a survivor, ready to swim, walk or fly. I want courage like that, poised at the edge of my new life at Brighton Court.

The chatter is deafening, but I can't help but overhear an exchange behind me.

"So you're Carla?" The tone is rich and resonant, the kind of voice that inspires confidence. "My daughter sends you her congratulations. Deirdre O'Connell? You knew each other at college."

"Oh, Dee was so much fun! So you're the Doc. Don't you live somewhere out of town? In Franklin? How is Dee?"

"She's fine. Big career in fitness and flat out with two kids or she'd be here. I'm new to town. Just moved in. Beautiful work, Carla."

"Why thank you, Doc O'Connell."

I glance behind to catch the owner of that delicious voice – the mystery "Doc" – I'm sure I know that name.

Just then a portly man in crimson trousers, a voluminous silk shirt and a flamboyant, multi-coloured vest rushes across and grabs Carla, pixie thin, with a nose ring, and leads her to a small podium in the corner.

I peer around. Do I know Doc O'Connell? I met hundreds of people in my old job at the tv network, and afterwards, Bart's associates.

All I see is a quick impression of someone more formally dressed, tall and distinguished, if a little wooden – an older man with a striking presence; somehow out of place. Formal. Yummy aftershave. Mint. Spice. And he's alone. A rush of excitement runs through me. Must be the champagne.

The speeches begin, first from the exuberant Patrick Lenihan, the gallery owner. He introduces Carla as "a bold and promising new artist" and gushes over her output. He advises us all to "buy up fast" before she becomes better known, and invites her to speak about her art.

"Birds are among the world's greatest survivors," Carla says. "They're quick, and, best of all, most avoid chaos by flying. Some say their ancestors were the dinosaurs, now extinct, but birds stayed safe and adapted, high in the treetops and down burrows at the edge of the seas. Imagine making your home on top of a light pole, like a wily seahawk, or in the eaves of a shopping centre when your forest disappears."

There's a hush in the room, every face turned towards Carla. "I got to know each of the birds I painted," she says. "That is, they tolerated me long enough to be photographed. As I committed them to canvas, I imagined their lives. 'Free fall' is my first exhibition."

Applause breaks out as she lowers her head, humble, and I clap loudest of all. I'm a survivor and an artist, in a way. I'll buy that seagull if I can afford it, to go beside my new front door. But Patrick, Carla and the waiter are rushed, and by the time I make it to them with my credit card out, Carla shakes her head. There's a red dot beneath the seagull. I look in vain for the tall man, but he's gone. I head home.

Chapter 2

Lucy

Next day, I drop into Jill's Frocks and Fancies. A magnificent glossy green gown in her shop window beckons me inside. It gestures from the mannequin, whispers possibilities – perhaps even a promise, so I enter the frock shop with a spring in my step.

It's cool and quiet in here, with a hint of fragrance – coconut and lime – probably from the gift candles for sale beside a tempting display of costume jewelry.

When I left Bart, my only emotions were anger and fear and exhaustion. I've survived, but now I'm ready to thrive, and one thing is for certain. I am tired of being the invisible support person. Maybe if I'd taken more care of my appearance over the years, Bart and I would still be together – not that I miss him.

So much in my life is wonderful – my friendship with Donna, my lovely apartment, the excitement of exploring my new neighborhood, good health, and … my beautiful diamond rings. I thought I'd have to sell them, but so far, so good. I flutter my fingers so they sparkle. I do love my diamonds. They're my forcefield, my portable manufacturers of rainbows. Did I mention I love rainbows? Actually, I love everything about life. Never mind the divorce. The trick is to stay in the game, and now that I'm almost settled again, I'm ready to play – no apologies.

I always dressed well at the network, but with motherhood, gardening, and then using paints and glue all day for my shabby chic business, I was often in stained overalls. Glamor makes no sense when you're busy unpacking for people, either, but these days, in my new life, when I'm not at work, I want to look good.

I don't ever want to be the woman Bart discarded, to always look in the mirror and feel rejected. Somebody has to stand up for me. It's time to honor myself. To make the most of myself.

I raise my head to catch the eye of the attendant. She's a mature woman, not unlike myself, in glasses with heavy frames and with an instant smile. A potential accomplice, maybe even a friend. I could offer to do hair and make-up presentations for her customers. Why not? My life now is about the future, with all its possibilities. My past can only enrich it.

But first things first. I smile back at her in expectation, because dressing for success is an art and a joy. I should know – makeup artist to the stars. At least I was until the great Bart Hardenburg monopolized me for himself for a few decades, then ditched me for his assistant. But none of that now. I've moved on.

"Welcome," she says, as she approaches. "I'm Jill. How may I help you today?"

"You're Jill! I love your boutique." I give her my warmest, most dazzling smile. Moving to Brighton Court is my fresh start and I've given myself permission to celebrate, to spend some of the money I've earned working with Donna. My attorney says my divorce settlement could take another few months, but she's making progress. I'm going to be okay.

I sigh and smile again as I scan Jill's racks of exclusive attire, so artfully combined with scarves, belts and bags. I can barely wait to try a few; to find a treasure or two to mix and match with the outfits I retrieved from the house, the best of my classics. The possibilities practically sing.

I pounce on a purple evening purse. It's Donna's favorite color. She'll love it. I place it on the counter, buy it for her, then keep browsing.

"Such a gorgeous shop, Jill!" I say, then drop my pitch and volume, conspiratorially, and face the glossy green winner in the window. "I'm in love with this gown already."

I reach out to caress its three-quarter sleeve, the sheen of it almost iridescent. The fabric is heavy with quality, the gown's cut and color magnificent. I'm sure it will fit.

"It's a one-off," says Jill. "A Georg K."

"Yes," I say. Will Jill be a bore? To place a gown in a window and refuse to undress the mannequin for a potential customer amounts to false advertising.

Jill's glance drops to my fingers and I wiggle them obligingly until the rainbows sparkle. The gown will be exorbitant, but diamonds speak. I suck in my waist and stand tall as Jill surveys me with a fixed smile.

"I'm sure it's my size," I say. "Georg's gowns are a marvel." I have actually seen some before, at the network, back before everything. I can be an aspiring Georg K owner. There's no law against it.

But still Jill hesitates. I give her my extra bright smile.

"It may take me a few moments to arrange, Mrs ..."

"Of course. Please just call me Lucy." I step deeper into the shop, survey the skirts and trousers, run my hand along the rack of blouses, in various shades of color. I hesitate. Necklines are so challenging these days, but these cuts are clever.

I pull out a scarlet silk number, of the exact fabric of the dress in the window; another Georg K. I check the size and price – eye watering – before glancing back at Jill, who maneuvers the mannequin closer and starts to unscrew its arm. Good.

I pluck out another blouse, in a soft lilac, and another, in a sumptuous orangey red. I frown at the prices, then smile. The future is wide open.

A gleaming red convertible pulls up outside, an older man in the passenger seat. Fit. Broad shoulders. He's definitely familiar. I stare. He smiles a little self-consciously. Intriguing. Very appealing.

Jill clears her throat, the gorgeous green gown over her arm.

"Shall I place this in the change room for you?"

"Oh, yes. Thank you so much, Jill. I thought for a moment I saw someone I knew."

"Of course. And would you like to try these as well?"

"Yes. No. Actually, would you have this blouse in a paler pink, please? I love the little bow at the neck."

"I may have one out the back. Shall I go check?"

"Please."

I watch the man get out of the car. He's tall, in long gray trousers, a tailored navy jacket with brass buttons, and a gray-blue tie. Better and better. My pulse jumps. A man who knows how to dress is rare in this world. Perhaps he has a club and visits frequently. Perhaps he owns a club. Or two.

Maybe uptown is full of tall, eligible men. Regrettably, he disappears into one of the coffee shops. Still, if I'm quick with the gown, I might catch him when he emerges. I zoom towards the changeroom and am out of my clothes and shoes in moments.

The emerald gown is a dream; the satin silk slides over my skin like a waterfall. And the color and fit are perfect. I whip back the curtain and stride towards the door, the fabric whispering around my ankles.

Jill runs after me.

"Oh there you are, Jill," I say. "Would you help me with this zipper, please?"

Up goes the zipper, and the fabric snugs against my waist and settles in a heavy swish, as if it's alive and begging me for the last, treasured dance with the king of the prom. Perfection. This dress belongs with glass slippers, at a ball.

"I love it! I love your boutique! Would you have some high heels I could try it with? I only ever shop in my flats."

"Of course."

Jill disappears again as I back up, twisting and peering at myself in the mirror between the racks. The back of the dress is divine, with a v-line so deep and wide it shows off my shoulder blades. There's much to be said for our backs – covered and invisible for most of our lives. As long as we remain upright, the back divulges few clues to the actual state of our front.

I begin to laugh at my own joke when – smack! I'm staggering, tripping on the hem of the gown. I grasp at space to avoid falling, and find warmth, fine linen and, beneath it, a firm physique. Mint. Spice. Definitely not Jill.

Blue sports jacket, white shirt, gray tie. It's him! An apologetic smile; a smile of concern, of interest. A strong, steadying hand on my upper arm, and then at my waist. Heaven. It's been a while.

"I'm sorry," the man says, regrettably removing his hand and stepping backwards. It's him; the man with the red convertible, the appreciator of art. Be still, my heart! "The coffees. The dress. No. Have I burned you?"

"Yes. No. I don't know."

Burned me with his hand, yes, but most of the coffee is on the long hem and Jill's polished floor boards.

"Oh Dirk!"

"Jill," he says. "Sorry. Slammed right into your customer here. And the dress. I'll make it up to you. To both of you." As his glance finds my face, I rearrange it. Joyous pleasure is probably inappropriate. I clap my fingers to my smile, then slowly let them drop.

I remember this silence. Dirk's eyes linger, on the curve of my cheek, my neck and decolletage and up to my lips and briefly, not too briefly, on my eyes. His are gray with blue flecks – shocked. Interested. They duck away, down to the spreading darkness on the fabric, and back to my waist.

I turn to Jill, treating the stranger to a glimpse of the extravagant scoop of back, so perfectly framed in this gown. It's my best side, at least in this exquisite dress.

"Magnificent," he says. "Devastated."

I study him. His comment is general, about the gown, not me, but the words are thrilling.

Jill, one high heel dangling from each hand, shakes her head slowly.

"I meant well, Jill," he says. "I brought you coffee."

"Thank you, Dirk."

Oh. Perhaps they're married. Maybe he owns the shop. I clear my throat.

"Would you undo the zip for me, please, ah … Dirk? I'm Lucy, by the way. Lucy Beston."

"Of course, Lucy," he said. "Anything."

I pull my hair to the front to allow him full access. If his hand hesitates a little as the zip slides down, the warmth of his fingers is more than welcome. Perhaps it's residual heat from the coffee, but everything about this morning is unfolding exactly as it should. Despite everything – don't mention my Ex and the Minx, nor Phoebe – life is a dream. A good one.

Chapter 3

Dirk

APPOINTMENTS: *Lunch with Jamison*

Not my best day. With Millie gone two years, I'd finally agreed to retire early and relocate to the city, closer to my children. I'm still getting into the swing of my new life – and now I've spilled coffee on a stranger in Jill's frock shop.

Won't mention it to the kids. Jamison and Dee are so grown up they now boss me around. Jamison asked me to collect his car after its overnight service; insisted I take a spin in his shiny red convertible, so I visited my sister at her dress store.

The last payment from selling my family medical practice in Franklin came through yesterday, so I wanted to tell Jill in person I'm cancelling her debt to me.

Unfortunately, I had trouble starting Jamison's fancy car. The kid at the service desk told me I didn't actually need a key, and when he fiddled with my phone and the engine started up by itself, my old face was as red as the car.

I still had time to drive to Jill's boutique, surprise her with the good news, and then meet Jamison at his business with the car. He's promised me lunch in return.

My mistake was to overdo the whole Jill thing. I got take-out coffees for us before dropping in.

I drop in, alright – drop coffee on Jill's classy customer.

I don't generally notice women – Millie was my one and only – but I'd be lying if I pretended this one didn't catch my eye, so … shapely. In one of Jill's best gowns – emerald green, sleek as an otter – she reminds me of Elizabeth Taylor.

The coffee lands on the full skirt and I breathe a sigh of relief, glad I avoid giving her beautiful bare back third degree burns. Jill's horrified. She loves her stock.

Flush with cash for the first time in my life, I take the easy way out – fish out some notes and hand them over to the customer – to let her buy the dress and get it dry-cleaned. She hands the cash to Jill. Win. Always feels good to do the right thing.

Okay. I see the price tag when I helped the lady with the zipper. Expensive, but all of Jill's stock is expensive. Accidents like this must happen from time to time in retail. Jamison calls it risk management. They even happen in medicine, though I worked like a demon to keep my patients as healthy as possible and heal them fast. Sure kept me busy. Too busy. Whole decades went by while I wasn't looking.

Jill frowns at me. She always was a terrible sulk.

Her customer flashes her extraordinary eyes all the way down me and up again, then gives me full beam. Are they violet, or deep green? When she flutters her eyelashes, she has me stuttering like a teenager.

Those eyes are quicksilver. She masks her shock; replaces it with something else – curiosity? A calculation? I've met thousands of people. As a family practice doctor, I never saw them at their best. For sure, no patient was ever dressed in a gown this alluring; more like farm overalls. And they were in pain, or sad. This woman's in great health and raring to go … somewhere. With me?

I tear my eyes away from hers; stare down at the eye-catching waistline of the outfit. Frying pan to fire. The woman whips out her phone and asks for mine. Sends herself a message so she has my number; says she'll pay me back if the stain comes out.

The customer – Lucy – rushes to the changeroom; dress swishing. Then she sticks her head out from behind the change room curtain and dazzles me with a smile.

"You're far too generous, Dirk," she says. How does she know my name? Oh yeah. Jill mentioned it. Should I worry?

"No need to dry clean it," Lucy says, her voice musical as an actor's. "Let me at least pay half. I was going to buy it anyway, and perhaps I can remove the stains myself."

"No, please," I say. I want to see her smile again. "Allow me. And coffee. Let me bring you a fresh coffee, too. Jill?"

"Thank you, Dirk," says Jill, cleaning cloth in hand, down on her knees. "It's the least you can do."

"Oh, Dirk, thank you," says the woman from behind the change room curtain. "Perfect! Skim latte. One sugar. My only vice."

Vice. The word has connotations. This Lucy has a voice like artisanal honey – with a hint of double meaning. I smile. I need to get it out of there – fast – so I go to get fresh coffees, including the one for her.

Back at the coffee shop, there's a queue. I survey the cakes, then change my mind. The last thing Jill needs is more sticky food on her merchandise.

Time is ticking. My parking spot is for fifteen minutes only and the parking enforcement officers are merciless here, so close to downtown, but I've given my word. Besides, what's the price of a parking ticket compared to everything else?

But when I return, I can't believe it. The woman, Lucy, is sitting in Jamison's car – sure, she matches the thing; racy – but …

She looks great there – as if she belongs. Audacious. But as I open my mouth to protest – again, that utterly distracting smile.

She's done something with her hair that shows off her neck; twisted it up and secured it with … a pencil?

"Dirk!" she says as she springs out and holds out her hand for her coffee. "Don't be alarmed. I saved you a parking fine."

She accompanies me back into Jill's store, as if I'm on a tv show with her and she's the elegant hostess, all glamor and ease, and I'm the witless interviewee, being wheeled in for a quick exchange. Is that it? Have I seen her on tv? Never watch it, though I was interviewed once, way, way back, before the illegal tackle that cracked my head against the goal post, that moment that changed everything.

Back inside the store, Jill takes her coffee. She's unusually quiet while Lucy beckons me across to the shirts.

As we sip our drinks, Lucy asks my opinion. I know nothing about fashion, beyond what Jill's told me over the years, about stock and the changing seasons. Long sleeves. Short sleeves. No sleeves.

"What colors match my eyes, please, Dirk?" Lucy says.

Seriously? Still, makes a nice change from staring at bruises and bandages and scars and everything else under the sun. And now that I'm retired, with too much time on my hands and not enough ways to spend it, why not stay a few minutes?

Chapter 4

Lucy

"Do you really like this pale pink?" I ask the delectable Dirk as I hold it up beneath my chin. He's strikingly handsome in that older man way, a little silvery at the temples, a few lines on his face, still fit. I'm sure we've met before, long before last night at the gallery. I must remember to phone Donna and tell her she was right. They do exist – classic silver foxes, or at least one of them, this one – right here near Brighton Court.

I'm having such a good day, I give him a tiny wink from behind the curve of the hanger. "I thought maybe the red was a little more … exciting."

"Whatever you think," he says. What a keeper! He even knows what to say!

"No really," I say. "I'm asking you. I value your opinion. You clearly have excellent taste in cars. Nobody would disagree."

He blushes. He's bashful. He checks to see if anyone heard my compliment. He's adorable.

"Actually, the car is …"

"Or how about the blue?" I drop my voice. I'm having fun for the first time in months, maybe years. "It matches your eyes, Dirk. We could go somewhere, just you and me." So maybe I'm a bit forceful; taking a risk, but life is for living.

"It's a beautiful day," I press my point. "You, me and that car. We can stop at a supermarket or a delicatessen. We could picnic. Do you like rosé? Or Chablis? Is there a fish shop nearby? We can buy oysters. I adore them with Sauvignon Blanc. How about you? I'm sure you have your own favorite combinations."

He's speechless. I've caught him off guard.

"Oh," I say. "You don't like picnics? Of course not; not with those fine clothes. Chairs and tables were invented for good reason. Tell you what; you help me decide on these blouses, and I'll buy lunch for you at a restaurant – somewhere near the coast, somewhere with a view. Call it my way of thanking you for your generosity with the dress. Isn't it beautiful?"

"It's a beautiful dress."

I stop talking and just smile at him. I love his eyes, blue gray, similar to the tie, and they're all over me, like a curious, soft, rare moth. It's a great sign. What a day! I knew moving into this district was sensible. Day one and I am on my way.

"Well, now. Thank you but no. I have other plans, Lucy."

"Oh, of course you do, a busy man like you. We'll take a raincheck. You have my number. Any day you're free for lunch, message me. Simple as that."

I try to dazzle him with my smile again, then turn my attention back to the blouses. I'll buy a couple and keep Jill happy. I sense some disapproval on her part. Shame. I'd prefer an ally.

Dirk and Jill can't be a couple. They haven't touched each other once.

Chapter 5

Dirk

That Lucy gives me the distinct impression she's flirting with me. She's beautiful and she's classy, just like Jamison's crazy, racy car. She's way too high voltage for someone like me – a cynic – but when she turns away from me I'm disappointed.

Can I rearrange my day? Though I love my son, l see him every week, and lunch with Lucy could be fun. I want to gaze into those magnificent eyes over a cold glass of white wine, to find out more about her, to forget …

"Thanks so much for dropping in – twice," Jill says as I pull my gaze away from the woman and hunt for the car keys. Oh. That's right. It starts without a key. Ingenious. Confusing.

"And for your absolute generosity with that dress and my customer here, the lucky Lucy."

"Isn't Dirk lovely," says Lucy, just loud enough for me to hear. It's flattering to imagine she's interested in me. At my age!

"How do you two know each other?" Lucy asks Jill.

Time rushes on. I'll be late for my lunch with Jamison. He's a stickler for keeping appointments, so I head towards the door, ready to do battle with a few more features of the car.

"Take care," calls Jill. She stares at Lucy, and carefully raises one eyebrow with her glance back at me. I know that look. It's a clear warning.

"Of course," I say. "You too." Jill's always had my best interests at heart. She's been right before about things; kept me out of trouble now and then, but I'm a grown man with my own ideas and good sense.

"Delighted to meet you Lucy," I say, if only to remind Jill she's not my keeper. Yes, I've kept a clear eye out for Jill since her no-good husband left her with two sons to raise alone, and yes, I funded this business to keep her on her feet. It's what any good brother would do if they had the means.

"Promise you'll call me?" Lucy says. Her touch on my arm is soft and more welcome than I want to admit. Nobody touches me like that now; nobody has for years.

"I owe you," says Lucy, all doe eyes. "I am definitely paying you back if this stain comes out." It's endearingly coquettish, but surely she realizes I'm wise to women like her.

"Don't worry about it." I mean it. Life is short. Jill's whole stock value is like play money to me now the practice is sold. And after losing Millie, and realizing how the decades fly past, money seems like the least important thing in the world.

It's only as I get back in the car, work out how to start it again and head up the street towards Jamison's business that I see a parking infringement officer booking another car. Okay. So Lucy saved me a fine.

Her perfume lingers in the car all the way to Jamison's building. It reminds me of something from my childhood, of my grandmother's garden. Of orange blossoms and ripe peaches, warmed from the sun, of high summer. I haven't thought of her in years. But the fragrance has other associations – temptations. Night gardens. Something exotic and slightly dangerous.

I never daydream like this. I'll be late. I park underneath and take the elevator to the twentieth floor before I realize I forgot to give Jill the good news I'm cancelling her loan.

But it's Lucy I can't get out of my head as the elevator whooshes skywards – her elegance, her eyes.

"So do you want one, Dad?" Jamison is waiting for me in reception.

"What's that?"

"A convertible. Do you want one?"

"Never had much interest in fancy cars, son. Gives me a workout just getting in and out of the thing. Never realized how out of shape I was."

"Come on, Dad. You're not that old and you're as fit as I am. You know it was fun to drive." His smile is convincing, but I shrug. Cars have never been a priority. Not sure what my priorities are just now. I'm a fish out of water, living in the city – no more patients, no more Millie.

Despite his crisp suit and confident air, Jamison's on edge. Is this about me? Or about his business? I never understood finance. Smoke and mirrors. From what I see, he and his partners take people's money, move it around, and give a few bucks back now and then.

I study my son, the image of myself at that age, good looking, even if I say so myself; upstanding, a great sportsman. Like me, Jamison also bent to the books, made the most of his education, worked hard and made a name for himself.

Sure, my business was family medicine in Franklin, Millie's home town, and Jamison is now a partner in this fancy company, but I can't fault my boy. Jamison stepped up when Millie died, joined forces with Jill and Dee to convince me to move to the city. He's the one who found me my new place, top floor in an older block of apartments. Jamison even found the invisible Mrs West to keep the place clean and cook a few meals for me each week. All that is appreciated.

Jamison tells his receptionist we'll be gone for an hour or two. I never had that luxury. Sandwiches in the clinic for me, every day for thirty years, except on Sundays. That's all over now.

Jamison's club is full of people like him – still a shock for me. I'm used to actual cowboys – old fashioned, salt of the earth people, in home-knitted sweaters and worn-out jeans. These men, with their perfect white smiles, are in slick suits. They nod or wave at Jamison and he smiles back, all confidence.

I'm as uncomfortable here as I was in Franklin, for different reasons, but Jamison seems at ease. I follow him to a table by the window and try to find something plain enough on the menu to order.

Chapter 6

Lucy

TO DO:
Wash gown
Invite Donna for dinner

The dress is deliciously heavy in its big, glossy bag, with Donna's purple evening purse and two of Jill's blouses wrapped in tissue tucked in beside it – the ones that delectable Dirk liked best.

Jill actually smiled when she rang up my purchases, though it may have been from habit. I resolve to visit her frock shop again soon. Best to keep on her good side. She seems to know that wonderful man very well. Perhaps he'll visit her again.

It's on the tip of my tongue to offer to model for Jill. Surely she has fashion parades each season. Or I could make a lamp or two for her as gifts, then ask if she'd like to stock them. Better still, I could offer makeovers for her customers. I'll never forget the skills of my first profession, at the network.

I swing the shiny bag as I leave Jill's, and saunter down the hill, delighted with my morning. I've worked hard to pick myself up and start again. Sure, I have my down days. Who doesn't? But I know how to smile, and I'm prepared to fake it till I make it. When I smile, others smile back, and before I know it, my own smile is genuine.

I find my door key and stand tall as I survey Brighton Court and my apartment, on the left, three floors up. I smile up at my kitchen window. The whole apartment might be small, but it has plenty of light and a great view of the street.

I stop to unlock the front door of the apartments. As I stoop to grab the silky ribbon handles of Jill's classy bag once more, my diamonds sparkle in the sunshine, all six of them. Even counting them calms my mind. They remind me that love exists, as solid as my mother's love for me and her mother's love for her.

For a moment, I am seven years old again – back at my mother's hospital bed. She'd twisted the loose rings around her frail fingers and promised me they'd be mine one day, when I turned twenty one.

And they were, her glittering promise that her love would never really leave me.

The memories are vivid – of her warm arm around me on the edge of the hospital bed, bony but fiercely strong as she hugged me. She'd pull out a coloring book and new pencils, full of glitter, and together, on the big tray on wheels, we'd color. Every page had a rainbow, and I sat and colored and colored – rainbows and butterflies and fairies and ladybugs and flowers.

I still hear her voice beside me, reverberating in my chest, as she told me how much joy I'd brought her, how much beauty there is in the world if only we care to notice it – rainbows in spiderwebs, brave plants taking root in ugly walls of concrete, a bright leaf on a wet gray pavement, a message from a friend, a smile from a stranger.

Back then, I didn't understand that this was her way of saying goodbye, of passing on the things she'd loved most about the world – her attitude of gratitude, with a handful of sparkles.

Now, in the sunshine outside Brighton Court, I wiggle my fingers and flashes of light shoot out like stage lights. I smile and head upstairs, wondering if I've unpacked the stain remover. I'll wash the dress immediately – gently – to remove the coffee. It's a perfect day to lay it out on a towel beside an open window beneath the clearest of skies, to dry.

I phone Donna.

"Lucy!" she says. "Was that you who sent the flowers, or a secret admirer?"

"How else do I thank you for letting me live with you for so long?"

"You didn't have to do that."

"But wait, there's more. I love my new neighborhood. And I've met someone already."

"No!"

"An actual, real gentleman."

"Am I talking to Lucy-who-swore-off-men-forever?"

"I never said that. You're the one who prefers dogs. And I found the most beautiful boutique. I bought you something."

"More flowers?"

"Nope. An evening purse. We're going out on the town."

"Already? Aren't you exhausted from moving house?"

"Well, we don't have to go right now, but when can you come and see my new place? I love it. I owe you a meal or fifty, and now there's this gift. It's your favorite color."

Chapter 7

Dirk

I eat too much at lunch. Jamison presses the full three courses plus wine on me, and then a coffee. Dee will be furious. My children are opposites, each pulling me in a separate direction when it comes to health and fitness.

Jamison invites me back to his office. For a moment, I think he's going to usher me into the big room, the boardroom, near reception, but one of the partners rushes past, the tall one, Brent Leverstone – reminds me of a shark.

Last time I was here, Jamison introduced us, and the man was all charm, but it's clear he's too busy this time, or maybe he disapproves of long lunches.

Jamison frowns. He insists I borrow his car for another few days; says he's heading off to a conference and will catch a cab to the airport.

He's on edge.

"Everything okay, son?" I say.

"Yeah. Nothing for you to worry about."

I go to question him further, but he's checking his watch. My job is to get out of there and let him get on with whatever's preoccupying him. I make a mental note to quiz him harder next time. He's too young to have so many frown lines.

A faint trace of Lucy's perfume still lingers in the car's dark leather upholstery – alluring, tantalizing; like fruit punch with too much alcohol. It's as unforgettable as the woman herself. Amusing. Exciting. Probably trouble. All I can think of is the shock in her eyes just after I slammed into her with the hot drink, the full softness of her; and the shape of her back as I loosened the zipper of the stained gown.

She was like some kind of mermaid in that slippery green dress, shapely as a figurehead on a pirate ship. Lucy's danger. She's a temptress.

In the rear vision mirror, I catch my reflection, eyebrows up. I still can't believe Lucy's audacity in "saving me the parking fine." Outrageous. But helpful.

I must work out how to set the car alarm to repel other intruders. Takes a while to learn all the features of a new car, especially one like this.

At the lights, I pull out my phone and make a note to read over the full manual. It's a mistake. My phone also carries the trace of Lucy's perfume. I plunge it back into my pocket, and frown.

Just then, it rings. Lucy? My heart quickens as a female voice comes through the car's speakers.

It's Jill.

"You have no clue, Dirk," she says. "That woman. Lucy. She will eat you alive. Men can be so childish. And I saw you in that car. What is that?"

"It's Jamison's," I say.

"It's bait, Dirk. You'll find new fish in the sea, alright, but they won't be the right kind of fish. Lucy's a piranha."

"Pretty sure piranhas are freshwater fish, Jill."

"Don't be pedantic. You know what I mean. Or maybe Lucy's exactly what you and Jamison have in mind. You might think you want someone like Lucy, but she's not who you need. Not after everything you've been through."

I'm silent.

"Don't get me wrong, Dirk. You're a generous man. Too generous. I've benefited myself, of course I have, and I'm more than grateful."

I grunt.

"Maybe I'm being too protective, Dirk," she says. "I can't quite put my finger on what worries me about Lucy, but you get a feel for them after a few years – the ones who really can't afford what I have to offer. They try on my clothes to test the sizes, then go home and search for them online. They cheat me of sales. I have to pay rent. I invest in my stock. I'm not a free fitting service."

"Of course not, Jill."

"To be fair, Lucy did buy a few things. I love my customers, but you'd think some women had nothing better to do than shop – half their luck."

I consider reminding her of the loan, and telling her I'm cancelling it, but a bus roars past too close and there's some kind of alarm blinking at me on the side mirror. I have to concentrate.

"I suppose I shouldn't be so quick to judge Lucy," Jill says.

"I liked being asked my opinion about those shirts," I say.

"Blouses. But when she pulled out the leopard skin one, she actually growled at you. I don't want you making a fool of yourself."

Am I a fool? Would it matter? Don't I deserve to live a bit? Over lunch, Jamison told me to lighten up. It's not easy after a lifetime of caring for other people's ills. Fool or bore? I'm floundering.

I clear my throat.

"Jill, about your loan …"

"Gotta go, Dirk. Customers."

The sun is out. It lights up the line of beaches heading north and south. Lucy mentioned a coastal restaurant. How long since I enjoyed a long lunch, a lunch with wine, a lunch with a beautiful woman? Decades.

Despite Jamison urging me over lunch to get out and enjoy life, Jill may be right to warn me. Lucy's a distraction, and I don't do surprises. These days I'm a creature of habit; of order; of logic and control and routine. It's the only way. It's everything. Especially now.

I drive and think of Jill and her debt to me, and her boys, my nephews – young Lachlan and Cameron – almost as tall as I am now, with their own aspirations and idiosyncrasies.

The sun starts to set, glowing behind the tall buildings of the city, and I turn the sleek red car back towards my apartment. The day may be over, "but the night is young" I hear myself say, and allow myself a smile.

Ping. It's a message from her, no doubt – from Lucy. It will be a suggestion for dinner. She won't take "no" for an answer. I ignore it. Mrs West will have placed my dinner in my apartment's oven, on a timer. My table place will be set, overlooking the city skyline; a small, healthy, covered salad waiting for me in the refrigerator; a suitable bottle of accompanying wine, uncorked; my favorite glass beside it on the table. I like my new living arrangements. At least I've liked them until this evening.

My telephone pings again. I don't like messages. Nobody messages me. It has to be Lucy. Already she is nagging me, though to be fair, the phone always pings twice.

Or it could be Jill again. Occasionally one of the boys breaks an arm or leg, and she'll want a referral, a quick fix from one of my old medical colleagues.

Then the phone rings and a panel lights up on a screen. Lucy's face is all over the dashboard, alarmingly engaging, even more beautiful than I remember, and I have nowhere to hide. I had no idea Jamison's car did this. Technology has gone too far. I stab at a button on the steering wheel to make her go away; to cancel the call; to give her a busy signal – anything to make her disappear, but unfortunately I've pressed the wrong tab – fog lights are on. What?

"Dirk?" Lucy says, and punctuates her greeting with another smile. Her father must have been an orthodontist. My heart jumps and quivers, and I stop just in time for a red light.

"Yes." It comes out more gruffly than I intend, but I don't need this woman in my life. Jill was right. The sooner Lucy realizes it the better. This car, this woman – high octane.

Lucy's smile drops a notch. I must have scowled. I'm ashamed. I'm not cruel. I just don't like to waste my time; nor hers.

"Look, Lucy," I say. "Nothing personal. I'm busy."

"Of course you are," she says, eyes bright as an amusement park. She shields them with her long lashes, dims them, contrite. Then her words rush out like snowmelt down a mountain. "So sorry to interrupt you. You're busy. I knew it. How extraordinary that we should agree so well already, Dirk. I just wanted to thank you for paying for the dress this morning. I won't keep you, though you might be interested to know that the coffee washed out of it perfectly. I have the gown on now, and it's as good as brand new. You see? Thank you. You were very generous, Dirk, but I really must pay you back."

"The stain. Oh. Good. Right. Fine. No need to pay me back."

There's silence.

Surely she'll argue.

"It was my fault," I say, surprising myself. Now I don't want the conversation to end. There's music in her voice, a lilt. She's engaging; not that I'm looking for an engagement.

"No. Not at all," she says. "I rang to let you know that I realize I was at least fifty per cent to blame. I was walking backwards – never a good idea. And I must pay …"

"No," I say abruptly, aiming for a firm tone of disinterest to make her go away. I search again for some way of ending the call, but Lucy pushes her own phone away from herself and holds it up high, to show me the dress. Even as the traffic lights turn green, the screen hijacks my attention. The gown stands out from her waist as she gives it a twirl. There's a glimpse of creamy shoulders and that stunning V at the back, all but bare.

"I need to focus on driving," I say, gruff. This Lucy is reeling me in like a fish, like Jill warned; showing herself off like bait. And I am the kingfish, ready to chase her all the way.

The headlights turn on automatically, still set on fog. No idea how to fix them.

"Well, you're so busy, I won't keep you." And she's gone, just like that; the dashboard blank – devastatingly empty – the vision of Lucy in the gown a phantom behind my eyes, set to haunt me.

My apartment is peaceful and still as I enter and toss the keys in the wide brass bowl on the hall table. This is usually my favorite part of the day. I inhale deeply. There's a strong aroma of beef casserole with a faint underlay of cleaning fluids. Fresh lilies stand tall on the sideboard.

I loosen my tie and undo the top two buttons. I slip off my shoes and place them on the rack in the hall cupboard to air, then survey my domain. Everything is in its proper place. It's calm. Peaceful; exactly how I like it – so why am I so restless? I pull out my phone, stare at the blank screen and frown. The scent of Lucy is all but gone. Not so the memory of her smile, nor the vision of her in Jill's green gown.

I pad across the soft new carpet and into the kitchen, where I serve myself the perfect portion of dinner and take it to my dining table.

The city lights twinkle. Usually I press the button and music fills my apartment, Greig or Rachmaninoff or Beethoven, but my head rings with

Lucy's words. If she doesn't want an affair, what does she want? Worse, what doesn't she want?

I lift my fork, then drop it. It clatters on the table. I pull out my phone again and study her message.

It's an emoji, the one with hands together, supposedly in thanks, but surprisingly like a prayer. Is that all? And, if it is a prayer, what exactly is her wish?

Chapter 8

Lucy

I'm reluctant to take off the dress. I love it. I give another twirl. Too bad if Dirk is uninterested for now. It's a little sad I couldn't keep him on the phone longer, but there's no point coming on too strong.

I try the dress with several pairs of shoes, high heels and higher; with a silver belt, and a gold one; and with various evening bags, shawls, scarves and jackets.

I replay the day's events, sort the facts.

Dirk is generous. If that car is any indication, he's wealthy. He cares enough about Jill to bring her coffee, perhaps every day. That would be lucky. Coffee drinkers are creatures of habit.

I wander past Jill's a few times each morning for the next week, but see no sign of Dirk's gleaming red car. Maybe he has multiple cars. Maybe he's travelling. A man like Dirk belongs in Paris, New York and London now and then – with me. Maybe even Geneva. Money seems to be no object.

My unpacking work takes me to another part of the city I've never visited before, a place of jackhammers and tall, clanking metal cranes, where urban renewal sees new towers under construction beside others, gleaming in their fresh completion.

I find a car space, my second-hand little green hatchback conspicuously different to all the builders' macho trucks.

The cranes are already at work hauling up materials. Blowtorches flash sparks off enormous steel beams as they're welded into place. Jackhammers pound.

I check the address Donna gave me and walk a couple more blocks, handing the banana from my lunch bag to a person who clearly spent his night on the street.

One more block and I find the apartment building, brand spanking new. I buzz the number on the shiny panel.

Donna lets me into the gleaming foyer and I head on up in the elevator. She's already busy in the master bedroom, unpacking box after box of high-heeled shoes into a rack that runs the length of a mirrored wall. Every wall in this walk-in closet is mirrored, creating an infinity of Donnas, amplifying her delight as I hand over her gift.

"Can you stop for a moment, and open it?" I ask.

"Sure. I think there's an armchair or two in place out there. The dining table is in, but not the chairs. Wait till you see the view. I have to keep my back to it, this place is up so high! You better do the living room accessories once all the sofas are in."

I agree. It's no hardship for me to sit this high in the sky, to watch another couple of towers take shape beside us. We won't break for long. It takes a team all day to unpack a whole household, especially for a place this nice.

Donna loves the purse. Unpacking people's possessions is a strange experience, but sometimes we see things we love. It's given Donna and me expensive taste. I'm so thrilled she loves the evening bag. She actually hugs it to her chest before she puts the strap over her shoulder and retreats to the dressing room to admire it from all sides. I follow her in.

"I found it in a boutique right near my new place last week, Donna. You must come and visit me. Oh, and I had an adventure, but you'll have to wait until lunch to hear all about it."

"Can't wait!" she says. "Can you do the kids' bedrooms?"

"Sure."

I wonder about their lives, all these strangers destined for the homes we unpack. There are two children in this household; a boy and girl, each with their own bedroom and ensuite. Judging by the mix of pink and denim, the girl is probably a tween, and the boy is younger, still reading picture books – about bulldozers and trucks and fire engines and space.

I come to a pencil case, and start to set up a little chair and table for him, and add a small stack of his coloring books.

It sends me back to childhood as I work, my hands busy now unpacking toys and setting them on a shelf beside the books.

My Mom and I never finished all the coloring books she had with her in the hospital. I had to complete them without her, not truly understanding she was never coming home. I was lucky, surrounded by caring neighbors – and my father did his best to be everything to me; to be both parents.

Turned out coloring so carefully on paper lent itself to drawing faces, which led me to painting actual faces. By middle school, I was sculpting voluptuous lips and deep and fascinating eyes on myself and my friends.

Never mind simply curling hair and straightening it and covering up blemishes. Beside that row of school washbasins, I practically invented contouring before it became a social media sensation. I graduated, got the job at the tv network, fell in love with Bart and then had my own little girl to cherish, my baby Phoebe.

I was only seven when my mother died, but I reached twenty one before my father died. At least he died doing what he loved – playing squash.

His attorney gave me a key and a number and the address of a bank vault in Seattle.

Back then, Bart called on me all my time to do his hair and makeup, and it wasn't until Phoebe left school, that I remembered that key.

Bart was wearing toupees by then, so no longer needed me for his hair before he went on air. He still needed me for his "invisible" makeup, but I drew the line at giving him injections. I just couldn't do it.

While he was recovering from plastic surgery, I took that trip to Seattle, drove up in my little van. I sourced more old furniture and upholstery for my shabby chic business on the way, along with a few more lamp bases, and finally visited the bank.

Ahead of me, a woman with a howling baby waited in line for the teller. She rocked and jiggled her bundle, and I offered to help, but just then, a man in a black jacket stepped away from the window and she pulled out her card and spoke to the teller. The baby patted at the glass screen and quietened, and I studied the posters, of boats and happy families and European holiday destinations.

Butterflies rose in my stomach as I stepped forward and slid the key and documents under the barrier. The teller stared at them, then called a supervisor. They both demanded identification, and when I produced it, the manager beckoned me aside, towards a door, and made a phone call as I waited in a red faux leather chair.

The manager disappeared as a man with a blank face and a gun stood guard. He returned with a metal box and faced the keyhole towards me.

Inside the box were half a dozen tiny old boxes and an envelope bearing my name, in a shaky script; inside, a simple sheet of paper, folded twice, and a message.

My darling Lucy,
Wishing you rainbows day and night. Be happy.
Love always,
Mother

My fingers trembled as I opened the first box – tissue paper, creamy with age, and inside it, an elegant, old-fashioned ring set with three diamonds, already transforming the ordinary room with its icy fire and light. I slid it onto the middle finger of my left hand. It fit perfectly, outshining even Bart's ring, the bold solitaire – our wedding ring. In the box at the bank were all the rings I'd admired and played with on my mother's fingers. So many memories came back to me as I slipped each one onto my own fingers. I haven't taken them off since.

People say diamonds are inanimate things, too white and too cold, but to me, they're close to magic. They cheer me up. How I would love to continue the tradition and pass these rings to my own daughter one day – if only she'd agree to see me.

That these diamonds exist for me beyond my mother, beyond the tragic shrinking of her body, is almost miraculous. They hold the moment she slipped them off her frail fingers and left them as a glittering promise to me that her love would never really leave me.

Well, Bart made the same promise when we married. Shame he didn't keep it. But life moves on.

Chapter 9

Dirk

I stare at my reflection in my shaving mirror, mercifully small, revealing only the parts of myself I need to see. No parsley stuck in my teeth. No whiskers missed. Graying temples and hair neat enough, even if it's longer than Millie ever liked it.

Fifty pushups? Done. And the fifty sit ups, yes, though they nearly killed me. My daughter, Dee, is an exercise scientist – tells me every time I see her that if I don't use my muscles, I'll lose them.

Yes, I know a doctor should be healthy, but my patients were always in worse shape than I was. I focused on them, not myself.

Breakfast is over, my bowl placed neatly in the dishwasher. Teeth, shave, hair. Now to iron the shirt and retrieve the paper.

Millie always did the ironing. Jamison tells me I can request online that Mrs West do it each week, but I don't mind the task. There's a sense of satisfaction in ironing out wrinkles. If only there were irons for faces.

Steam rises as I press the hot metal against the fabric and release the fresh smell of the laundered cotton. Millie taught me to iron after her diagnosis.

"You'll need to know," she'd said in her earnest voice. She'd been wrong, and she'd been right, but now it's part of my routine, the routine that holds me together now she's gone.

"You won't want to be one of those sad old men, unkempt."

"Unkempt," I tell my reflection in the tall mirror, and snort. I pat my stomach, draw myself to my full height and frown.

Jamison offered me a role in his business, but what can an old, burnt-out country doctor offer a slick city funds manager? Jamison uses his height and breadth well; moves and shakes it with the big end of town time after time, so he says. He inherited my build, but what do I know about money?

"It's a people business, Dad," Jamison told me yesterday over lunch. "Same as treating their sicknesses. People want solutions, answers, reassurance. They want to know where to park their money, and I give them options. Tell them what they need to hear. I'm just a money doctor with a talent for IT. You could do it with your eyes closed. You're still smart, Dad. You could learn about our product offerings."

"I'll think about it."

If my days are a little too long and a little too empty without my practice, I don't plan to dwell on it.

I snort again at my reflection. Self-pity's the worst, and self-pity about self-pity is beyond fruitless. The sun has risen, the newspaper awaits me – real paper, the sort you can flip through all day if you wish – down at the gate. I'll have time to read every word, maybe even finish the cryptic crossword. I nailed it last Tuesday.

Lunch with the old boys at the club at noon will be followed by a long walk home, with all the world's best crime novels to greet me on my return. It's choir night tonight, too, with Walt, my old buddy from college. Tomorrow is film night at my old alma mater, for people like me, people they hope will leave a bequest one day. They also invite me to student art exhibitions and plays – daytime affairs that suit me if I'm free. I'm usually free. There's still too much time on my hands, but at least there are options here in the city, so close to downtown. People who claim their lives are boring are boring people.

I turn on one heel, grab my keys, let the apartment door click shut behind me, and spring down the stairs – straight into something, someone – warm and fragrant and altogether far too soft and silky for comfort.

"Oooff!"

In the stairwell, the heavy bundle of human drops backwards below me, a slo-mo future fracture for sure, but I grab it, grab her – it's a her – lest she tumble.

She finds her footing in silver slippered toes. In the crook of her arm is a newspaper, white against the lavish crimson silk of her gown. Her hair is lush and tousled as she shakes her head rapidly, like shampoo commercials I remember from my childhood. Shot with silver, the lustrous waves of it settle around her shoulders, around her curves as she grabs at the stair rail with bejewelled fingers.

I remember those diamonds. It's her. Lucy. Impossible. What are the odds? Is she stalking me, or does she live here, too, at Brighton Court? Is Lucy the new tenant, below me?

I drink her in like a long cool, welcome glass of tonic; this vision. She's every bit as striking as she was in Jill's shop. Surprises are rare in my life these days. I thought I'd seen most things; done most things.

I close my eyes, open them, refocus on a mark on the wall that needs repainting. It's a shame tenants drag their furniture up and down without enough care for the shared spaces.

"Excu ..." she begins.

"No, no. Excuse me. My fault entirely," I say. Jamison or Dee would say "my bad" but such phrases never slide easily off my own tongue. "I wasn't looking where ... is that my paper?"

"Oh. Is this yours?" Lucy's voice is rich and modulated, amusement lurking just below the surface, a trained thing, on a leash. Is my new neighbor a retired diva or movie star? She's nobody I recognise, yet she's riveting, a vision.

"I wondered whose it was," she says. "I was just going to scan the headlines, then pop it back."

"That's theft." My smile is prim. I hate myself for it, but really ...

"Borrow it?" she says.

"Without permission."

She mirrors my tight smile, pins it on, and blinks. Several times. But the newspaper, she holds steady beneath her elbow, cradled like a cartridge. She narrows her eyes until her scrutiny sears me – a million accusations poised, unspoken, right there between us in the stairwell.

I know I'm a privileged old white male. I could spare a newspaper, but if I'm not poor and I'm not popular, I can live with that.

The fact is, Lucy is stealing my newspaper. It's always a risk when you live in an apartment – Jamison and Dee insisted I move here when I was still too weak from grief to fight the idea – and here I am, hard up against outright theft, and here's the thief – far too beautiful, if dishevelled, and she probably knows it.

Lucy. What kind of woman wears lipstick at this hour of the morning? Millie would have disapproved. Millie isn't here.

I've already heard the day's headlines on the radio news during my workout, but if I back down now, she'll steal my paper every morning. And do I really want her at my door every second day, inventing excuses to borrow milk or sugar, or beg an egg?

I hold out my hand for my paper, face blank, expectant, insistent.

Far too slowly she releases her hand from the railing. Theatrically, she touches the end of the roll, tenderly encircled it with those elegant fingers, withdraws it from under her elbow and holds it out to me, like a reluctant peace pipe.

I catch my breath. She reveals the tops of her fingers, encrusted with that telltale flash, the unmistakable sparkle of too many diamonds.

My friend Walt is a top divorce lawyer, the subject of fortune hunters never far from his conversation, and this Lucy exhibits all the warning signs he loves to discuss. Jill was right. My new neighbor is a gold digger if ever I've seen one; a merry widow or a serial divorcee out on the chase again for someone just like me. Well, I may not be habitually wise to women like this, but I will be fully on my guard.

As if she's read my mind and the challenge is on, Lucy flashes me the most dazzling of smiles. "I'm at number Forty One if you'd care to drop the paper at my door when you're done with it. Reuse, recycle, share and care, all of that."

She chortles, as if life is some sort of fun game, as if we're naughty children. And she is up and around me and gone in a swishy puff of silk and velvet and fruity perfume and sparkles, like a genie – fruity and exotic and far too feminine for comfort. A vision of one pale, slim ankle in a silver slipper stays with me.

The paper, still warm from her body, is motionless in my hand like a baton in a running race halted mid-flight. I stare at it, gaze down the stairs, and up them past the number on her door, then slowly mount the steps beyond Forty One, and retreat into my apartment.

Chapter 10

Lucy

Living here at Brighton Court, I will need to buy myself a little old lady shopping cart for sure. I've only bought a few small things, for my parties, but the bags are so heavy I worry my arms have stretched by two inches and my knees have compacted like a telescope.

There's a dull "thunk" as I deposit my groceries at the front door of Brighton Court and contemplate the lack of an elevator. So much for the olde worlde charm. I should have forked out more for a place in a newer building where I could just push a button.

For a moment I consider opening the bourbon and taking a little swig, for strength, but it's not a good look, and Silver Fox could turn up at any moment. The fact I saw him out walking yesterday at about this time might have had something to do with my choice of time to go shopping. People who exercise tend to have routines, and yes, I'd love to run into him again.

I contemplate whether to leave the bourbon and coke and mineral water at the mercy of passersby; or the beer, cider and champagne. The caviar must go in the refrigerator soon, even on such a perfect day, but, along with the corn chips, their weight is neither here nor there.

I settle on carting up the champagne – essential for my home-warming. Back downstairs again and facing the other bags, I'm thrilled to see Dirk emerge from the front door in dark gray exercise gear. He attempts to stride past, but I give him a cheery wave; one he can't possibly ignore.

Dirk almost smiles, then sees my bags. He deliberates. Does he have bad knees?

Success. He turns towards me. I am all for women's lib – I am fully liberated now that Bart is in my past, but my groceries are simply too heavy to deal with now I no longer have a drive-in garage leading straight to the kitchen and pantry. I can't dwell on what I've lost, nor the fact that the Minx will now be enjoying all these luxuries and more. I sigh, push the past way, way back behind me, and focus on the moment.

Thank goodness. Dirk lifts my heart as deftly as he lifts my shopping bags. He even sends me up the stairs ahead of him, like a gentleman, and perhaps I sway a little more than necessary.

At my door, I turn, and he bumps my shoulder as he sets my bags down.

"My apologies," he says. Adorably polite.

"My fault," I say. "And what a thing to do to you when you've been so kind. Would you like to come in now, for a coffee? I'd really like to pay you back for being so chivalrous about the gown." I gesture at my closed front door. My apartment is clean and tidy and welcoming, and so am I, but Dirk backs away as if I'm a wild animal. What is wrong with the man?

"Or just drop in for a drink this evening," I say. "Six o'clock."

"I have another commitment."

"Then have a coffee now."

"I should continue my walk." He is so formal – stiff with politeness. Is he shy? Or does he think this is some kind of trap?

"Coffee's not compulsory, Dirk. I'm having one. You might like one, too. I appreciate your help with my heavy bags. You could sit for a moment, and then walk."

He hesitates. I turn and throw open my door, and sure enough, he follows me inside with both bags. He sets them on the narrow kitchen bench.

"Milk? Sugar? I'm sorry I haven't made any brownies yet. Do you like them?"

"I don't need brownies, Lucy."

"So I'm guessing you like your coffee black?"

He stares at me and nods.

"It's not a marriage proposal, Dirk."

I pull down two blue and brown mugs, hand-turned, from the potter in my old neighborhood, slightly off round.

"I brought these with me to remind me how impossible perfection can be to achieve. I love it that they're not quite right. What did you bring with you from your old life?"

"Not much. Mostly clothes. My children arranged it all."

"Lucky you." There's silence. Do I tell this man my daughter's still not speaking to me? Something about him instills trust.

"I'm afraid my daughter avoids me," I say. "According to Phoebe, I 'broke' my marriage and 'lost' her childhood home." He raises his eyebrows. He doesn't rush in, doesn't judge.

"She may be half right," I say. "But that doesn't bring it all back, does it?"

"No."

"I'm sorry," I say. "This has nothing to do with you. It's just that I loved my old house and neighborhood. Maybe too much." He nods, as if seriously considering my words. I sigh. I'm glad I told him. Until this minute, only Donna has known my woes. He hasn't walked away, hasn't condemned me, hasn't tried to tell me everything will be okay. I flash him a grateful smile and change the subject. I open a packet of exotic Italian cookies dipped in chocolate, pour them into a bowl, and load all of it onto a tray.

"Here," I say, as I pick up the tray. "Let's take these into the living room. I think you have a similar bay window? I adore this architecture. So gracious. So solid. I chose this place ahead of one with an elevator, just for the pleasure of admiring this room every day."

"My daughter, Dee, is an exercise scientist," he says. "She chose this place precisely because it doesn't have an elevator. In her view, it will prolong my life to have to use the stairs every day."

"Well, that's good news for me, too."

My living room is so charming it lifts my heart. I'm not keen on the pale blue walls, but renters can't change such things. I'd choose a rich white, but soon I'll make some lamps to lift it. I'm thinking of warm crimsons and pinks. Supplies are still in boxes in the spare bedroom.

"So, Dirk," I say as I hand him his black coffee. "What do you want more of in life?"

He is silent a long time. Maybe he's depressed. Or is he an ax murderer, considering his next victim? I don't actually know him, after all.

"Don't tell me you're a sad old cynic, Dirk? Is there nothing that brings you satisfaction? Or do you love silence?"

"Silence is underrated, Lucy."

I almost choke on my coffee. And there I was, thinking I was cheering him up with a little conversation.

"On the contrary, communication is vital." I lift my chin to challenge him.

"You may be right." He holds my gaze, a slight flush on his cheek, perhaps from the strain of bringing up my groceries. When I stare back, my heart flips and stills and flaps. He is serious, this Dirk. My hot neighbor may be a deeply sincere man, and possibly just as sad. Does nothing bring him joy?

I offer him the plate of cookies and he selects the smallest one, with the least chocolate. I grab the largest and turn the thick chocolate end towards my lips, holding his gaze.

He turns to me, and as we chomp at the same time, he closes his eyes and smiles. I swallow and sigh.

"These cookies are masterpieces," I say. "They've been making them the same way in Italy for hundreds of years because they got it right. Don't you agree?"

When he nods and reaches for another, I'm as glad as if I've been coaxing a toddler to eat, or encouraging a stray to become my pet, or a heartbroken man to open himself up to love again. Because I know it in my bones – it is Dirk who will bring me joy.

But I don't tell Donna. I hold the secret inside me. It's just an idea, after all, and I'm a grown woman. I know how love can be elusive. I've just watched it evaporate and turn my ex-husband into a stranger.

Next night, Donna joins me for dinner. I give her a full three-course dinner, silver candlesticks and all.

"Can't thank you enough for saving my life, Donna, for taking me in, for feeding me, and giving me the job."

"That's what friends are for," says Donna as she serves herself more baked vegetables. "Although I really only did it 'cause I like your baked dinners."

"Ha ha…"

"So are you happy now? Apart from your relationship with Phoebe, and you know I'm working on that for you. I'm no ordinary Godmother."

"That's true."

I stand up and give her a hug, then clear away the dinner plates, ready for dessert.

"Donna, my friend, you are amazing. Thank you."

"So are you?"

"Happy? Happy to have found this place, for sure."

"I know you, Lucy. You won't be happy until there's another man in your life."

"I'm only just divorced! What I really want is security. I never want to be thrown out of my own home ever again. I need to buy my own place, Donna, like you did."

"What kind of place?"

"A place like this. Exactly like this. I wouldn't even have to move again. It'd be perfect."

Chapter 11

Dirk

Walt greets me at choir rehearsal in his usual, hearty way, with the same huge handshake, a slap on the back and a laugh like we're teenagers again; like he's dreamed up some new game I can't refuse; like life's for living.

It was Walt who got me onto the soccer team back in college, goalie, Walt who convinced me to take my medical exams again the year I failed – after the head injury – and Walt whose recent endorsement got me to move back to the city again from Franklin when the rest of the family forcefully suggested it.

"Why the heck not, Dirk, old boy?" he said. "Why stay in the middle of nowhere and drown in misery? You never actually liked the place."

That's the trouble with Walt. He remembers everything. I'd forgotten I only moved to Franklin cause Millie was in love with her family home and thought it the best place to raise our family. She was right. At least the kids had a textbook childhood – all bike-riding and jumping in the leaves, and snow fights and ponies. But they were in college themselves before we knew it, the big house almost empty, and Millie slowly signing out.

Walt's friendship was a lifeline, and the minute I moved back to the city, he hauled me into this Christmas choir.

"Nothing to it, Dirk," he'd said. "All you gotta do is turn up and open your mouth."

It's been a bit more than that, like learning parts, but at least the rest of the choir made me welcome. That first rehearsal, I worried they'd mob me like Millie's friends, all doe eyes and sympathy, but city folk are different. Everyone smiled and sang, and then rushed away, back to their busy lives. They left Walt and me to stack the chairs.

I'll admit I like our rehearsals, turning my brain off for a couple of hours to follow the conductor's baton, and Walt is mischievous as ever afterwards.

"Come on, Dirk," he says. "One for the road. Rhonda doesn't mind. Likes it when I leave her in peace a little longer. New bar. Fancy."

He takes me by the arm and steers me away, two blocks behind the church hall, and there it is, the lights behind the bottles glowing like honey, beckoning us inside, and a young crowd in there; city people, dressed in black, tossing back expensive wines and whiskies.

"Just one," I say. "Something red" and he's back a few minutes later with one of those fancy glasses without a stem, as if wine and wine glasses have only just been invented.

A waiter turns up with a small black dish of green olives, and Walt dives straight in. I pick one up, admire the glossy orb, stick it in my mouth and wince at the salty assault, even stronger when my teeth pierce the skin.

"Met anyone yet?" he says.

"Only if you count the woman I spilled coffee on a few days ago. In Jill's store – Jill was not impressed."

"Ah Jill. Your sister. How's she doing?"

"Store's looking great. Boys are giving her the runaround."

"You're a good man, Dirk. Gonna go sort 'em out?"

I shrug. My own children brought themselves up, or Millie was a magician. Either way, I wasn't there to see it, almost always busy in my practice or at the hospital handling decades of need; a flow of illnesses and injuries that never stopped. I loved my work – healing the injured and improving lives was a great privilege when the treatments were effective – but I was over it by the time I sold my clinic.

"You're doing it again, Dirk."

"Huh?"

"Going silent on me."

"Oh. That."

"Where'd you go? You thinking about that woman?"

"What woman?"

"The one in Jill's store."

"No. I wasn't."

"Well?"

"Lucky I didn't burn her. Turns out she lives in the same building, at Brighton Court. Can you believe it? Gave me coffee earlier today."

"No way! She following you? Watch out, man."

"Why?"

"Retired doctor? Bachelor? Good looking? Flush with cash. You are eligible, my friend."

"Not interested."

Walt doesn't believe me. He gives me a nudge and laughs, and I down my wine and get up to go.

"Hey, Dirk."

Walt winks. I laugh and sit back down again.

Am I interested? I was a one-woman man, and with Millie gone, I don't know what I want. I tell Walt Lucy is divorced, and he asks whether she wears many rings.

"Well, now you mention it, Lucy does wear a lot of diamonds. So what?"

Walt shakes his head.

"Prognosis is bad, Dirk old boy. Watch it. Fortune hunter for sure. But no reason you can't have a bit of fun. Play the field like in our olden days."

I never played the field. Millie zeroed in on me at college and we were an item. She stuck with me after the big head injury, too, even when my sporting career was shot. Helped me through my medical degree, with all those hours of study. We were married and raising Jamison and Dee in that big old country house before I noticed.

Next day is Thursday. Dee insists I meet her at ten for a catch up once a week at her gym, for a free workout, as well as on Sundays for a family lunch. My grandchildren give me more of a workout than all of Dee's shiny machines, that's for sure. Baby bootcamp. I turn up and they jump all over me.

"So, how are you, Dad?" Dee says. She's wearing a blazer over her fancy gym clothes. She tells me about a promotion; something to do with her now managing several gyms; beyond consulting and giving classes. I'm proud of her.

"Dad?"

I raise my eyebrows. What had she asked me? How am I?

"That's my question, Dee. How are you?"

"Actually, anyone can ask it of anyone else, and there's no right or wrong answer."

I try hard never to ask myself how I am. That was the whole point of moving to the city, to get away from that question, to get away from all that pity. Millie's friends were everywhere in Franklin. I was drowning in their sympathy – couldn't take any more of it.

After Millie, my silences alarmed everyone, especially the patients.

I'd refused to take time off – couldn't stand the empty house, and knew that my patients still needed my care. So I ran my usual, slightly out of control clinic, with urgent extras and all the old faithfuls keeping me busy. And I nodded and smiled and prodded and peered and tapped and listened and kept prescribing as usual, but occasionally, I'd stop in the middle of a consultation.

"Doc? Everything okay?" they'd say. It happened once. And then again. The receptionists started knocking on my door. Cases ran over time. There was standing room only in the waiting room. Someone must have contacted Jamison and Dee, and next thing I knew they were both at my door, the two of them, successful youngish professionals, not accepting silence and not accepting "no".

Yes, I'd been forced to admit. I'd been drowning in grief, surrounded by the never-ending needs of others and smothered by the sympathy of Millie's many friends – couldn't go anywhere in Franklin without being recognised, without having my loss reflected in everyone else's sad faces.

So, I'd agreed. The only way forward for Dirk "the Doc" O'Connell, after a lifetime of serving his community, was to sell my practice and move away – to make a fresh start, in the city, close to my loving, insistent children and sister.

So I moved. But now I'm a stranger in a strange land, in a city I barely recognize, so changed it is, with its new freeways and tunnels and high-rise buildings and fancy precincts. But at least friends of Millie no longer lurk at every corner offering me casseroles. They were so thoughtful, but they kept reminding me of my loss.

Fresh vistas carry no memories. Strangers never ask about Millie. Nor do they even know I was a doctor. There are no impromptu conversations about bunions, bad backs or rumbling coughs that refuse to clear. I'm a free man.

"Dad?"

"I've joined a choir."

"Oh, that's great, Dad. I didn't know you could sing."

"I didn't know either. Walt insisted. You remember my friend Walt? From college. He convinced me there are never enough baritones and all I have to do is turn up each week and open my mouth."

Dee laughs. I crack a smile and she seems pleased, pushes her hand across the table and puts it over mine, warm and pleasant. And then she holds hers up in the air.

It takes me a while to register. A high five. I've high fived hundreds of miserable children, summoned their bravery when their broken limbs were finally encased in plaster, forced them to smile through their tears.

I high-five Dee back, hating the realization I'm no longer the Doc, the one to make others smile.

"Still super serious, Dad."

"Do I have to apologize?"

"No. We all just want you to be happy."

"Kind. Thanks. I'm not unhappy."

"Not the same as being happy, Dad. How's the apartment?"

"Still great. Thanks. Clean. Quiet. Comfortable. Everything's in order, thank you. Housekeeper leaves me food and does most of the laundry. I make my own toast and eggs; order takeout. I'm not starving, as you can see. And the cherry pie was the best I've ever tasted."

"What cherry pie?"

"Mrs West's, I guess. Oh, Carla sends you her best wishes. I bought one of her paintings."

"That's great, Dad. Oh, did you hear about the fund-raiser for dementia research?"

"No?"

"You remember the Fontaines, don't you, Bettina and Raymond?" says Dee.

"Friends of Millie's, yes."

"Raymond died a year ago. Bettina's set up a foundation. There's a ball. Matt can't come. He has to go to the Caribbean for a conference first thing next morning. Will you come with me, Dad? It's no big deal. I know you still have a dinner suit. I made sure we packed it for you in case an event like this came up. Just say 'yes.'"

"When is it?" As if my calendar is full. As if there's anything in my life beyond sitting in my perfectly renovated, perfectly clean apartment and staring out the window, walking now and then, and catching up with my children, and choir once a week. I'm still not used to it. My life was a whirlwind. Now it's too quiet.

"A week from Thursday. I'll text you the details. It's at the Town Hall."

"Okay."

"Maybe get a haircut, Dad?"

"What's wrong with it?" I pat the back of my head and Dee shakes her head and laughs.

"Just get a haircut. Please?"

I nod. I might or I might not. Millie used to cut my hair, and one of her friends did it ahead of her funeral; all over me with her pity and powder and polished pink fingernails, as if she could step right in where Millie left off. She meant well, but it was too soon, and she reminded me too much of Millie. I shudder and shut out the memories.

Chapter 12

Lucy

My fridge is overflowing with tiny cakes I've baked for my neighbors. It's a way of breaking the ice. I'll follow by inviting them to a drinks party.

First stop, the apartment beneath me. An older lady with tight, dyed brunette curls and gold-rimmed glasses opens the door wide, all smiles.

"Yes?"

"I'm Lucy Beston, your new neighbor," I say as I hold out the Saran wrapped paper plate, laden with finger foods.

"Oh. How marvelous," she says. "I love it when new residents introduce themselves. So civilized, don't you think? I'm Mrs B. Would you like to come in for a few moments? Sorry the place is a mess."

It's anything but messy, the orange kitchen benches and lime green tiles in perfect condition – clean and bright. A stack of lime-green saucepans graces the shelf beside the stove, along with a purple fondue set.

"I love your kitchen," I say.

"Mr B and I remodelled it in 1973 when we moved in," she said. "We looked after it, and now it's back in fashion. Coffee?"

"Thank you."

She places my plate on a shiny purple tray and takes her mission brown percolator off the stove. Even her coffee cups are 1970s, small and squat, and decorated in geometric brown and orange triangles.

"These are so retro, Mrs B. Amazing."

"This set was a wedding gift from Mr B's parents. They're still perfectly serviceable. I wash and wipe by hand, very carefully. I listen to the radio as I do it. My things are special, so I take extra care. They remind me of Lenny. And we never had children, so there's that."

There's a little silence as she loads the matching milk and sugar bowl onto the tray and carries it into her front room. The wallpaper, carpet and furniture match the coffee cups, all triangles and arches in brown and yellow and orange – alarmingly bright.

"So you've been in Brighton Court all this time?"

"I love it here," she says. "It's good and solid. Most of my friends have moved now, or died, it's true, but I'm happy here. Now tell me about you, Lucy Beston."

"Oh. I only moved in a week or two ago, but I can see exactly why you love it. It's such a lovely area, so many good local shops, the bus service, the little bit of yard, though truly, it needs some work."

"Good luck with that. Professor No stops everything."

"Who's that?"

"Ignatius Raynor. Apartment One. I shouldn't be so rude, but really, if you think my apartment is old fashioned, you should see his."

"Well, I don't think your place is old fashioned. As you say, all these colors are the latest again. As for Apartment One, I'm actually on my way down there next."

"If he opens the door to you."

"What's his story?"

"He must be about ninety nine by now, which is admirable, but he keeps to himself. The only time any of us hear from him is when he vetoes another thing the rest of us want."

"Like what?"

"Better lighting in the halls, new carpet, an intercom at the front door – it's downright dangerous leaving the place open to anyone. But you name it, he says 'no.'"

"Why is that?"

"Oh, you don't want to cross Professor No. He has a number of degrees, in law and engineering, so he says, and he can recite every city ordinance ever invented. Plenty of brains but no common sense. Nothing wrong with his mind, even if his hearing and eyesight aren't the best. I shouldn't be negative, but Professor No is as stubborn and mean as they come."

"I wasn't even sure anyone lived down there. The blinds are always drawn."

"He lives down there alright. Gets his groceries delivered once a month. Goes to show you can live forever on a box of eggs and onions and oranges and flour and rice and a side of beef."

"Oh." I'm not sure I want to discuss another neighbor in so much detail, especially as he's not here to defend himself, so I steer the conversation back to the building. "Well, I miss my old garden and am itching to trim back the vines and see what else is there. He'd actually get more winter sunlight. Surely he wouldn't object."

"You go right on ahead and suggest it, Lucy, and see what happens. I don't bother with him anymore. Now, tell me about you. You seem familiar. If you don't mind my asking, are you on your own? I haven't noticed a Mr Beston, you see. You can tell me to mind my own business."

"Oh. I am on my own now, yes." Something makes me want to hold back the whole of my "story" as Mrs B calls it. Mrs B for Mrs Busybody, perhaps, though she seems kindly enough. Mrs B for Mrs Broadcast.

"Fresh start?" She fishes.

"Exactly," I say, and beam back at her.

"Mmm."

I smile into my silence and she sits and sips her coffee, foiled but still friendly.

"Well, these little cakes are delectable, Lucy. I can see you must be an excellent entertainer."

"So glad you like them, Mrs B. I can tell we'll get along fine. Are you happy with your lamps? I could make you a side lamp to match your decor."

"Really?" She looks up at the amber light fitting hanging from the center of the ceiling. "A little orange side lamp?"

"I collect retro materials. I have a few that would match your wallpaper. I could show you some samples."

"Well, that would be very kind."

"Tomorrow? Or this afternoon?"

"I'm playing bridge this afternoon. But tomorrow – great. And if you have any questions about Brighton Court or the neighborhood, just ask. You've met Dr Dirk O'Connell, in the penthouse? A real doctor. Imagine."

I nod and hope my cheeks don't flush. Mrs B doesn't need to know the depth of my interest in our esteemed neighbor.

If she notices, she doesn't quiz me on it, mercifully. She just goes on to give me a rundown on the other residents – a teacher with a rich lawyer boyfriend, a nursing student, a songwriter who might or might not smoke pot or maybe it's incense, and someone called Felicity she knows nothing about.

Good for Felicity, I think, as I take my leave. It's lovely to have an ally, but I might watch what I say. I skip Davey's door – he's always out in the mornings, and besides, Mrs B told me he's a chef. He'll hardly need more food.

I rap on a few other doors, but nobody answers. It's a working day. They're probably out.

Two more flights down and I'm below the level of the road. I open the door to the garden and peer out, but the growth is so thick on this side it's hard to see beyond it. Besides, I want to give my final mini cupcakes to Professor No.

Back inside, the number One on the dark-panelled door hasn't seen polish in fifty years. It blends into the dark wood panelling, such an invitation to a shabby chic practitioner like myself. Sinister. Could Mrs B be right about our neighbor? I've done the make-up of thousands of strangers, and there weren't very many I couldn't charm.

I hold out my remaining plate and rap at the door.

I know he's in there. There's a thunk and clunk, thunk and clunk, as if he has a limp and a cane. I can practically hear him breathing as he peers out the tiny glass hole.

I smile and hold out the plate.

"Professor Raynor?" I say, loudly. "I'm Lucy Beston, new at Number Forty One. Just saying hello with some little cakes."

There's more breathing, but no movement. After about a minute, I place the plate on the floor outside the door.

"I'll leave them here for you. Bye." With a smile and a wave, I step away and find the door into the garden again.

It's a beautiful day. I'm so grateful to Donna for sharing her job with me. Working casually allows for so much flexibility. She's given me a couple of quiet weeks to find my feet at my own place, before I duck all over the city again to pack and unpack the lives of others.

There's sunshine up there somewhere, beyond the thicket of ivy and overgrown bushes. It's rare to have so many mature trees so close to downtown – a couple of oaks and three pines. I push my way through to a side fence and then along the back fence past lilac and dogwood. I peer through the winter branches. I'm sure I see roses, tall and unpruned, back towards Brighton Court, where the undergrowth thins. This would be a sun trap if I could just trim some of it back.

I bark my shin on a block of concrete. It's a structure, a rounded arch of seating around a circular table. Yes. There's a rose garden behind what might have been a vegetable patch, the unpruned stems tangling way above my head.

Such a shame it's all a mess. I am itching to get into it, to prune back the thicket of Virginia creeper and ivy that filters out so much sunshine, but I left my gloves and clippers behind. Mistake. The Ex and the Minx won't have a clue what to do with them.

I'm just contemplating making another raid on the forever home when the twitch of a faded, drawn curtain catches my eye.

It whisks back, exposing a bald and frowning Professor Raynor, his fist high, and shaking.

I plant a smile firmly on my face and wave back, then turn away to continue exploring.

He wrenches open the window.

"Stop," he says. "You can't go there."

"Pretty sure this is common property. You're not the only resident, Professor Raynor. We all want to enjoy this space."

"'No resident shall garden without the permission of other residents,'" he recites, as if it's one of the ten commandments.

"So that's how this mess got here," I say. "You'd actually have more winter sun if I pruned back these vines. Nobody could object. I won't tell, if you don't." I give him my biggest wink.

He humphs, slams the window closed, whisks the curtain closed and disappears, so I continue.

A few minutes later, the back door creaks open. The bent old man emerges, scowling.

"You can't do that," he says.

"Arrest me," I say. We stare at each other until I throw back my head and laugh, and I catch him hiding a smile.

"Why don't you want this space improved?" I say. "Look, there's a beautiful old table with benches. We could put a pizza oven over there. Give me a few moments and we can sit and chat."

I push back some branches, and use one foot to sweep off decades worth of twigs and leaves to expose the circular garden setting. The land falls away towards the other side fence. There's definitely space for some vegetables, if I can only prune back the chaos.

"This could be lovely," I say. "Here. You can sit on my apron." I haul it off and lay it on the bench.

He's silent. He inches forwards with his stick. I go to help him and he almost hits me with it.

At last he takes a seat and glares. He is pale and trembling – maybe with rage. Or Parkinson's.

"You can see what used to be here. It's lovely. We could have picnics down here. Children can kick a ball without losing it. And you could come out any time and enjoy the sunshine and some company."

"Don't patronize me, young lady. I know what used to be here."

"'Young lady.' You flatter me, Mr Raynor." I'd love to ask him how he became so grumpy, but maybe it's just gravity pulling down the edges of his mouth.

"I think that's a magnolia, and are they camellias way back there along the other fence?"

He nods.

"Mrs B tells me you've lived here all your life. She says you know everything."

He harrumphs.

"How about that pizza oven?" I say. "They're great fun."

He shakes his head and I smile, not scared of an academic. I did the make-up for plenty of them when I worked for the network; shy experts commenting on this and that, fronting up for their five minutes of fame. Under all that importance, they're as vain as the rest of us.

"I suppose you know your nickname."

He narrows his eyes.

"We could always prove Mrs B wrong," I say companionably, and let my comment hover in the patches of sunlight that dance and shift as a faint breeze moves through the garden.

Chapter 13

Lucy

The following Monday, I'm laden with grocery bags as I pass Jill's. On impulse, I turn around and step back into her boutique. I rest my bags beside the counter and admire her window treatment, the green gown Dirk bought me now replaced with an off-the-shoulder orange jumpsuit in a stretchy kind of fabric. It's eye-catching, but not my style.

Jill's on the phone as I enter. She lifts her head but I shake mine. "Just browsing," I mouth with a wave, and she nods and continues her conversation, her voice low and urgent.

I busy myself examining her rack of dark trousers, all surprisingly similar yet marvelously different.

"Yes, an ice cream cake," Jill says. "But no, no tattoos. There are standards. An eighteenth is a formal occasion. It's not all about you. It's about family, too. If you get a tattoo; no cake and no party. Do you understand?"

She places the phone on the counter with a "tsk".

"Teen troubles?" I say, but Jill fails to open up.

"My apologies," says Jill. "I don't normally make personal calls when I have customers."

"But teenage boys," I say. "I hear they're like puppies, aren't they – all action, very messy, but beneath all of that, utterly adorable."

Jill refuses to agree. I toy with the idea of telling her about my Phoebe. At least her boys are talking to her.

I linger, tinker with her evening purses. Even though it's coffee time, Dirk fails to show up. A shame.

"That green gown," I say. "The divine Georg K. Would you have some earrings to match?"

Jill warms up. She slides out a drawer beneath a display cabinet and there they are – row upon row of sparkling bangles and bracelets and necklaces and earrings. I dive on a pair of faux emerald earrings with large pearl droplets, Vermeer style. My eyes water at the price, but my relationship with Jill is important. She's clearly on great terms with Dirk, and I'd love to see more of both of them. They're part of my new life.

"I must have them," I say.

They're expensive, but a great additional investment given the gown. They'll complement each other beautifully. Better still, Jill's mouth softens.

Just then I notice the flyers on the counter, each with a lavish golden bow in the top corner. Something about a fundraiser for dementia research. Perfect! I pick one up and place it in the bag with the new earrings. I love a ball, and it's an excellent cause. I'll be able to wear my new green gown and matching earrings! Fortunately I still have some savings from my shabby chic sales. Spending is always a temptation, and I have to watch my outgoings.

I walk back down the street on Cloud Nine. Perhaps I'll invite Dirk to join me at the ball. Surely he invests in good causes, too.

I smile at a young woman walking three dogs, but she's wearing earphones and doesn't notice me. How do the young ever expect to meet anyone if they block real conversations?

That reminds me, I must invite some of the neighbors for drinks. I've heard them, but not met them all. There's someone with a noisy motorbike who revs and leaves before dawn – Davey, maybe – and there's been the tinkling of a piano, occasional voices in the stairwell, phones ringing, snatches of radio or television and a few banging doors on windy days, but apart from Dirk and Mrs B, they're complete strangers.

I'll ask Jill to drinks, too, and maybe even the lovely people from the delicatessen and that Patrick fellow from the gallery. I'm so lucky to have such excellent shops nearby.

If only Phoebe could see my new arrangements. She still hasn't visited. I'd invite her to the ball, too, though we haven't spoken since that terrible call when I had to tell her I'd left her father. She seems to have blocked my number; cancelled me.

Sudden tears scald my eyes. They form and drop of their own accord, blinding me, but I keep walking. It's not hard to put one foot in front of the other – it's all one can ever do – so I continue, my bags heavy, the handles cutting into my fingers. It's not far now, and then there'll be all those steps, but exercise and a task are exactly what I need.

My shoulders slump, and not just from the weight of my shopping.

I allow myself a genuine sob or two, let those salty tears roll down like breakers at the beach, let them tumble down my face in runnels. I give a great sniff. My neighborhood's a blur and my face is a mess, but it's not as if there's anyone around to notice them.

But I'm wrong. A tall figure looms close and I flinch. It's broad daylight. I thought this neighborhood was safe. Is this the end?

"Allow me to carry those bags." Thank goodness. It's Dirk, the gentleman.

"Oh."

"My daughter says it's sexist to offer, but I just think it's common sense. Helpful. Neighborly."

"You're very kind, Dirk, and I won't say no," I say, but keep my face averted. I can't remember if this eyeliner runs. He takes both bags and I reach for a tissue and give a quick dab.

But with his long legs, Dirk's a quick walker, and he's already up the stairs and dropping my shopping at Forty One. He tries to dash up to his apartment and away, as if the last thing he wants is my gratitude or another friendly invitation. Well, he won't get away with it. I've caught up with him. I'm planning a cocktail party, and Dirk is added to the mental invitation list.

"So, chivalry is not dead," I say.

"I'd do it for anyone."

"You're lying, Dirk. I can see the street from my kitchen window. I've never once seen you carry up anyone else's groceries. Thank you. You're a treasure."

He stares at all my shopping bags, hiding a blush. Sweetie.

"No, I'm not an alcoholic," I say. "I'm planning a party. Just
something small – pre-dinner drinks – to meet the neighbors, a few at a
time. Can you join me?"

"When?"

"Are you free this Saturday evening? I'm all for seizing the day. I
won't be able to find a time that suits everyone. I'm about to go and slide
a few little notes under the other doors."

"I …" He seems reluctant.

"You must join us. The more the merrier."

Still he holds back. I can't force the man to be sociable.

"It's no big deal, Dirk. At least let me thank you for helping with my
shopping now and then. One drink. One peanut, or an olive if you're
allergic. Are the neighbors so awful?"

"I haven't met many actually."

"Perfect. We'll see who turns up. Nice to get to know each other a little
better, don't you think?"

Chapter 14

Dirk

Does Lucy mean her party will allow us to get to know the neighbors, or does she mean we'll get to know each other better?

Already she's bossing me around. I like my solitude. I'm content in my silent apartment. I shrug. According to Jill, Lucy's a vulture and I'm carrion. Jill reads trash fiction. It's how she sees the world. According to Jill, since Lucy's a single woman, she must be a gold digger, and since I am single, I am the gold, or something silver. Silver wolf or something.

I haven't pointed out the hypocrisy. Jill's been single for a decade and I don't see her out chasing men.

Well, if Lucy and I are a literary cliche about to happen, there's only one answer to her invitation.

"Yes. Thank you," I say. "That would be lovely."

I think about Lucy's party for the rest of the week. What do I wear? And what do I bring? Millie would have baked something, like cheese sticks, but that's not happening.

I would bring a bottle of wine, but I know for sure that Lucy hardly needs more alcohol. I've carried up all those clinking bottles.

I decide to bring her a small bunch of flowers, nothing meaningful, nothing "language of flowers" – just something cheerful. She seems to like color.

I catch her on Thursday morning, slipping something under my door, and I swing it open. There's her fragrance again, fresh and fruity and floral.

On the carpet between us is the invitation to her drinks party, beautifully written on a creamy, textured card. Lucy is class.

We bend together to pick it up and she laughs as we bump awkwardly. She snatches it up ahead of me, straightens and hands it across.

"You're sure you want to invite an old widower," I say. "We're not much fun, but according to Jill, we're very interesting to single women."

"What. You think I'm going to woo you with cocktails and caviar, Doc O'Connell? You should be so lucky."

There's silence as we size each other up.

"You are a proud man, Dirk," she says. "It's no weakness to enjoy a little company now and then."

Her eyes dance. She is laughing at me.

"My son says it's good for me to mingle. My daughter says exercise is better."

"We could exercise together; make them both happy," says Lucy. "Walking works for me. I'm in excellent health." She spins on the spot on my doorstep like a ballerina, and laughs. Joy sparkles off her like dew in the sunshine. Lucy has star quality. Why isn't this woman on the silver screen? Maybe she was once. I'm about to ask, when Lucy fires her own question.

"So how did you end up east in Franklin for most of your life, when the rest of your family lives here in the west?"

I stare at her, tongue tied. My patients never asked me about myself, and Millie already knew everything. I'm in no hurry to open up to her. If I share the bedrock of it, she might turn it around and use it against me. Kids did that in school. I smile. Let her wonder.

"See you on Saturday, Lucy," I say, enigmatic.

"You're not afraid of me are you, Dirk? You could let someone in, you know."

"Let you in, you mean."

"Would that be so bad?"

If that isn't mischief in her eyes, then I have no experience with human beings, and that certainly isn't true.

"Well, see you at my party," she says, and she's back off down the stairs with her handful of cream envelopes. She hums as she stops and posts another under a door and another. Quietly, I close my own door and lift the envelope to my nose. Yes. Smells like Lucy, like juicy fruit, like a summer night, like fun.

Chapter 15

Lucy

Is there time to make some lamps ahead of my party? The boxes sit and stare at me. It will make a mess. Bart and I had a five-car garage – enough space for my lamp workbench and all of my shabby chic furniture in all stages of renovation.

I sigh. I need to get the Lucy's Lamps business going again, making my lamps and marketing them. I gained quite a following before my life was turned upside down, with custom orders and a steady stream of buyers. I love my work with Donna, but it's just a way of paying the bills. My lamps are a passion. Everyone needs more light in their life, and a bit more fun. A quirky lamp cheers up everyone.

Who knows how long it will take for the settlement to come through. Besides, I want to make Mrs B's orange lamp, and the elegant ones for Jill. She needs one in the back corner near the changing rooms. I've designed it already in my mind – a feminine little shade in a shiny mid-blue, with silver tassels, on a black stand.

I make an easy meal of baked beans on toast and a cup of tea, then find the materials and spread them out on the kitchen bench. Nothing to it, really, though the glue smell is not ideal with the simple dinner… I take it into the living room to enjoy, then fish out more materials and make five more lampshades before midnight, all in different colors.

The orange one with lime green pompoms is so eye-catching, I decide to make another in reverse colors, to go with it. I must keep an eye out for some more black bases.

Next day, I go hunting for stray bases in thrift stores and pick up some bargains, nabbing some gardening gloves and new clippers while I'm at it. That evening, I make a couple of adjustments to the pompoms on one of Mrs B's shades, then plug in all my new lamps to take a photo for Instagram – but there's a "phut" and all my lights go out.

I stumble to my door, grasp for the key on its hook, and stare out into a pitch black stairwell. All around me, neighbors' doors open. I wish I'd thought to bring a flashlight. I know exactly where to find them back at … I almost said "home" but Brighton Court is my home now.

"So sorry," I call out into the stairwell. "My fault. I think."

"Lucy?" It's Dirk.

"Yes."

"Are you alright?"

"Is Davey there?" It's a voice I don't recognise, soft, with an Irish lilt to it.

"Who's that?"

"Amaryllis. Ask Davey. He fixed the fuses last time."

"I'm trying to study!" It's another voice, a young woman.

"What about my lesson plans?" says another stranger.

"We've got visitors for dinner and the oven's going cold." It's an older woman. She doesn't sound happy.

"Sorry!" I sing out again. "I'll phone an electrician. Any recommendations?"

"S'okay. Davey here. I'm onto it."

"While you're all here, I'm Lucy in number Forty One and you're all invited to drinks on Saturday night from six o'clock. Did you get your invitations? Spread the word. Everyone at Brighton Court is welcome, with Plus Ones."

"Hmmph."

"Thanks."

At least some of the voices are warm.

"Do I bring something?" It's the woman with the accent again.

"Just yourselves."

I'm about to close the door when a flashlight illuminates the stairwell above me, as if we're on the set of a television crime series.

"Lucy?"

It's Dirk. "Need one of these?"

"I do, actually. Thank you so much." He gives me one of his flashlights, warm from his hand, then leans in close, so deliciously close my heart jolts. Will he kiss me in this darkness? I'm ready. I lean in and tilt my face to his.

"There's orange fluff on the side of your nose," he says.

I step back, blush and rub it off. Yes. A bit of pompom.

"Oh. I've been making Lucy's Lamps. I was testing them. Stupid. I must have overloaded the circuits or something."

"Happened to me, too, two days after I moved in. It's Brighton Court, not you. This is an old building."

"Who is Davey, Dirk? What's he doing? I guess I'd better come and learn how to fix the lights if they go out this often."

"Good idea."

I follow Dirk down the stairs, as if we're children in an Enid Blyton adventure, down and down below the entrance level, down to where it's spooky, with clanking pipes and mysterious old panels of switches. I creep closer to Dirk, close enough to smell his aftershave and a trace of moth repellent in his suit coat, close enough for a cuddle, but all the lights blink back on again, and all the magic evaporates.

I introduce myself to Davey, apologise, and go to hand the flashlight back to Dirk, but he presses it back into my hand and closes his fingers around mine.

"Keep it," he says, his voice so low and close it's my heart that lights up.

Davey shows us a switchboard and points at the place that shows the problem started at Forty One.

"Did you use a power board?" he says.

"A big one. It's my business. Cottage industry. Lucy's Lamps."

Suddenly, we're plunged back into darkness.

"That'll be one of your lamps. Short circuit. Get a few boards with trip switches, will you? Can you go and unplug them all now?"

Dirk accompanies me up the stairs.

"Need a hand?"

"You're so kind, Dirk. I know, you'd 'do it for anyone' but it doesn't mean I'm not grateful."

He laughs and stays silent, but he smiles down at me and I'm sure of it. There's a buzz between us, a little spark, an excellent development. Dirk is almost flirting.

When the lights flicker back on again, and stay on, he comments on my handiwork, my lamps, my hobby-come-business that made me a reasonable income after Bart insisted I stop working for the network – so I could work exclusively for him, as it turned out. Until he found someone better; someone even more compliant.

"Quite unusual lamps," says Dirk.

"Are you being rude about them?"

"They're quirky. I like them."

"This one's for Jill. Would you like one, too? Swap you one for the flashlight."

"They're a bit …"

"Creative? Unique? Interesting? Gorgeous? They're works of art, Dirk. They're quite popular. They sell quite well. What's your favorite color? I custom make them in all colors, shapes and sizes. Show me your place and we'll come up with something you love."

"Now?"

"Why not?"

"Not now. Another time, maybe."

"Okay. But you'll still join me for drinks this weekend?"

"That's the plan."

On Saturday evening, I twist my hair into a chignon and pin it in place with a simple mother-of-pearl clasp with three diamantes. My new cream silk blouse and dark pencil skirt stare back at me in the full-length oval mirror – demure, perfect good taste.

There's that little patter of nerves I always get before hosting a party. All is cleaned and ready. Will anyone turn up?

My mother's carriage clock strikes six, then a quarter past, and ticks on in the silence.

I rotate the gin and whisky bottles around and around on the shelves, adjust the champagne glasses for the fourteenth time, sigh and stare out the window. Nobody has RSVPd. How rude. I invited Dirk in person, and left the little notes under his and everyone else's doors. Jill at least

declined on the spot. Donna is upstate for a dog show. How could thirty
two households be so uniformly inconsiderate?

I know some of the neighbors are home. As I prepared the finger food,
the appetizers and cheese plate, I heard gentle creaks, their feet in the
corridors, snatches of conversation, muted radio and television
broadcasts, someone practicing a violin, out of tune, repetitive. It brought
back memories of my own childhood resisting piano scales, of my
Phoebe with her shiny, squeaky clarinet.

Phoebe didn't even acknowledge the invitation I sent her by
phone. Perhaps she's changed her number, dropped me forever. Was I so
dreadful a mother? I'm so ready to find out, to apologize, to see it all
from my daughter's point of view. We'd been so close, flesh of my flesh,
the weight of her in my arms and on my lap, her tiny hand in mine, so
keen to cuddle and learn from me, then the sharing of clothes and
handbags, even teaching her to drive. We got through all of that. I
thought we'd be best friends forever, my dream baby, a model child and
a teen without too many tantrums. So what did I do wrong?

Chapter 16

Dirk

I remove the portion of Mrs West's baked chicken from the oven and serve it for myself with a potato salad with dill, an excellent accompaniment.

It's been days since I heard from Lucy, not that I'm counting.

I select the music – Chopin – calm. What music would Lucy enjoy? Something brash and fun no doubt – ragtime, for dancing, or brassy big band, or even rock'n'roll.

A memory of a thumping good time arises unbidden, of a party back when Millie and I were students, back before everything – a fifties party, with the women all in full skirts that swirled out and showed their legs the faster we twirled them. We men had slicked back our hair, and our skinny ties swung out as we danced in our short-sleeved shirts and stovepipe trousers. *Rock Around the Clock*. We drank too much, deafened by music cranked up on a huge stereo, slaves to the beat. The only thing to eat were cubes of cheese, and the next day was a nightmare. I wonder what's happened to all those people. I know about Millie and Raymond of course. Both gone now. Walt and some of the boys are still friends.

On my gleaming dining table, the chicken cools. Potato salad clags in my throat. Though I eat it every Saturday night, I'm suddenly tired of it, and for the first time, it's far too quiet in here.

Saturday. Something. Saturday drinks. My neighbor's party! Lucy invited me in person and followed up with a card. What time did she say? Six? It's seven o'clock now, and I have no bunch of flowers for her, nothing.

The one night I had a decent invitation, I've blown it. I wouldn't have minded meeting a few neighbors. The only ones I've met so far are Lucy and Davey, and now I've stood Lucy up. It's beyond stupid. It's rude.

Outside my apartment, dusk has settled around the building and light rain begins to drizzle. I settle on a navy polo neck and jeans, the kind of thing Jamison might wear on a golfing weekend with business associates. I'm grateful I don't have to drive anywhere. I pluck the white roses from the vase on the dining table Mrs West left for me earlier in the week.

I stand and check myself in the long mirror. Is it rude to arrive so late? I can invent an excuse but it's best to get on with it and apologize. I rush down the stairs.

I stop outside Lucy's door. It's suspiciously quiet. I lift my hand but hesitate, knuckles poised.

When it swings open, a rush of welcome smells assails me – of cooking, the kind my cardiologist would forbid – of perfume and bubble bath and chocolate cherries in liquor – of mysterious alluring scents which beg to be explored.

Lucy stands, hand on the door, as if shocked to see me. She is beautifully attired, elegant as the hostess, but for an instant her expression is bleak, then unreadable, and a moment later, her smile is back and she is supremely in command, poised.

I hand over the roses. I regret not taking a moment to wrap the stems. They drip. But I wanted to get on with it. I'm late enough already.

Lucy's delighted. She takes them from me, and dips her face towards the blooms and inhales deeply, giving me a glimpse of the skin of the back of her neck, so achingly elegant I shiver. She whips her eyes to mine, smiles, then leads me into her kitchen where she grabs a vase, adds water, plunges the stems deep inside and sets them on a side table where an ornate mirror doubles their volume. She places her fingers inside my elbow – an intimate gesture – and drags me forwards.

Lucy's apartment is generously furnished, mostly with classic, old-fashioned pieces recovered in bright fabrics. There's a chaise lounge, a Persian rug, and three of her lamps in the corner, quirky. Interesting.

"I'm so glad you'll catch the last of the twilight, my second favorite time of day," she says. "Sunset is the greatest show on earth, don't you think?" Her eyes are magnetic. Lucy is a flame and I am the moth.

But there's something very wrong. Am I the only one here? Jill was right. I am entrapped.

"Drink? I've just opened the champagne. Won't you join me?"

"Just one." I've come this far. "Am I really your only guest, Lucy, or am I so late that everyone else has left?"

"They're very rude. Or very busy. Or very forgetful." She cocks her head and presses the stem of a fine glass into my hand, tapping her own to it so it rings in the silence. She pulls me down beside her on the couch, her eyes to the large window. Deep lavender clouds soften the view of jagged, dark buildings. Lines of streetlights dot the distant hills, and more and more lit windows pierce the darkness, with, here and there, the blue-black flicker of television screens and a few early Christmas lights.

"Sorry I'm so late, Lucy. I'm not accustomed to receiving invitations from beautiful women."

"Oh. Too charming by far, Dirk; Dr Suave. You'd be on everyone's invitation list, I have no doubt." Her eyes dance as she takes a long sip.

"You're wrong," I say as I match her sip and take another sip of my own, the cold bubbles sharp on my palate. "I keep to myself."

"Something to eat?" She's up and back beside me with one of the silver trays. There are blinis with smoked salmon and dill. My favorite. The tray is full. I take one, and even though I've eaten, it's good. I reach for another.

"Tell me about Brighton Court," she says as she refills my glass. The last of the sunset glints off the buildings, changes to a burnt orange. She stares out at the view, making it easier for me to talk. Millie was good at mixing. I don't do small talk.

"What you see is what you get," I say.

"Sorry?"

"Post war, modern, walk up, no elevator. Solid. Excellent position, close to shops and transport, not too far from all the buzz of downtown. Perfect for an old widower like me."

"Mmmm."

"It was all Jill, Jamison and Dee's idea, and my friend Walt's, but I like it." Lucy's such a good listener, I'm talking again without thinking. I never spoke much, busy listening deeply to my patients. Living alone now, I barely need my voice anymore. I clear my throat. Words don't come to me.

"Great choice," she says. "I love it here." She taps her glass against mine again, and holds my eyes. Her laughter is like rain on new leaves, like glitter on a Christmas tree, like something sweet, something I've missed, like fresh air or a summer storm after a long drought. I want to hear her laugh again and again.

Her hand is on my arm. Without thinking, I flex my bicep and her eyes widen.

It's on the tip of my tongue to tell her about Millie, and now, about Jamison's unexpected invitation that I invest in his business. Lucy is a brilliant listener, all dark eyes and subtle nods.

"Winning is about defence as much as attack; about foreseeing the risks and avoiding them," I say to myself as much as to her. It's hard to stay on my guard. Lucy is the star here, and I am a comet, drawn closer and closer into her orbit.

"More champagne?" She's already poured it, before I can object, and it twins perfectly with the blini. I eat more.

"Tell me about yourself," I say. Millie would be proud of me.

"Oh. What you see is what you get."

It's such an invitation. Who could resist running their eyes over her, the poise, the curves, her grace, her hair and makeup – so subtle yet so alluring – her smile so ready to widen into a laugh, for me, about me, who knows? I don't care.

The talk flows. I've never thought of myself as a conversationalist, but Lucy has me talking about all kinds of things, about travel and food and wine and sport. No, I don't do much of any of them anymore, but she brings back treasured memories.

"But tell me about you," I try again. This time it's me who stands to top up our glasses.

"Do you know, we could walk together sometimes," she says.

This is what Jill warned me about. Lucy is definitely reeling me in.

"Well, it could be fun," she tries again. "You know you need me."

"Absolutely not. You'll tell me what I can and can't eat and drink, and then redecorate. Run a mile..."

"That's exactly the point, Dirk. You can't run a mile. But you could. With me as your personal trainer, everything is possible."

"Everything? That's false advertising."

"Trust me."

"Over my dead body."

"Exactly."

"I'm fine, thank you. I already have a personal trainer."

"Of course you do, a man like you."

I don't tell her it's my daughter. Let her think what she wants about me. Let her think I'm a silver wolf. Or is it fox?

I stand and offer her the spread of cheeses and fruit and nuts. She takes some cashews and insists I sit on the couch again beside her. It's an elaborate, ornate puffy blue thing with stripes and a carved wooden frame, painted gold.

Outside, it's growing dark, the lights of the city blinking on. Inside, the room is elegant in pale pinks and pale greens. The three small, rose-red lamps in the corner cast a warm glow.

"Beautiful room," I say.

"I salvaged this sofa from my shabby chic business. I had to give up the rest of my projects. Except the lamps, of course. So glad you like them."

I nod.

"I haven't given Jill or Mrs B their lamps yet. I'd hoped they'd come to my party."

The sofa is slightly outrageous, gilded and Georgian, ornate rather than functional.

"I love being creative, reworking old lamp frames and bases and giving them an extra life; and it's a nice little earner. You can follow Lucy's Lamps on Instagram, Dirk." She whips out her phone and flicks through to show me photo after photo of whimsical side lamps of all shapes and colors, some with tassels, some with fringes, others with bobbles.

"Very creative," I say. "I avoid social media. I was a country doctor."

"Hmmm," she says. "I can see why you'd hide. But you're not practicing now. You could learn something new, Doc."

I'm relieved I don't have to explain that I already knew enough about all my patients.

"Let's try ten questions, Dirk," she says, as if it's a dare. "If you don't like me after ten questions, I'll leave you alone."

"I have no idea what you're talking about."

"I'll go first. Here's a question: What do you miss most about your life before Brighton Court? I'll tell you my answer. I miss my rosebuds, the white ones, in springtime. My rose bushes lined the drive and the front fence, and the curving path to the front steps. When the first white blossom burst out, I knew all the rest would soon follow. I miss that garden more than anything."

I see it then, in my mind – Lucy's fine house, and her loss. You'd never know she'd lost a thing from the way she carries herself, like some kind of princess, in love with every moment, as if life is just a lark.

I'm about to ask her why she left her last home, but she speaks first.

"It's your turn, Dirk. Tell me just one thing you miss about life before Brighton Court."

Millie's the obvious one, but I'm not going there. Maybe it's because Lucy mentioned the scent of roses, but my mind pitches further back; way, way back in time to my grandmother's orchard, and the fragrance of orange blossom in the evenings, the night turning violet and velvet around me as I watched the slim petals drop, white on the dark grass. When did I last smell those citrus trees? Fifty years ago? More? But they are real again, here in this elegant room with Lucy beside me, waiting for my words, and I am innocent as a small boy, with all my life ahead of me.

Lucy's face is expectant in the soft glow as the night grows darker. She's reading me.

"Orange blossoms," I say. I clear my throat, defensive, but I'm no longer small. She doesn't have to understand. I press on. "The last time I saw my grandmother was in her orchard. We waved goodbye and we never went back."

"Here? Out west?"

I nod. Lucy waits for more.

"My grandparents owned a ranch. My father was a cowboy, but his big brother got all the land when our grandparents died, so Dad bought a truck and packed us in; little Jill, my mom and me, and we drove east.

Dad made our life in the Midwest, driving that truck here, there and everywhere."

"Did he miss the land?"

"Never said so, not that he ever said much. He was away most of the time, and when he wasn't, he was lecturing Jill and me to work harder at school and make the most of all the opportunities he never had. But that loss was always there, as if our own life was being lived on the sidelines and the real world was back at the ranch and in that sweet orchard."

"Is that why you've come back west?"

"Dee, Jamison and Jill insisted when Millie died."

"Your wife died?"

I nod and wait for the wave of grief to hit me again, but for once it hovers way out on the dark horizon and stays away. I breathe.

"I'm sorry," she says.

"Don't bake me casseroles," I say.

She almost chokes on her champagne, sees I'm serious, and answers.

"I already told you, I'm not much of a cook. So you came west to avoid casseroles?"

I nod.

"I was tired of running into Millie's friends and all my old patients."

Her eyes have softened, as if she might understand.

"You're still a doctor?"

"Was. I just sold the practice. Fresh start."

"Great place for a fresh start, Dirk, Brighton Court. Great location. Particularly great neighbors." She touches her glass against mine again and we laugh.

"But what about your own friends in Franklin? Don't you miss them?"

I shrug. Some died. Mostly my friends were Millie's friends. I worked all the time. Is this why I've come west? To learn to actually live? Maybe to learn to love. Dee keeps suggesting it.

"Do you know, Dirk; I feel like I know you; like I've seen you before somewhere. Like maybe we knew each other when we were younger. Were you always a country doctor?"

"It was never my dream," I say. "I started out playing soccer, a goalie. I was good. Got myself a college scholarship."

"Here?"

Suddenly Lucy's hand hovers in my hair. I like it there. To my surprise, I neither flinch nor move away.

"You were on tv, weren't you?" she says, her voice low and fast. "I worked at Network Eight, behind the scenes. Hair and makeup. I got less than five minutes with each person, but I had a feeling we'd met before, Dirk."

I nod.

"Bad head injury," I say.

"You'd blacked out for days," she says. "You were a star, Dirk! Dirk 'the doc' O'Connell. D.O'C. Amazing! Sports champ. College scholarships galore. Top of the class. You saved that impossible goal for the nation when we beat Brazil. Hit your head on the goal post. We replayed that scene for days promoting your interview. Everyone worried you'd die, and when you came to, days later, everyone wanted your story, and our network got the scoop. I did your make-up. I was new. You were one of my first real challenges. I was a bit in awe, to be honest. I wound a big, white fake bandage over your scar. Do you remember that?"

I nod slowly. I find her in my memory – cheer leader cute, and very professional. Very effective with me. I scared myself with my own scar, but she made me presentable in no time flat.

"So, you went ahead and made your initials a reality – became a real doctor. That's so impressive. Fancy a star like you turning up here, at Brighton Court!"

Her fingers are back in my hair, gentle, skilled, like a hairdresser, a make-up artist – someone accustomed to having her way with people's hair and faces. She leans closer, so close, her fingers in my hair, gentle, insistent. She finds it, and runs a finger along the old scar, almost reverently. Her dark eyes search mine. I want to lean towards her, to brush my lips against hers, to wipe the pity right off them. Yes, I was frustrated when it happened – angry with myself. I'd been top of my game, with all the strength and confidence every young man takes for granted. I lost it all – the promise of my skills and team leadership – in one head-cracking moment. The disbelief, the shame of it, the shadows … they lingered for years.

But I picked myself up after that injury. I made a new life for myself –
not the one I would have chosen, but one I'm proud enough of.

She's watching me closely, waiting, her fruity perfume tantalizing, her
eyes on mine, on my lips.

I've misread Lucy. It's not pity. It's admiration.

Chapter 17

Dirk

I am never impetuous. But I do it. I lean forwards and capture the fullness of Lucy's lower lip, warm and sweet with her wine, and draw it between my own, as sparks and fireworks shoot through my body.

She breaks away and retrieves her glass. I want more.

The shadow of her touch on my scalp lingers, so intimate in this elegant room, so welcome. Nobody touches me like this. The broken kiss floats between us through too much distance. I want more.

Decades fall away, and memories return. Of the much younger Lucy, so much more glamorous than the nurses and doctors who'd been tending to my wound, though equally serious, equally professional in the too-bright room, brandishing her brushes and potions.

"I asked you out," I say. "Before that interview, way back then. You never gave me an answer."

Lucy busies herself at her dining table.

"You were amazing," she says. "Such a star. Everyone wanted you to recover. You were quite the hero, Dirk O'Connell. Do you know, I'm actually blushing. I had a crush on you. So did half the State. And I would have gone out with you, but we had a code of conduct at the network. And Bart, my ex-husband, had just cornered me for himself.

Codes of conduct never applied to him. Still don't. Besides, you disappeared."

"Soccer was never going to last forever. Too many injuries. So I went back to the books and got my medical degree."

"Do you miss being a doctor? Will you start up another clinic?"

I shake my head. She's waiting, but I won't go there – all the sleepless nights, the never-ending need, the Christmases I had to leave my family's table to tend to the injured; the senseless pain of people who repeated the same mistakes over and over. I could never work hard enough to cure all the world's ills. I gave it my best, but every death felt like my failure.

"It's a wonder Jamison and Dee want me anywhere nearby, that we have any kind of relationship at all. I knew what it was like to grow up with an absent father – his truck was his home – and I still went ahead and worked throughout most of Jamison and Dee's childhoods."

Lucy moves closer to me on the couch. She bridges the distance between us. Her hand hovers like a butterfly, pale against my forearm, but I warn her away with my eyes, and she leans away again.

"I'm sorry if my questions bother you," she says.

"There's no law against asking questions. Some say 'the unexamined life' is not worth living."

She nods. "Socrates," she says. "Friend of yours?" Her eyes dance, challenging me, laughing at me.

I want to grab her and pull her close. I want her fingers back in my hair, her hands all over me. But she's a neighbor. So much could go wrong, and if it does, we'd still have to see each other every day.

So instead, I stand and hold out my hand for a formal shake. Even after all that champagne, I can trust my own self-discipline.

The dusk darkens to magenta and exits, and I must do the same.

"Excellent sunset you put on for me," I say, attempting banter. It's not very good.

"I expect you'd have seen it too," she counters. "Or are you on the sunrise side?"

"Sunrise," I say.

Her eyes dance over my face, her smile a question I won't ask. I'm not offering anyone a sunrise. Not yet.

I place my empty glass on her windowsill. I stayed for just one – one bottle, I see – and it is high time I left. I've already leaned far too close to this flame. I won't mention it to Jill.

"Take some blinis, Dirk," she insists, and presses another full tray into my hands. "Can't let them spoil."

It's only when I'm back in my own place that I realize what she's done. I'll have to return her silver tray. This Lucy is exactly the kind of woman Jill warned me about, a predator. But maybe I want to be caught.

Back inside my own apartment, it is too quiet, too neat; my furniture too perfect. Imagine Lucy remembering me from way back then, from that television interview, when my soccer career collapsed. I shake my head and touch my scar, flat now, and practically invisible.

Lucy already knows too much about me. What I regret is not asking her more about herself.

Chapter 18

Lucy

When I let Dirk out, he's apologetic. His eyes duck back to me, as if he fears he's offending me, as if he's reluctant to leave. Perhaps he's uncomfortable alone with me. Does he think I tricked him into attending, and only invited him?

It's not the first time I've hosted parties when most invitees fail to show, so I don't mind. Bart's colleagues, the journalists, were notoriously fickle. They'd either be too busy filing their next story, or out elsewhere, at some media event or free show, downing more free alcohol.

I'm just about to turn off my lamps when there's a quiet knock at my front door.

Did Dirk have a change of heart, or leave something behind? I open it with a smile, to a tiny woman with long white hair and pale purple glasses, the lenses thick as coke bottles.

She pushes one pale hand out to me, tentatively. In her other, she cradles an ornate bottle of something the color of lemonade.

"Amaryllis Logan," she says in a breathy whisper as she hands it over. "From Thirty Three. I hope I'm not too late?"

"Not at all, Amaryllis. Come right in."

She hands over the bottle.

"Elderflower wine," she says. "I make it myself. It's alcoholic, just a little."

"Amazing! Can I pour you some?"

She nods, and exclaims over my apartment and my lamps, so I ask her what colors she likes and promise to make her one. Everything about Amaryllis is tiny, but her joy is unmistakable.

"There's nothing like a handmade gift, is there?" she says, and we toast the thought. Her wine is slightly fizzy, not too sweet and not too sour. It's delicately delicious.

Over the next hour, I learn more about Brighton Court, and about her. A popular book reviewer, Amaryllis plays a small Celtic harp and sings along – ancient songs. She even composes new ones, with her own lyrics.

"Please don't take it personally I arrived so late," she says, her voice quiet. "I usually don't turn up until a party is almost over. I'm an introvert. Too much company upsets me for days, but a quiet conversation is lovely, don't you think?"

She clams up as she studies my décor, nodding with conviction.

"I love what you've done in here," she says.

"How long have you lived at Brighton Court, Amaryllis?"

"All my life," she says.

Before I can ask her about who lived here before me, and how it was decorated, she questions me again.

"What brought you to Brighton Court, Lucy, a stylish woman like you?"

I laugh and thank her for the compliment and shake my head.

"I'm no model. I started taking more care of my appearance when I became invisible," I say.

"Invisible?"

The alcohol and Amaryllis's earnest, agreeable company loosen my tongue. Donna knows me through and through, knows everything, but Amaryllis is a neighbor, maybe a new friend. I hope so. It's the first time I've voiced my experience like this, put words around my losses.

"I just got divorced, Amaryllis. This is my fresh start. I love it here. I'm just renting, but if I could, I'd buy this place. I absolutely love it."

"Brighton Court is special. You said you felt invisible?"

She's listening, waiting. Do I share my story with this kind stranger? She's a gentle person. I begin.

"I became invisible somewhere between the birth of my daughter, Phoebe and her graduation. She and Bart were always out, Phoebe with school and friends, and Bart with who knew who, his suit bag on the hanger and briefcase at the door, or not."

Phoebe had always been so happy to sit in my lap for a story, or to have her hair done, or to go try on dresses with me and test them for twirl, or make chocolate cakes with me and lick the bowl.

Then Phoebe's eyes became hard, in high school, and she'd rather be anywhere than at home with me.

"One night when neither Bart nor Phoebe was home, I was so beyond sad, I got angry with myself. I'd been so busy making their lives easy, my own life had disappeared. I was an endless support system for my husband and child. If I'd been a heroine in a novel, nobody would have bothered to read it. What a waste of a beautiful life!

"I'd once had dreams. I just couldn't remember what they were. I ran on auto all day in a blur of chores, then zoned out on pay tv. No wonder Bart and Phoebe were bored with me. I bored myself.

"Meal times once anchored us. Around our table, we'd swap news of challenges and triumphs and laughter and tears. But those times became erratic. I'd have to guess at their news from their accusations and demands."

"Demands?"

"Like 'We're out of eggs, Mom,' or 'Who ate the last of the peanut butter?' or 'I'll need four shirts for this trip.'"

"You're not a slave, Lucy," said Amaryllis.

"I was the ghost who made everything possible."

"That makes me so sad for you."

I pull up. Have I said too much?

"Don't be sad for me. I've had this beautiful fresh start."

She smiles at me, sincere, expectant.

"Once I realized I was invisible, I thought long and hard, and in my large and clean and silent house, I searched through my cupboards. No wonder I'd become invisible to my most beloved people in the world. My clothes were old and worn and faded and out of date, and the woman in the mirror was sad and ordinary."

"You are not sad and ordinary, Lucy."

"Oh no. I took action straight away. I went to the largest mall I could find, in the centre of town, and found a hairdresser who could do my hair immediately. I gave that hairdresser complete freedom. I surrendered utterly as I lay my head back in the basin. The warmth of the water down my scalp; the tropical smell of the shampoo; the head massage under his firm fingers. I sighed out loud.

"It was so strange to see my own wet head, slick as a seal's when I sat and stared at the mirror. I was a make-up artist at a tv network before I became a housewife. I'd transformed so many others in my early career, and now, this stranger in a black cloak stared back at me with big, serious eyes, high cheek bones, expressive mouth and my skin still smooth enough. Smooth enough for what, though? I smiled at myself. I sat higher in my chair. I realized; Bart didn't know what he was missing. But by then, it was too late for our marriage."

There's an awkward silence.

"I should go," she says.

"No. No. Please, Amaryllis. Tell me how you make your wine."

It's a long process. Amaryllis tells me she gathers the berries from a friend she visits every year in the east during the fall, then there's the right amount of sugar, testing acidity, the temperature … It's interesting, but I stifle a yawn.

"I'm boring you."

"Not at all, Amaryllis."

"Oh. Look at the time. I probably should have given you the short version. Not everyone is as passionate about elderberry wine as I am. But you know, I do love the idea that you can bottle the sunshine."

"And it tastes so good! You must show me."

"Not tonight. I need to get back to Merlin."

"Oh?"

"My old cat. He frets if I'm gone too long. You must come down and meet him. Any time. I'm always home, except in September when I pick the berries."

I clean up and turn out the lights, aglow with my new friendships. I love to think that Dirk is above me – a fine, fit, upstanding, *attractive*, retired doctor – and Amaryllis below; so interesting and welcoming.

In the quiet hours of the night, in my apartment, my mind drifts. I'm not used to living alone. In those first few months after fleeing Bart, I lived with Donna. On her sofa, rolling up my bedding and stashing it underneath each morning. We took turns cooking, washing and sorting our clothes, shopping.

If I wanted to rant and rave about Bart, Donna ranted with me, and nodded without stop. If I wanted silence, she was fine with that, too, or we'd chat about our working day, about the lives we'd unpacked, guessing at the details. I should have married Donna, we joked, more than once, and in that way of friends. I even worked out when it was time to leave, though she never said a word.

By then, along with the money from the sale of my shabby chic furniture van, I'd saved enough for rent, and was accustomed to living in a smaller space, without my workshop – so many projects half-finished, more shabby than chic. My life had shrunk. My needs became simpler. Food, shelter, money to live on, and working out how to reconnect with Phoebe.

In the darkness, I drag my mind to the present, to the generous proportions of these rooms, the ceiling rose above me in the centre of the room, the ornate light fitting. It glows like a pearl, like a milky opal. Calm.

I wonder who else has lived in this apartment. It's more than eighty years old, and unlike Dirk's perfectly renovated penthouse, many of the features are original. I love the old bones of this place, the polished floorboards, and especially the window seat where I often sit and stare at the busy view, of so many other buildings and windows, some with the blue and white flicker of television screens, others with Christmas lights winking. Some are empty or dark – the residents deep in the slumber that evades me. Some are lit with the romantic golden glow of side lamps like the ones I make, while others are bright with white lights, like workshops, dance studios and offices.

I tiptoe out to the living room and peer out. A full moon stares across the city, huge and sombre, and I perch on the wooden window seat, my shadow streaming out into the moon, a ghostly silhouette. I put out my arms as if to spook myself, but I can only laugh. There is nothing sinister about this room, and though I miss Phoebe, and the glory years of Bart's

and my marriage, and my years with my parents – all too short – I am
full of hope about the future, now that I've found this new home at
Brighton Court.

I will make a cover for this seat, once I paint the room. The dark timber
of the seat is ominous, a little dented and stained.

It's only then that it occurs to me that the window seat might open, and
in the darkness, I prise open the heavy lid. It's completely black inside, a
cavern. I am thrilled. Tomorrow, I will move my lamp-making tools
from the spare bedroom and fit them all into this bonus space. Yes, I
miss my old workbench, purpose built by Delta Kitchens, a network
sponsor, with drawers for my tools and fabric and a mighty expanse of
flat space for cutting, but the floor will have to do. I've been kneeling on
a rolled-up towel.

I tiptoe back to bed and sleep without dreams.

Early next morning, when I open the seat, I find three dead moths, a
shrivelled-up spider, the torn corner of a yellowed newspaper from 1979
and a rusty paperclip. I wipe it all out with a damp sponge and let it dry.
It is only as I am settling the heavy portable glue gun into the rear corner
that I notice the flooring wobbles.

Loath to damage my tools, or lose glue sticks and other supplies into
the gap that opens, I peer further inside, and discover a whole floorboard
loose. Curious, I wiggle it back and forth then give it a bang and a yank
and it is free, the space beneath it dragging my attention deeper. If only I
could see around corners. Gingerly I reach inside. There's something
there, velvety and heavy. It falls away from my flailing fingers and my
heart rate spikes. It can't be a rat. It's cold. My stomach jumps. A dead
rat?

I can't resist. I reach inside again and extend my whole body as far as I
can, the edge of the window box hard against my ribs. If it is a dead rat, I
want it out of there. I manage to pinch an edge of the thing and draw it
closer, and closer again, until I can reach my fingers around it. It's
awkward and surprisingly heavy. I haul it up and out and sit, the deep
grey pouch in my lap.

I untie the string and unfold the edges of the old cloth and gasp. They
shine and wink like a school of fish in the early morning light –

teaspoons of every shape and size, chinking as I turn them over in my hands. Why were they hidden? Who lived here? A thief?

Chapter 19

Lucy

I'm out walking next day when I spot a taller man, just like my handsome neighbor. He's way ahead of me again, up the hill, so I quicken my pace.

It's my lucky day. The traffic lights go red and the man in the coat is stuck for a few minutes while I catch up.

I'm puffing when I reach him, elated it really is Dirk.

"Well, hello, neighbor," I say, and he turns to me and breaks into a smile. "Where are you going, Doc?"

"Nowhere in particular. Thanks for the drinks the other night."

"Glad you enjoyed yourself," I say. "Don't you just love this neighborhood? So many old trees. How are you liking it?"

"Fine. What is this? An inquisition?"

"It's called 'conversation,' Dirk. It won't kill you. I'll leave you alone if you want. We don't need to walk the same way."

"No, no. I've never been good at small talk."

"It doesn't have to be 'small.' We can go deep, Dirk O'Connell. Ten questions, remember? The big ones. Like 'what brings you the most joy.' That's an important one, don't you think?"

"Hmmm. Joy. Hard to define. Never thought about it."

"But it matters."

"What? You think life is about chasing joy?"

"Oh wow. You've skipped straight to the meaning of life. That's the really big one."

"Alright. So we'll backtrack to joy. What brings you the most joy, Lucy?"

"That's cheating, making me go first, but I'll tell you, because for me, that's the easiest question of all. Just about everything brings me joy. Like walking here with you, getting to know you better."

He stares at me as if I just made it up. Old cynic.

"Dirk, I feel joy from the moment I wake and stretch and see the sun has risen again, to the moment I'm back in bed at the end of a full day, warm and cosy and drowsy, with a good book. I'll never stop if I tell you everything that brings me joy. I love to talk – that's evident – I love my first mouthful of cereal in the morning, my first sip of coffee, laughing with friends, walking. I truly do. You already know I love roses. I love Brighton Court, the way those apartments have held so many other lives – I actually found some old silver teaspoons hidden in my apartment last night. Can you imagine? Now it's your turn."

"Okay. I guess my kids are okay. Yes. They turned the love around somewhere. Maybe when they knew they'd lose their mom. I never thought I'd see them care so much. And afterwards, after Millie died, they didn't just keep in touch. Dee practically moved in with me. I kept working, like a maniac, trying to block everything out, and she quietly cleared out all Millie's things. Millie was everywhere; always had been. Jamison came out every second weekend to help. Jamison and Dee talked about me as if I wasn't there. I wasn't really. The clinic was my retreat, my salvation. Nothing there changed. Phone kept ringing. I'd get home and Dee would force me to eat something, and they'd talk about the future, toss up ideas."

"I'm pleased for you, Dirk."

"You're pleased for me?"

"I'm jealous, really."

"Jealous?"

I frown. I can't help it. My chin actually wobbles. I think I'm going to cry.

Dirk, the gentleman, slows his pace, touches my wrist, brings his gaze to mine, drops his voice, conspiratorially.

"Do you want to sit, Lucy? Need to talk about this? Want a coffee? Or a drink?"

It's four o'clock in the afternoon. One minute I was striding along beside him, and now I'm a mess. How did he know I'd like to sit? My legs have crumpled. I want to curl up in a ball and howl.

He leads me into a wine bar, to a booth in the corner.

"Coffee? Wine?"

"Rosé, please. Just one. Rose-colored glasses and all that."

While he's at the bar, I pull a tissue out of my bag and clean myself up. The tears have stopped. I blow my nose, check my reflection in the little circular mirror Bart and I bought in Paris, a lifetime away. I'd hurl it under a bus but it's too useful and it's not every day a woman in love goes to Paris. The darkness is a mercy. I snap the mirror shut as Dirk returns with two large, stemmed glasses, one glowing ruby red, and the other, pale pink."

"I'm all ears," he says, as he slides my glass across the dark table. We tap our glasses together. I could get used to this, deep and meaningful conversations with my handsome neighbor, but I'm still not sure I should confide. I've only had three sips and the wine will loosen my tongue.

"You said you'd had a gutful of other people's problems, Dirk. I can see why your patients loved you. You're even more attractive when you stop and listen. Everyone in Franklin would have been lining up to confess. Not only their broken toes, but their broken hearts. Doctor Hot."

For the first time ever, he actually laughs; a deep belly laugh that fills the room. I love it. He actually twinkles at me and leans closer, then taps his glass against mine.

"What are we toasting?" I ask.

"Friendship?" he says. "This is not a consultation."

I sip a bit more. Okay. So maybe I gulped it a bit, and let the wine soften my defences, let my stiff shoulders drop until I lean a little closer to him. I feel safe with this man. I will let the monster out of the cage.

I hold his gaze.

"You've raised beautiful children, Dirk. My Phoebe's not like that. She doesn't want to know me. Blames me – for everything. She's all anger and accusations. I never knew she held so much hate in her heart."

"You know that's a stage that will likely pass."

"Doesn't seem to be passing any time soon."

"Sorry to hear it, Lucy, truly I am."

"I know why you were in demand, why your phone never stopped. You're a truly caring human being, Dirk. And you passed that on to your children."

He shrugs, turns the conversation back to me.

"Are you still in touch?" he asks.

"She never returns my messages, blocks my calls. She's in college. I guess she's busy."

He nods at me, ready for more.

"It's so hard, Dirk. Nobody wants to be in the firing line of rage. I've endured enough suffering lately. I only want to focus on joy, because these days Phoebe brings me everything but. I don't know what to do. I gave her my new address, to invite her over and offer her a drink or a meal. She ignores me. I try to stay in touch, but it's so hard.

"If that's a question, it's not my place to tell anyone what to do, but I can say from experience that anger is a symptom of grief, and that it dissipates."

"How long does it take?"

"I'm sorry I can't tell you. Everyone's different, Lucy. We're complex creatures. You've heard of the five stages of grief? Denial, anger, bargaining, depression, and acceptance."

"She has to go through all of that before she'll see me?"

"Maybe."

"Tell me some good news stories, Dirk. You must have seen plenty of patients go through things like this."

"Confidential."

"I'm not interested in the details of who they are. Help me, Dirk." It's out there on the table between us, the black cloud that settles on me too often, that sucks the joy out of everything.

"Maybe I'm just selfish, like she is," I say. "Maybe I passed that on. You were right about me the first time you met me. I'm divorced, but it wasn't my fault. I guess every divorcee says that. I don't think it was my fault. Maybe I was too selfish, maybe I crowded Phoebe, was too doting, and ignored Bart and his needs. And then I started my shabby chic business, and then the lamps. It kept me busy, scouring places for old lamp bases and material for recovering, and then giving workshops. People love to be creative."

He just nods at me, so I take another sip of wine and continue.

"I thought Phoebe would want more space in middle school and high school, more time with her friends like most teens. And I was there for her, after school and on weekends. I went to all her school concerts, so proud of her. I drove her places, gave her opportunities, hosted parties for her and her friends, baked healthy food for her playdates. I thought I did everything right. I certainly tried. And we were so close; closer than sisters. And now there's nothing."

"They're beautiful memories, Lucy."

I nod. I reach across the table and place my fingers beneath his hand, and he squeezes them. The words of the Beatles' song run through my brain, and I slip out of my side of the booth and into his, and I nestle beside him, so I can hold his hand properly, and be comforted.

He lets me rest my head against his arm, and he brings his own arm up and around my shoulders, until I'm safe as a cherished baby. I could get used to this.

A little warning bell sounds, deep inside me – that Dirk is a professional carer, that he really would do the same for anyone, that it isn't safe to fall in love, because I've just explained how much it hurts to lose somebody you love. And I never, ever, want to go there again. I'd be safer falling in love with my diamonds – my tiny beacons, so permanent in this changing world, so constant, so reliably brilliant.

Dirk walks me to my door. No kiss this time, but he's respectful. Attentive. I lean in and give him a hug and he hugs me in return, then springs back, and we smile at each other. He actually dips his head to his hand in a kind of salute as he backs away, still smiling.

I let myself in. I hang my coat on the hook, place my keys in the bowl on the hall table, and wander into the living room to gaze out at the city lights. It's peaceful in here.

Beyond the joy of getting to know my neighbors a little better, I love my apartment. I want to stay here forever.

Speaking with Dirk about Phoebe has calmed me.

Chapter 20

Dirk

Her hair is fragrant as she lets me hold her. Lucy Beston. My neighbor. Even in this dark corner, her diamonds sparkle in the dim light.

What have I done? I don't need another dependent. I'm finally doing alright; escaped the never-ending needs of too many patients in my family practice; got out of the home Millie worshipped, and all its demands. My housekeeper cooks my dinners. I see my old friends and children regularly. I have a new life.

Lucy is silent and her head becomes heavier. She has fallen asleep beside me. I sip my wine and think of how brittle she is; how all the chirpy talk about joy, the fun with hairstyles and makeup and elegant clothes is a mere facade. Beneath it all, Lucy Beston is as vulnerable as we all are, deep inside, and I smile. Humans. We're all just humans: Fantastic, complicated, treacherous, loving, lashing out, creative, stubborn humans. I shake my head and sip more wine, and swirl the many flavors around my tongue – bitter, sweet, metallic, musky, fruity, mellow, sharp.

Beside me, fast asleep, Lucy is vulnerable. I must be more careful. I hope I haven't led her on. There's nothing date-like about this, is there? We'd both walked miles. We were ready for a rest. That's all this is. A brief rest on a friendly, neighborhood walk.

She murmurs in her sleep. Is she faking it? She's smart. Jill is right, I should be on my guard.

I'm new to this, being single.

Lucy moves her head, then wakes and stiffens. She moves away from me, embarrassed.

"Oh no! Did I fall asleep? On you, Dirk? I'm so embarrassed! Did I drool?" She retreats to her side of the table. "Can I order us pizza or something? Or more wine?"

"I think I'll walk home now, Lucy."

"Of course." She wraps her scarf back around her neck, and at the door, I hold out her coat for her.

"Such a gentleman, Dirk. I'm really sorry I fell asleep on you. That's terrible."

"Relax," I say. "Sorry to be such boring company."

"Don't be ridiculous, Dirk. It was just such a weight off my mind, to talk about, you know, my … daughter."

I'm on my guard. Maybe it's all an act. Jill says the diamonds should be a warning to me; that Lucy has targeted me and if I let her under my skin she'll get a bull's eye – "a sweet and unsuspecting widower" is what Jill calls me.

Just then, Lucy's chin wobbles. Can she fake tears that well? She pushes a fingertip to her eyes and blinks.

"I'm so sorry, Dirk. I hate this vulnerability, the treachery of my emotions, cracking me wide open, letting out my grief for all the world to see. Does this pain ever go away?"

"It's okay," I say.

She's silent as we walk home. I let her slide her hand under my arm. It's companionable. There's nothing seductive about it. Jill doesn't know what she's talking about, and I'm no fool. Lucy lets go of me as we approach Brighton Court. At her door, she turns to me.

"I really can't thank you enough, Dirk." This Lucy is serious. She tries to smile, reaches up to cup my forearms in her gloved hands and squeezes. "I owe you. Brownies?"

"I thought you said you'd get me fit if we walked together. Brownies will cancel it out."

"Healthy brownies, then. Did you know you can make them with avocado? And beetroot. You can! I like baking. Give them to your children if you don't want them."

"Okay. Good night." My smile costs nothing. It's neighborly, nothing more.

Mrs West has been here. It's lasagne, her Tuesday specialty and the aroma fills the spaces, makes it feel like home. The place is spotless. I peer in the oven and refrigerator, hoping for more of that cherry pie. No luck.

There's an old-fashioned envelope in the middle of the dining table, propped against the vase of white flowers. It has a pale harlequin pattern all over it, and it's embossed with a huge gold, old-fashioned "RFF" in the top left hand corner. It's not my birthday.

I'm intrigued, and turn the envelope over, then sit back, remembering Jamison's comment about the fundraising ball for old Raymond, Rest In Peace. I've already agreed to attend, with Dee, but I use the mother-of-pearl and silver letter opener and slide out the thick, cream-colored card, the same pastel artwork outlined in a gold frame on the cover.

The lettering inside is also gold.

"Please join us for the launch of the Raymond Fontaine Foundation, honoring my late husband and raising money for medical research in his memory. Bettina Fontaine."

I exhale through pursed lips. Jamison must have given Bettina my new address. I hate charity events. This one is five hundred dollars a head. If people just donated the money and didn't bother with the venue and drinks and food, there'd be so much more money to go around.

But then I remember Raymond, diagnosed far too early with dementia, an old occasional lunch pal who could always be relied upon to share a few tips and jokes about the world when I needed alternative views to my father's.

My name appears below: "Doctor Dirk O'Connell plus one."

"Plus one" – that old chestnut. Bettina is a good sort. She made contact when Millie died. I wouldn't flatter myself to say she's interested in me, but I want her to be in no doubt that just because we're both single, we don't belong together, like a pair of old shoes. Bettina is admirable. Raymond worked in Big Pharma, and Bettina was once a chemist who transferred into sales before she and Raymond became an item. Bettina on the loose …

"Plus one." The words haunt me.

It's ages since I've gone to an event like this. Millie loved them. She'd go on the organising committees.

I'm about to throw the invitation in the trash, when I rest it back against the vase instead. Bettina at least deserves a hand-written apology. She and Raymond were a wonderful couple. Though I'd never be romantically interested in her – nor anyone else, ever again – I feel for her loss. And it's an honorable cause.

I could just make a donation. It's what I usually do.

A vision of Lucy in the emerald green ball gown emerges and won't go away. I ignore it.

The lasagne waits. I need dinner. I don't need more of Lucy in my life any more than I need Bettina.

Chapter 21

Lucy

When Linda from the network calls, I'm surprised. It's the first time I've heard from any of them. I guess that's what happens when you leave your old life behind. Does Linda even know about the divorce? Of course she must. News like that travels fast in tv land, I remember.

"We're doing a feature on ReUse," says Linda.

"Oh. That'll be great publicity for them! Thank you."

"We'd really like to round it out. They told us all about your generous donation, and Violetta wants to interview you."

"I don't think …"

"You know Violetta, Lucy. She's insisting. Think of the audience. ReUse will really benefit from your gift. Unless …"

I roll my eyes. An uneasy weight shifts in my gut. But what's the worst that could happen? Can I overlook my own personal humiliation for the sake of the charity?

"I've never been really comfortable in front of the camera, Linda. We're off-stage support, you and me."

"Come on, Lucy. It's for the charity, isn't it? We've filmed your shabby chic pieces – stunning by the way, you're so talented. Linda might ask you about your techniques. The viewers would be interested."

She might. Or she might not.

I know what Linda's doing, calming me down and buttering me up, but I do want ReUse to benefit from my gift. We might as well maximize the impact through the free publicity. Violetta's morning show attracts a big audience, and they're exactly the people who might want to pick up nice furniture at reasonable prices.

"As long as it's about the furniture and the charity. Okay." And as long as I don't have to see my Ex and the Minx.

Linda gives me the time slot. Phew. It's far earlier in the day than current affairs, Bart's specialty. I should be safe.

I barely sleep, remembering my old life. I'm uneasy, imagining what Violetta might do to me on screen. I get there in good time, assuming they'll send me in to get my hair and make-up done, but there's none of that. They leave me on a plastic chair until the last minute. I almost chicken out, but see that Chad's still on Violetta's team, filming. I'd love to hear about his kids. He was expecting another when I left.

Chad and I are good friends. We'd always catch up when I was around. He's filmed my old garden over many years, and all the Christmas backdrops using our own tree. He's watched Phoebe grow up.

Chad and I used to shake our heads between Violetta's victims, the never-ending stream of innocents, awe-struck in her presence, rabbits in the headlights.

I hated how Violetta would keep her cool as she'd impale them with her questions; make them squirm. Some never even realized, even a few politicians. Violetta showed up their duplicity, the fools.

I glance at my watch. Surely it's time for a break on set. But Chad gestures to me, headset on, plugged into the network, a creature of the machine, like Violetta. At least I'm wise to her. I even admire her, the way she carved out a place for herself and has kept it so long in this sexist industry.

I agreed to come along, but I wasn't expecting to be a focus of the story. I'm not prepared. If I'd realized they weren't going to show me the courtesy of doing my makeup for me, I could have done my own – armored up. I know how to use makeup like a shield.

I've been working overtime for Donna and Freya – haven't even had my hair styled in a while. I was hoping to be in the background of a shoot, a two-second cross over with a smile. Seems the network has other ideas.

I used to think that daytime tv was honorable – a lifeline of news and world affairs delivered to people trapped in their homes or in hospital beds. Chad always joked it was just window dressing between the ads.

I fear I'm about to see it laid bare. As Violetta beckons me across and an assistant wires me for sound, she leans back, at ease on her fancy sofa. She fixes me with the smile of a snake as my stomach disappears. Daytime tv is gladiatorial.

Chad points at the low chair opposite Violetta, and gives me a wry smile. It's probably the only program in America that still broadcasts live. There's no escape.

Violetta is pencil thin, perfectly dressed and coiffed, the high collar concealing her age. She's using all the tricks. I don't blame her – just wish I'd made my own preparations more carefully. Violetta is a star in her own right. If she'd been given a chance in Bart's roles, she'd be strutting the world stage, maybe even making a difference. Instead, she takes her bitterness out on those she interviews.

But I am here for the charity, ready to help them maximize their coverage. I may have nothing much left to lose, but I am no loser. If I go down, I do not go down alone.

I sit, straighten my back, and stare at the camera, but it's already rolling. Thanks for nothing, Chad, showing me stooped.

"Welcome, Lucy," says Violetta, with the slightest shake of her head, as if I'm pathetic.

"Thank you, Violetta," I say, with my own fake smile. I'm down, but not out. Not yet.

"You and Bart and Phoebe were the darlings of daytime tv for decades," she says. "Our viewers celebrated the change of seasons in your garden; Easter, Christmases and so much of your redecorating." She pauses as Chad's team shows replays of old footage of my beloved home, of Phoebe as a baby. The tech team has artfully edited Bart out. He's still on the payroll. Of course.

Thanks for nothing, bringing Phoebe into it. I did not agree to this.

"So why didn't you fight for your marriage?" says Violetta, and she settles back with her death stare. So that's how this is going to be. Okay. I'm no pushover.

"It takes two to make a relationship work, Violetta," I say.

"Did you focus too much on your shabby chic business and let yourself go?"

She is miming pity as Chad's lens drills into my face. She nods to make me nod, but I refuse.

"You won't ask Bart Hardenburg the same questions, will you, Violotta, because he's still on the network payroll," I say.

Violetta blinks. I push on, mindful of the timing.

"I am not guilty and I am not a victim – not Bart's, not yours, not anyone's," I say, perfectly composed.

"Difficult women lose their husbands," Violetta shoots back.

"Selfish men create difficult women," I parry.

"Lucy, what do you say to the rumors you're an alcoholic and a drug addict?"

"I'd say you invented that rumor right now, Violetta, because this interview isn't going how you planned. This shoot is supposed to be about the ReUse charity, which gifts good quality furniture to people in need, so that something can be salvaged from failed relationships and other tragedies. I am here to help benefit people who are bravely remaking their lives," I say. "And even if I was addicted to drugs and alcohol, which I'm not, there are programs available for people who need help, and many of your viewers will be bravely receiving therapy. How dare you try to shame me and shame them, Violetta?"

"You've let yourself go." Violetta tries to interject, but I'm on a roll.

"If you're trying to humiliate me so that viewers, mostly other women, are shamed into buying more beauty products, then you are despicable. Beauty comes from within, Violetta, and when your behaviour is ugly, you let all of us down."

"Unstable," says Violetta, and she gives the camera her sad eyes.

Chad is hyperventilating, gesticulating wildly, pointing at the crew to run the next ad, predictably, an anti-wrinkle treatment with some kind of pink plastic wand.

"Please," Violetta hisses at me.

"The charity is the only reason I'm here," I say. "You get off my back and I'll get off yours. How dare you attack me like this. Have some decency. You should be ashamed."

Her eyes flash anger and sudden self-control as Chad's fingers go up again – four, three, two, one.

"So Lucy, how do you spend your time now that you've lost your home and husband and business? And how about Phoebe? How does she feel about all this?"

I see red.

"How dare you bring our child into this, Violetta? This has nothing to do with her!" I stare into the camera. "This network exploits staff and viewers," I say and Violetta locks eyes with Chad and talks over the top of me, shaking her head.

Even with the five-second delay, most viewers will have heard me fight back. I'm so angry, I could explode. How could I ever have thought this industry was glamorous? Violetta talks to the camera.

"So sad to see our colleague reduced to this. When did you start receiving therapy, Lucy, and speaking of therapy, viewers, take a look at this beachfront health resort."

Chad is at my shoulder, hoisting me out of the chair and shaking his head. They can't get me out of there soon enough.

Chapter 22

Lucy

Harrowing, texts Donna. *Evil. Don't watch the replays.*
That bad, huh? I respond. Great. I knew it. Public humiliation.
Yup. Sorry, kid.
Should have known better.
Donna sends me a crazy face emoji.
Need a day off?
No way. I want to be so busy I can't think about anything but packing tape.
Donna promises me triple shifts for the next two days. If I had time to think, I'd wonder whether I should hide my face, but I haven't done anything wrong. Instead, I'll lift my chin.

The network uses their allegations as a banner for two days, with clips of me looking pathetic, but I comfort myself that the initial interview was live, and I know that some people saw the full thing.

Somewhere in that blur of busy-ness, there's a knock on my door. It's Amaryllis with more elderberry wine, her eyes large behind the lenses, all concern and sympathy.

"I knew you looked familiar, Lucy, but I couldn't think where I'd seen you before. Were you married to Bart Hardenburg?"

I nod and let her in.

"No wine now, though, please, Amaryllis. Feeling a bit fragile."

"Of course you are," she says. "I only ever turn on the tv to see the weather, but they kept replaying bits of that interview. You were so strong. Violetta is awful. I've written to the network in protest."

"Thank you."

"I'm here if you want to talk about it. And if you don't want to talk, that's okay, too. I want you to know I'm here for you."

She's so soft and gentle, her mauve clothes all draped about her. She looks like a stalk of lavender.

"Come and see my lamps, Amaryllis. I'd like to make one for you. We can talk about shapes and colors."

She chooses a bell shaped shade, and loves the idea of a fringe of transparent pale pink beads. I find myself spilling the whole story as she flips through my fabrics.

"When Phoebe reached high school and began to spend more time with her friends, I had time on my hands. I picked up a job with a local hairdresser, coloring hair, but I was so tired at the end of the day, and after a week, Bart fixed me with his ice blue eyes and told me he earned enough for all of us and needed me at home. I tried to tell him it wasn't about the money. It was about being part of the wider world, but he told me to get a hobby.

"I gave up the job; did a course in stained glass, but cut my fingers; in oil painting, but had no talent and hated the smell; and then settled on upholstery. Suddenly, life had more purpose. I specialised in found objects – bringing old furniture to life again with simple repairs and swathes of bright fabric. I love a glue gun, Amaryllis! I found all the best fabric suppliers, and then started using the offcuts to re-cover lampshades."

"They're beautiful. You truly have a talent, Lucy."

I nod.

"They were a hit at school fundraisers. Everyone wanted one. Then one wet weekend when Bart was away, Phoebe showed me how to use photos of my creations to make my own website, and Lucy's Lamps was born, trading on e-Bay. I started creating lamps to order. I still love my taglines. 'Focus and flair' and 'light up your life.' But Bart wasn't pleased. Not that he ever said so, but I'd had decades of deciphering the narrowing of his eyes."

"The private life of a public star…"

"Oh, Amaryllis. It was almost a relief when I found someone else's lipstick on Bart's collar," I say. "Bart had already accused me of paranoia, of listening at keyholes and eavesdropping. If I asked him what was happening at work, he'd snap an answer that put me in the wrong, as if I had no right to ask."

I shake my head, remembering. Amaryllis seems perfectly happy to hear how my life disintegrated – slowly at first, and then in an avalanche.

"The Minx – his personal assistant – would turn up at the house with some papers to be signed. I'd invite her in. I thought of her as a friendly colleague. What a blind fool I was! We'd swap news about the network – harmless chatter – while I stapled and glued my furniture. It was insidious, Mishelle's encroachment. I'd offer to make her a coffee, and she'd tell me to keep my gloves on, and she'd do it. Bart appreciated her visits. That's an understatement."

Amaryllis nods.

"I should have been more suspicious, but Bart was a celebrity. Everywhere we went, people wanted selfies with him. He adored the attention, but it didn't mean I had to be worried, to feel insecure about our beautiful family, did it? Everyone knew he was my husband. It didn't stop the Minx. Next thing I knew, he announced she was going with him to New York, to help with social media for his next set of interviews.

"After that first trip, I asked him if I should be worried, and all he did was laugh, as if our marriage was rock solid and I'd made the funniest joke. Or maybe it was a laugh of delight, that he should be so lucky that Mishelle, more than three decades younger, would be interested in him.

"There were so many trips – to Toronto, to South East Asia, accompanying senators. Mishelle was in our home office almost every day, helping tee up the interviews, the accommodation, the flights. And then she was in our bedroom – selecting appropriate shirts and ties and jackets for his interviews; and shopping with him for whatever else was needed; something Bart and I used to do together. They'd be in the living room surrounded by shopping bags, feet up, elated, exhausted. Of course I'd invite her to stay for dinner, to find out about the next trip."

Amaryllis shakes her head.

"I'm so sorry, Lucy. You didn't deserve any of that. I'm so glad you've made a fresh start, and I think your lamps are amazing."

She turns to me and holds out her arms. She's as soft as she looks, like the petals of a flower. Somewhere under all the layers there's a strong centre, as she hugs me as if I matter.

I sigh and we exchange a smile as she steps back.

"I have some deadlines on my reviews, so I have to get back, but don't you ever feel alone, Lucy. You knock on my door any time you need to talk."

Just as she leaves, my phone lights up.

You did not deserve that, Mom, texts Phoebe. I'm so surprised, in a good way, that I sit down on the spot, in my hallway, and stare at my phone. It's real. I didn't imagine it.

Thank you, darling, I reply. *Nor did you. Sorry about that footage of you as a child.*

Not your fault, she texts. *I saw what they did to you. It's called victim shaming. We're learning about it in college…*

I'm about to reply, when she shoots me another message.

I'm sorry I victim shamed you, too. I've been mean to you, Mom. I cradle my phone to my chest. I want to phone her, to invite her over again and give her a hug. But this is our first real exchange since I left Bart. I don't want to chase her away again.

Darling, I text back. *You were hurting. I love you.*

Love you too, Mom.

I fist pump the air ten times. I almost phone Violetta to thank her, but I know that's ridiculous.

There's another knock on the door. This time it's Mrs B.

"Oh, Lucy. That was so unfair."

"The tv thing? Please come in, Mrs B. I have a gift for you."

"A gift?"

"You've made me feel so welcome here." I hope to shift the topic, but Mrs B is on to me and won't let go.

"I just knew you were famous. I thought I recognised you. Why didn't you tell me?"

"I'm not famous, Mrs B. Far from it. Bart is the famous one."

"Well, I used to admire his reports, but my opinion has changed. I'm switching stations. What was he like, as a person? Is that insensitive of me to ask? I think I had a bit of a crush on him way back, not that I ever told Mr B. He just seemed so authoritative. You're not on drugs, are you?"

"Of course not. She made all that up. Bart was great in the early years, Mrs B, especially when we first met and I fell completely under his spell. He turned up in the network hair and make-up studio, an exhausted District Attorney, about to be interviewed on Prime Time, our channel's most popular public affairs show. The director told me Bart looked 'scary,'" I tell Mrs B. "'If you don't clean him up, Lucy, viewers will think he's the criminal."

Mrs B's eyes widen.

"I was fresh out of beauty school. I knew about perms, and short back and sides for the military, but Bart was one of my first male cuts. He fell asleep at the washbowl, and I wondered about this powerful legal expert, helpless as a baby beneath my touch."

No amount of pain can destroy the wonder of our first moments together.

"Bart's appearance on the network was such a hit, they called him in as a regular to comment on criminal rulings. Off camera, he smouldered more each time I worked on him. One night, he grabbed my hand and insisted I go out with him after my shift, at half past nine at night."

Mrs raises her eyebrows.

"It was a whirlwind. I was just twenty when we married. As Bart's star rose, I made everything work behind the scenes. I found our first apartment, then moved us to our larger home on a big block of land – for privacy – and renovated it. Phoebe arrived, and I fell in love again, with my baby. Motherhood consumed me, and Bart extended his work travels. I closed my ears to rumors and kept myself busy."

"But the rumors were true?"

I nod.

"Well that's not your fault. And that Violetta …"

"It's okay, Mrs B. Brighton Court is my fresh start. Come and see what I made you."

Mrs B falls on the orange and lime lampshades as if they're babies. She practically coos.

"I adore them. You clever, clever person, Lucy! Bart doesn't know what he let go."

"You're right, Mrs B."

"Well, personally, I'm glad he let you go. I can't wait to try these in my apartment."

"Thanks for your visit, Mrs B."

"Thanks for the chat."

Two days later I get a call from Chad. My finger hesitates over the button, but I end up taking it.

"Thanks for nothing, Chad," I say.

"Not my idea," he says.

"But you went along with it. I thought we were friends. I wanted to ask about your family, but you just threw me into the snake pit."

"I'm sorry, Lucy. I just want you to know we pulled the banner."

"After two days, huh? Should I be grateful? Why did you pull it? Worried I'll sue?"

"We got hundreds of complaints and lost a big advertiser. Violetta's lost so many viewers she's being retrenched."

"Sorry to hear it, and not sorry. Violetta was brilliant. She was wasted on that show. I guess you're safe, are you? I know you have to feed your family. But don't call me again."

Chad sighs as if he's sorry. It's not enough.

Are you okay? texts Dirk.

I am okay, I text back.

Come and see me, he texts.

Yes, I text back, but I am flat out unpacking for strangers and tired at the end of each day. If he thinks I'm a drug addict, I don't really want to know.

My phone rings as I'm taking down the trash, and I grab it and stab at the green button, then put it on speaker so I have a spare hand.

It's Donna, thanking me for working so hard.

"Is that all, Donna? I'm grateful for the work. You know that."

"So tell me again about your hot neighbor," she says.

"Donna! We're far too old for this kind of conversation."

"Nonsense, girlfriend. I read 'later in life' romance and you're never too old. We're human, aren't we? Anything is possible."

"But not probable."

"The bait is not stale, Lucy. You're beautiful and smart and generous and attractive. Bart was an idiot."

"I agree with you there."

"You won't stay single for long. Go on. Tell me about that hottie neighbor? I can't believe what you told me about you meeting way back in the old days, when you were in your twenties. How good is that! What's his name?"

I check the stairwell, check no neighbors' doors are open, then whisper my response.

"Dr Dirk O'Connell MD." I blush. Just saying his whole name out loud gives me little flutters in my stomach. Do I have a crush on Dirk?

"A hot doc, huh? What's he look like?"

"Mature. Salt and pepper hair. He's considerate. Smart. Educated. A bit old-fashioned. Great body; tall and strong. Nicely groomed. Well, his hair's on the long side, but I can fix that. Lovely manners."

"And single."

"Yes. Widower. Couple of children; even a couple of grandchildren who adore him. I've seen them together here once. Coming in to visit. They're cuties."

"Children know."

"How would you know, Donna? You live with a pet."

"There's always family in seasoned romances. You don't get to that age without a grown-up child here or there."

"I love the way you want to fix me up with a new partner so quickly and you don't even have one yourself."

"Rex and I have been going steady for ten years."

"He's a dog."

"Uhuh. Loyal as they come."

"You're ridiculous, Donna."

"That's why you love me."

It's only as I'm inserting my key into my lock, that I see him. Dirk O'Connell passes me with a strange smile. Did he hear every word?

I rush inside, slam my door and lean against it, trying to hide my smile. Donna's right. I have a crush on my neighbor, and it gives me more of a thrill than I want to admit.

"What happened?" she says.

"I think he heard us," I say, and we laugh so hard my stomach aches.

Chapter 23

Dirk

Dee's excited about the ball; asks me if I've had a haircut. I haven't found a hairdresser. But I've dragged out the dinner suit, bow tie scrunched in a pocket, and ironed the pin-striped shirt. I slick back my hair and ignore her question.

I'm suspicious Dee wants to pair me up with Bettina. Matt's agreed to mind the children. I can't get out of this.

"Good of you to step up, Matt," I tell him at the door when I go to collect Dee.

"Pizza and ice cream. No complaints," Matt smiles. Dee is picky about what they eat – no sweet things; no fast food. "How's the apartment, Dirk?"

"Great. Thank you. Dee and Jamison chose well, and the housekeeper's just right. Haven't met her yet, but everything's in order."

"Excellent."

Dee appears in a pale blue dress. She's beautiful. I can say that. I'm proud of my daughter, proud of her career, proud of the way she juggles work and raising the children. House is a mess, but who cares? I can escape to my place when the noise and chaos gets too much.

"I'm meeting a few of the neighbors," I say.

"That's great to hear," she says. She flicks the back of my head and frowns. "No time for that haircut, Dad?"

"Ah. No." My hair looks fine from the front. I smooth it back.

"So. Any of them nice, your neighbors?"

"Single, do you mean?"

"Dad! Well, we make no secret of the fact you have our permission to move on. We know how devoted you were to Mom. It's just… You know, at the end, Mom insisted we not stand in your way. She wanted you to find someone new; to 'live a full life' is the way she put it. You know it's one of the last things she said to me."

There's silence in the car, Dee's words resounding. I know so many of my patients' children resisted their single parents marrying again. They feared being supplanted; feared the loss of their inheritance; wanted to preserve the memory of their lost parent and that relationship, as if nothing had changed.

I barely believe my own children can be so generous, so ready to let me move on.

When I park under the venue and turn off the engine, I pull Dee in for a hug. She fiddles with her evening purse and retrieves a tissue for each of us.

"Did I ever tell you how much I love you, Dee? How proud of you I am?" I hold her close in the elevator, my treasured daughter. Working in the health industry, she stays fit. My Dee deserves a great night out, and here she is with her miserable old Dad with the too-long hair, not Matt. It hits me. I should have insisted on minding the children myself and sent them both to this ball; let the two of them have a great night out together, at least for an hour or two. They could have made it an early night, so Matt's travel would work out.

"I want to babysit for you and Matt," I say, before I change my mind.

"Not tonight, you don't. But okay. Sometime soon. We'd all love that."

And she hugs me back, just as the elevator doors open and we step out into the biggest event I've attended in a long while. There are ice sculptures and mountains of food, the glint of jewels. A small orchestra pumps out classy, classical music and two waiters with full drinks trays descend upon us. Dee takes sparkling water and I take champagne. I need it. Socializing scares me. It was never easy for me, even with Millie right beside me, even with Dee here now – I was always better at one on one, and even then, the patients did most of the talking – but I know how to be polite. I scan the room for Bettina and other friends and acquaintances I haven't seen in years.

Is that a flash of emerald green? For a moment I think I recognise my neighbor, Lucy, in Jill's gown, the one I spilled coffee on, but the room is surging with gowns of every color, human flowers in a forest of black suits. There's a lot of small talk. Old friends exclaim over how beautiful Dee is as a grown up. They ask her about her husband and children and career. There are lots of "I remember when" and "looking after your father" comments, and nods of approval, as if I'm a wayward toddler.

Bettina appears at my other side, regal in a silver gown. This is her night.

"Now, how are you, Dirk?" she asks, and leans in close in a whoosh of expensive perfume, her fingers intimate on the inside of my wrist. Did she and Dee set us up? She's never been my type – admirable, of course, but I was never attracted to her.

"Very well, thank you, Bettina. Magnificent crowd you have here. Excellent initiative. You look …" – what was the right word? She is a widow. This is all about Raymond, too. "What a wonderful initiative. Stunning."

"Thank you, Dirk. There'll be positions on the Board, if you're interested."

"Kind of you to think of me. Feel free to send me details."

And she's gone, greeting others. I breathe more easily.

"Dad! This is brilliant," says Dee. "It's the 'who's who' of the healthcare and fitness industry. There's Grant, from Built, and Muraya. Awesome! I heard her speak at the CrossFit conference. I'll introduce you."

"I'm fine, thanks, Dee. You go mingle. Don't worry about me."

I grab another champagne flute and wander towards the food table. I'm halfway there when everything changes.

Chapter 24

Lucy

I'm so glad to be here, at the ball, after all. For a while, after that awful interview, I wanted to throw the invitation in the trash, worried people would recognize me and judge me. But why should I hide out? It's Violetta who should be ashamed of herself. Not me.

My new gown needs an outing. It's a year to the day since I found Bart in our bed with his secretary – such a cliche – and high time for our divorce settlement to be finalized. A cheery prospect. Do I want to remember this anniversary? No. But it's there, seared into my psyche – the ugliest of scars.

I hate feeling sorry for myself, and this glittering ball is the perfect place to forget my troubles.

There are couples everywhere, dressed in their best – friends greeting each other, introductions left, right and centre. A few lovely people admire my gown, some with smiles, a couple with scowls, their noses in the air, and several with actual compliments. I tell them I found it at Jill's Frocks and Fancies where I picked up the flyer about this ball, and I point at the matching earrings, swinging and shining just at the edge of my vision. I'll admit it. I feel beautiful. Knowing my daughter wants to see me again has me floating five inches off the floor. Life has never been more beautiful; whatever it is she wants of me.

I circulate, wondering if I'll recognise anyone, wondering if people will stare at me. This time I've done my hair and face with total care. I love this venue, the old Town Hall – so full of memories.

As the elevator doors open and another elegant couple emerges, I'm startled to recognize Dirk, his arm around a truly beautiful young woman, luminous in a blue sheath dress. Of course. Who was I to imagine Dirk would have any interest in me, someone closer to his own age? Older men have it so easy; distinguished until they die, especially if someone faithfully cares for them and they have a small fortune. Older women? We're obsolete. Dirk the Doc could have any woman in this room. And me? I can admit it. I'm only interested in Dirk. We haven't had a chance to speak since that horrendous interview. Dirk, shyer than he realizes. There's something so appealing about him, a generosity he doesn't even notice, and an honesty. Lovely manners. No wonder his children want to spend time with him. They share a genuine bereavement. That Millie must have been a saint. Even I miss her, and I never even met her.

I pull back my shoulders, stand tall and give myself the pep talk. Just because Bart gave me the flick and Violetta made it horrendously public, my life is far from over. I'm a survivor. I'm a thriver. I am actually Bart's greatest loss. His infatuation with his secretary is sure to fade. They should be ashamed of themselves. My mind pursues its usual route, climbing out of the chasm like a faithful donkey, one step at a time. The Minx is welcome to Bart. He snored. He never put his socks in the wash. He squeezed the toothpaste tube the wrong way.

Besides, they're stuck with each other now, at least until one of them betrays the other, which is highly likely given Bart's past behaviour. And me? I'm in the best gown in the room, bought for me by a true and highly attractive gentleman, never mind the whole accidental coffee spill.

The lighting dims. The musicians switch to soft jazz, my favorite.

I wriggle my fingers until my diamonds sparkle, and they pick up the light of every facet of every chandelier in the room, and there must be at least a dozen of them up there on the ornate ceiling. How many balls has this hall seen over a hundred years? How many hearts have grown and met and blossomed and broken beneath them, including the dear departed Raymond, late husband of our brave hostess, taking her tragedy square on the chin to make the world a better place? I must find the woman who dreamed this up and congratulate her. Forget all those fickle men who behave like Bart, dressed like penguins.

But I'm over near the dance floor when I see them, my Ex and that Minx, and they're so close you couldn't fit a platinum credit card between them.

It hits me like a soccer ball to my gut how besotted they are with each other, surrounded by that special golden glow, as attractive as a celebrity couple can be. And in contrast, how much I've lost – not just the husband I loved and cared for, but my beloved home of more than twenty years, and my own daughter, flesh of my flesh. My heart breaks all over again, shatters into smithereens.

And not one of my personal makeovers, nor my cheery, chatty chirpy neighborhood parties can ever make up for those losses. My heart is no diamond. It is broken in too many places. I am fundamentally damaged. The fractures run right through me. I am brittle beneath this gorgeous gown. It's only a front, a battle shield, thin as silk. Who am I fooling?

As Bart and the Minx swirl and frolic in front of me, their joy shimmers around them like gossamer, like phosphorescence, like moonbeams. I stand speechless – the saddest statue at the edge of the dance floor.

And then I see him on his own. Dirk. Handsome and slightly worn, like my favorite furniture – shabby chic. Dirk is a lifeline and I am drowning in despair, lonely and alone. I can't let my Ex see me like this. It's too pathetic, but more than that, I don't want this agony.

"Hold me," I say to Dirk as I rush towards him, touch him on the shoulder from behind, then slip in front to face him with a smile. Will he reject me? Will he be ashamed to be seen with me, that pathetic woman on Network Eight.

I reach for him, run both hands up the fine, cool wool of his dark suit, and join my fingers behind his neck.

A thousand thoughts run behind his eyes. Does he see me as a patient, a neighbor, the woman Bart rejected, a flirt, or drug dependent, as Violetta alleged?

I press myself against him; shameless in my need. Let the whole ballroom see us together. I have nothing more to lose.

Dirk's arms come around me slowly. Then he takes my right hand as if in a waltz as his other lands slowly, warm and dry and deliciously tentative, on the skin of my bare back, where the gown dips at my waist, an underrated part of the female anatomy, so sensitive I squirm involuntarily and press myself closer to him. Dirk is just the right shape for me. I don't let myself wonder whether any man would do. Dirk is perfect, my kind neighbor. I can apologize later, explain about my Ex; hope he'll understand.

"Dance with me," I whisper into his ear, and he inhales sharply. "Do it. Please. Now."

As he steers us onto the dance floor, past the Ex and the Minx, I drag on him, halt us, anchor us right beside them.

"Kiss me," I whisper. "Here. Now. Please. I'll owe you. I'll explain later. I …"

But his eyes have caught mine, and in those depths I see his own need.

Chapter 25

Dirk

If Jill is right, then Lucy was trouble the moment I saw her in Jill's shop, and I am an old fool. I can't believe I bought Lucy this gown. I've added kryptonite to the explosive that will destroy me. This room is full of younger women, yet Lucy is the siren in this gown, far too alluring, the belle of the ball, and she knows it. For all Bettina's efforts and honorable intentions, she is outshone by Lucy, my extraordinary neighbor. Jill told me about the interview, and I invited Lucy to visit me. I was ready to offer her referrals, but this is the first time we've caught spoken since that interview.

I can't take my eyes off Lucy, nor my hands, the traitors. I am not a demonstrative man, but I'm still a man.

Lucy's eyes entrap me. Is this guile or is it genuine? Jill saw the whole interview. She phoned me and told me about Lucy's divorce, her famous ex-husband, the drug and alcohol addictions. I told her it wouldn't be the first time the media got something wrong. I'd have thought Jill would have more sympathy, given the collapse of her own marriage.

I am a man who makes up his own mind about people. But this is not just about my mind. My whole body wants more of Lucy Beston. Still I hesitate.

How can I dare to love again and run the risk of loss? It nearly killed me when Millie died. The cardiologist blames age and lack of exercise – trapped as I was in my consulting rooms day in and day out – but I know the truth, and I want to dodge it. If I love again, and I lose my love, my old heart might crack for good.

Besides, even though I know Millie's gone for good, some of these people were at our wedding. In the same way as I keep expecting to run into Raymond, Millie is still in this room, so vivid in my memories. It's not that falling for Lucy would be a betrayal exactly – just that some part of me is still loyal to Millie. I actually thought I saw her in the crowd, but it was someone else with similar hair. I take a deep breath.

Every male eye in the room is on Lucy, elegance itself, never mind the whole Bart Hardenberg controversy. Fact is, Lucy could run through pathetic widowers like me at the rate of one a year; toss us out the moment she has a fresh diamond. Those jewels wink at me every time I see her. They warn me away.

But Lucy has pulled me in, literally. Of all the soft touches in this room, she's chosen me, and I'm ashamed to admit that my ego fist pumps sky high.

On the dance floor, the rhythm of the music forces us together. If we don't move with it, other couples will collide with us. She slips into my embrace as if she belongs with me, so close I can't help but admire the softest skin of her cheek, peachy against fine cheekbones that will never age. Those subtle crow's feet of experience beside her eyes, so expertly made up – they fascinate me. The creases deepen when she laughs … and suddenly I know that her laughter is infectious and I am addicted to it. I need her radiance to light up the core of my sad old soul.

Lucy and I are a matching pair. We're not young, but there's some future ahead of us, and we can make it a good one, a great one.

"Kiss me, Dirk." It's an order, urgent, and who am I to resist? Let the room see me as a fine old fool. Half of them could be her exes for all I know. She might have a reputation. But life is short. Millie taught me that. I've been alone long enough. Even Dee wants me to try again, or so she says.

The music slows as if it's my resistance, bending to Lucy's will, and to my own keening need. Beside us, dancing couples join each other, hold each other closer and sway.

Lucy tilts back her head and peers at me through lowered lashes. Is that a tear about to fall? She could be a star in an old black and white movie, Lauren Bacall. I know what Humphrey would do, and I play the part. My thumb and two fingers close on the soft skin of her chin as I bring my lips to hers. As I close my eyes, with her breath on my cheek, I let my lips find hers, warm and sweet and soft and all too willing.

There's a hum in her throat, the smallest of moans and it awakens a flame in me I thought had died. Lucy's hand is on my cheek, the gold of her rings as warm as her bare skin. Her diamonds glitter and sparkle as if they're alive, as if they're laughing at me as she pushes her fingers into the hair behind my neck to pull me closer, to deepen our kiss, and I am lost, lost in the shape of this woman.

In this deep winter of my soul, I am jolted, electrified. Beyond the activities of daily living, beyond my weekly meet-ups with my devoted, grown-up children and the little ones, and visits with Jill and her brood, and drinks with friends like Walt; beyond the polite pleasantries of passing others in the shops and streets and corridors of Brighton Court; beyond the comfort of my new apartment and the simple satisfactions of feeding my belly and reading good books; beyond my loyalty to the memory of Millie at her best, I am a man like any other. I am alive. Lucy's urgent kiss awakens something too long dormant. Desire. It scares me.

It is Jill who drags us apart. The music has ended. I don't care if we're causing a scene. I will stand by Lucy Beston.

"Bettina's about to speak, Dirk," she hisses, and glares at Lucy.

I won't have her rudeness.

"Do you remember Lucy, Jill? And this is your gown, remember? No coffee stains now. Lucy could model for you," I say. Jill gives one curt nod and holds her finger to her lips.

Lucy leans towards me again with a smile at Jill, forgiving the interruption. With a finger, she reaches up and gently wipes her lipstick from my lips, one eyebrow raised – a shared smile – then steps back with the rest of us for a better view of the stage as Bettina adjusts the microphone.

Chapter 26

Lucy

A model for Jill! Now there's a great idea. Dirk O'Connell stood up for me in front of disapproving Jill, and he's right. I'd be thrilled to model for Jill. An in-store fashion parade with a bit of a public profile might be just what she needs to bring in more customers. We could even make it a fundraiser like this one.

With all eyes on the stage, including Jill's, I move closer to Dirk and tuck my hand inside his arm. He doesn't object. His arm comes around me as if I'm cherished, and I close my eyes in gratitude.

"I can't thank you all enough for being here with me this evening," Bettina says. "Dementia stole Bernard, my beloved husband, but he was one of more than fifty million people worldwide with this terrible affliction. A new case is diagnosed every three minutes. Your generosity will help us all fight this disease, so invisible, so insidious. Please view the silent auction items. Wonderful volunteers have spent many hours and days and weeks arranging them, and your generosity will reward their efforts and ultimately reward us all. Enjoy this evening. Enjoy each other. Thank you."

There's a great round of applause and the music begins again.

Bettina is mobbed as she descends the stage. Dirk removes my hand and holds it.

"Thank you for the dance, Lucy," he says, and squeezes my fingers. I stare at him as if he's a hero, but he must have moved people out of his surgery thousands of times with just this technique.

"I must go congratulate Bettina," he says.

"Of course, Dirk. See you later."

And I do see him later, surrounded by people who seem to know him. That young man who seems so similar – is that his son? And is that his daughter? The slim young woman in the silver-blue sheath is back by his side.

I'd love to approach them, but Jill's glare holds me at bay. I'll work on her later. I don't own Dirk, but nor does she. I'm profoundly grateful to him for kissing me on the dance floor, in precisely the right place at the right time.

With the Minx and the Ex back at it, busting some moves, I turn away, retrieve my cloak with dignity, and make my way past the auction tables, towards the exit.

Chapter 27

Dirk

I'm surprised to glimpse the distinctive green gown in front of me on the grand old marble stairwell. Dee said she'd stay longer to pump hands, and Jamison will drop her home.

"Leaving early?" I say to Lucy, and she nods.

"I had an absolute ball tonight, Dirk. Thank you so much for the dance. You saved me. We were right next to my Ex and the … " Her voice trails off, but her expression says it all, until she covers her devastation with another bright smile. She's plucky, this Lucy, in her stunning green gown, but I heard her. My proud heart plummets.

"You used me to make your Ex jealous," I say. "And there I was, thinking my natural charm made me irresistible." I try to make a joke of it, as if a kiss means nothing. What century am I from? What a fool to read something into it, something like a future for us.

"Actually, I am attracted to you, Dirk."

"I see." I don't really. I'm old and jaded and cynical. What could the dazzling Lucy possibly see in me?

"You don't believe me, a handsome man like you?"

"Are you flirting with me, Lucy?"

"Just telling the truth."

"Then I better at least offer you a lift home."

"I'd love that, thank you."

I open the door for her and she slides in, her long gown rustling. I reach down and sweep a green length of it out of the path of the red door – red light, green light; my mind plays tricks with my attraction to her – then close it.

She is quiet in the car. I glance across at her, at the creamy gleam of her skin, and back to the road; work the gears as her perfume fills the car and my heart pounds. I must focus on the road.

It's unspoken, this thing between us, this awareness, as if my body can't ignore hers, as if Lucy has lodged in me like some kind of splinter, like an itch. She is there, as much a part of me now as my shadow.

Back at Brighton Court, I open the front door of the apartments for her and she goes ahead of me up the stairs, elegance itself. I can't take my eyes off her form, the sway of her body in the swish of green silk, and the glow of the skin of her bare back; such an invitation.

At her door, she asks me in, and my eyes drop to her neck, that tender place above her collar bone, one elegant green earring swinging above it. Softly, she smiles up at me, raises an eyebrow.

"Dirk?"

I grab both her hands.

"You're very beautiful, Lucy," I say. I run my thumbs across all her diamonds, then and step away.

"Why did you let go?" she asks.

Should I tell her? Her eyes sparkle as she waits for my answer.

"I have a friend who's a divorce lawyer, Lucy."

"So?"

"Don't you think you have enough diamonds?" I say it nicely. I smile.

She ignores me, stares at me – an admonishment, and I blink.

Lucy's past is irrelevant. If she goes through husbands at the rate of one a year, who am I to judge her? She's magnificent.

She examines her rings but has no answer. She brings her eyes back to mine, the suggestion of a dare right there; a challenge.

"One small glass of port, Dirk? That's all I'm suggesting." Her voice is low and reasonable. "It's been a wonderful evening. I'm not ready for it to end. Come in. You're always so, so serious."

Against my better judgement, I step inside. Those same alluring fragrances assail me. She keeps her place fresh and clean and inviting. Indirect lighting gives the spaces a warm glow. Knowing that Lucy made the lamps only makes them more enticing.

Lucy magics up a bowl of salted nuts and two tiny glasses. In her green gown, she's a genie, the creature of my dreams.

"Cheers."

Before I know it, she's reached up and undone my bow tie and top button, and I shake my head.

"Why not, Dirk?"

Because my pulse is racing, because my body remembers exactly where this leads, because Lucy may be all wiles and I'm a sucker.

She lights a couple of candles and we sit and stare at her view. There are far fewer city lights at this hour. We watch some of them blink off. It's mesmerizing, and she is warm beside me, her breath soft and sweet as we sip at the port. My lips remember hers. They have a life of their own.

"Thank you for being there," she says. "And for being here."

"For …?"

"I can't thank you enough for that kiss, Dirk. It was exactly what I needed."

"I'd do it for anyone," I say.

"Not that again! You really helped me out." And before I know it, she slips her hand inside my arm and presses closer to me. This time her kiss is chaste. She reaches up to my cheek, the fabric of her gown rustling, her perfume a delicious waft of temptation, but it's just a friendly peck, and I'm sorry when she leans away and regains a respectable distance.

"My Ex," she says, and sighs heavily.

"Which one?" I say. It's an attempt at a joke.

She inhales sharply, recoils from me. I don't understand why she stands and places her unfinished glass on the windowsill. She's waiting for me to leave.

I swirl the last of my port in the bottom of the tiny glass. It glows ruby red in Lucy's candlelight, the same color as her lamps with long beaded tassels in the corner.

I am dismissed, chastised – and strangely bereft. It was just meant to be banter. Was I unnecessarily cruel? For all her strength and guile, Lucy is vulnerable. I should know. It's not long since we shared the drink in the bar and she revealed the torment of her estrangement from her daughter, not to mention that horrific interview. Public shaming makes everyone vulnerable.

So now I am a different kind of fool. I have no evidence Lucy is a fortune hunter. She's only human, and I've insulted her. As I stumble out of there, out of that inviting haven where I had been so warmly invited, and up to my empty apartment with everything too neat and tidy, including my bed – too big and cold and lonely – I am ashamed.

Chapter 28

Lucy

Next morning, on my doorstep, wrapped in crisp white paper – roses. They're of every color, yellow and hot pink and red and amber and white with pale pink tips – my favorite.

I close my eyes, bury my nose in the waxy coolness of their petals and inhale deeply. Their lemony fragrance takes me right back to my beautiful home, in full summer, to all the jewels of my garden – in bloom around me, swaying in a breeze so mild and warm and gentle it's a caress.

There are tears in my eyes when I open them, and I gasp. Dirk is there, hands folded in front of him, contrite. He barely meets my eyes, but doesn't move away. He clears his throat.

"I owe you an apology," he says, and I stand straighter in my house gown. I meet his gaze and raise one eyebrow. I don't invite him in.

"Your past is none of my business," he says. "I transgressed"

Tears form in one eye and then the other, and as I dab them away, I realize I'm flashing my diamonds again. I shove my fist in my pocket.

Dirk fumbles in his own pocket and pulls out an ironed handkerchief, neatly folded. He hands it to me.

"The roses are beautiful, thank you," I say.

"I don't know the language of flowers," he says, as if he should. "But you said you like roses."

"I do. They're my favorite. Thank you. What did you want these roses to say?"

He clears his throat, lingers at my doorway.

Seconds pass. A minute; and I go to step back into my apartment, to put the flowers in water, but he reaches out, past the flowers, past my hand, and cups my wrist, gently, holds it a little too long. His hand is warm and dry and in control. I hold my breath.

"I was rude to you, Lucy. It was unforgivable. Your love life and marital status is none of my business."

I nod, not yet ready to fully forgive him. He insinuated I had many exes, and even if I did, how could he possibly think he would know the circumstances. However famous and respected the great doctor and former sports star might be, he has no more right to judge me than anyone else.

His head is bowed, his contrition seemingly genuine, and his words interrupt my thoughts.

"And I want to ask you a favor."

"What favor?" I am intrigued. Dr Dirk O'Connell has everything – the penthouse, a red convertible, an invisible housekeeper, two doting independent children and even some grandchildren. What could he possibly want that a retired doctor's savings can't buy?

He blushes, and then his words pour out.

"Every time I go home to Franklin I'm mobbed by old patients and Millie's friends, but if they see me with you, they might leave me alone."

"You want me as your bodyguard?" I laugh, astonished.

"That's one way of putting it."

"Or your fake date? A cunning plan. And why do you want to go back to Franklin?"

"I need to see the house again, to make a decision about selling it or letting it out. Need to check the garden. Dee and Jamison are far too busy, and you said you miss your roses. My roses need pruning."

I look him up and down. So serious.

"Millie's garden." My voice is steady.

He nods.

"But, there must be gardeners …"

"Please, Lucy."

"You want me to come with you to your late wife's garden and prune her roses, and to be your fake date just to keep away everyone who misses you and cares about you?"

"When you put it like that …"

"You should be ashamed. You should give me more roses, Dr Dirk O'Connell." I hold his gaze – deeply serious – but then I throw back my head and laugh, and the tension drops away. He shakes his head at me.

"Of course I'll come, Dirk, especially after a gift like this and your decent apology – which was welcome and called for, by the way. Everyone makes mistakes, but if you can admit them and apologize, you're a good man. I'm free as a bird today. I'll just put these in water and meet you in half an hour. Do you know, I just bought some new gloves and rose clippers? There are rose bushes right here at Brighton Court. I'm determined to get this garden under control again. You'll be able to play ball down there with your grandchildren, Dirk. And I want to install a pizza oven. Everyone will love that."

I consider mentioning the naysayer in Apartment One, but don't want to be a gossip. As we leave town, it's a joy to admire the changing view. Some days, good things happen. As we fly along the highway in the open topped sportscar with the heater roasting my toes, wisps of my hair escape my warm beanie and whip into my eyes. I shield them with one hand and steal a glance at Dirk, so handsome in his dark glasses and warm leather jacket.

He swears this car belongs to his son, but he drives it like he owns it, like a professional, like a lover, changing gears as we curve away off the highway and into narrower roads where the trees meet above the pavement and the fields have barns and cows, and horses in blankets nibble at cold grass, their breath all steam.

I haven't been out of the city for years. The air is fresh, if cold, the trees stark and bare, the fir trees the only exceptions, deep green sentinels.

Drifts of old snow hide in the shadows but there is warmth in the sun.

We slow as the roads narrow and the rush of wind and engine noise drops.

"How long were you in Franklin?"

"Thirty six years," he says. "Millie was born here. We met in college."

"What did Millie study?"

"Nursing."

"Ah, the old love story. Medical romance."

"Millie was blatant about our courtship. She came to a college in the city to find a doctor to bring back to her hometown, and I complied."

Was that all? Was Dirk bitter? He made it sound so clinical.

"What's it like, living in the country?"

"Everyone knows everything about everyone else, for better or worse."

"You don't make it sound very appealing."

He shrugs.

"Why are you asking?" he says. "Are you considering moving to the country?"

"Maybe," I say. "I'm only renting. My divorce is finalized. The money from the property sale will come through any day. I'll need to make some decisions."

I don't tell him Phoebe has finally agreed to meet me. She might not even turn up. I refuse to build up my hopes, but I know in my heart – I want to do the right thing by her, to give her some of the money from settlement, half of it, if I can spare that much. I'll need security – a roof over my head, and if I can keep Lucy's Lamps shining, I'll have enough to live on.

Dirk changes down another gear as we drive through an avenue of bare trees and into a pretty town, a few shops on either side – a pet shop, a grocer, a couple of banks, a bar, already open, a gas station and several hotels. Quaint wooden shops line the centre of the town, a hairdresser, some frock shops and a couple of home decoration and gift shops.

"Can we stop for a moment, please, Dirk?"

"Of course."

"I won't be long. I'll duck in and give them some Lucy's Lamps cards."

I'm just leaving the shop when Donna messages me with another assignment. That's fancy talk for another address and task. Usually unpacking. Sometimes packing. This time, the assignment is different. I inhale, check it again, hesitate, then push it out of my mind.

Chapter 29

Dirk

I haven't been back to Franklin since the funeral. It's a great time to visit – hardly anyone's on the street, thank goodness, not like last time I was here, saying goodbye.

I'm ready to see the house again. Maybe not ready to sell it. This house was Millie's. It *was* Millie. If she'd had other interests, like art or music or tutoring or sport, then selling it wouldn't be such a big deal. But selling it straight away would have been a betrayal. But time has passed.

I'm glad Lucy agreed to accompany me. I love that about her. She doesn't hold a grudge. She seems to have forgiven me for my tasteless comment about her diamonds. I'm relieved we can still be friends. Lucy is exactly the tonic I need today, bright company in her warm red hat and scarf and jaunty plaid jacket, and full of full of energy. She is out of the car to distribute her business cards before I can turn off the engine, and then ducks back in, beside me, all smiles.

"They're interested, Dirk! I'll email them photos when we get back. One of them said she'd host my lamp-covering workshop in spring!"

"Glad there's something in it for you, too, Lucy, this trip."

We accelerate away, slowly, past my old practice, the Family Doctor sign still prominent. Roger Tappy took it over. Lucy sees the sign and places her hand briefly on my leg, a friendly gesture – nothing suggestive about it.

"No regrets?"

I shake my head. My sigh is deep.

"I gave that practice everything, Lucy; my late nights and early mornings and everything in between, and nothing could stem the tide of misery – the illness and the injuries, accidental and self-inflicted."

Feels good to spell it out. Millie wouldn't have wanted to hear a word of it. Wanted to believe I loved my work.

"You okay about going home?"

"It's not my home anymore."

"But there must be so many memories."

"Of course." Lucy doesn't need to know they're not all good.

The white picket fence needs painting. Millie kept up all of that. She had the gardener and painter and electrician and plumber and cleaner and handyman and caterer on speed dial. She wasn't the queen of her home town for nothing. Her parents' home – which became ours – was the pride of the place, but it was old and quaint and the maintenance was never-ending.

I'm stiff when we get out of the car. Out of habit, I go around to the passenger side, open the door and hold out my hand … to Lucy.

She bounces out, all pink cheeks and excitement.

"Where can I start? You were right about these roses. They're so overgrown! It's the perfect time to prune them. I can't wait. You go in. I'll make a start. These will be gorgeous in spring. Go in. You don't need me in there with all your memories."

And she's through the gate with its rustic rose arbor, now all stems and thorns, and by the time I get to the front door, she's snipping away.

She's humming with contentment as I insert the old key and turn it and push open the door. Dee has already been here. She told me she cleared out Millie's things when she selected the main things I'd need in my new place.

The hatstand is empty. Millie had a hat for every occasion, even after hats became unfashionable.

The house is cold. Millie kept it toasty warm year round, never mind the expense. The long wooden corridor echoes with my footsteps. I peer into the sitting room, so much bigger without Millie's clutter, the generous simplicity of the architecture obvious. This was every bit her late father's house, the town carpenter, the old home made of the best wood available. Her mother told me the history every time she visited, and then she moved in with us, until the babies arrived and disturbed her rest. She moved out but visited all the time. She and Millie were a team, dreaming up never-ending home improvements as they minded the children and cooked our meals. Sometimes I wondered if I'd married Millie, her mother or even the house. We were all its slaves.

Movement catches my eye from the big window overlooking the garden, as Lucy stands and stretches and moves to the next rose bush, rubbing her back, then bending to the task again, all smiles and concentration. I'd guessed Lucy would be like Millie – afraid of the dirt – but I was wrong.

The children's rooms are empty, except for the beds and dressing tables, all period pieces Millie found somewhere. The place is a museum. We can sell it with the furniture, or rent it out as an upmarket boutique getaway, though that's not my preference. I'm done with the maintenance. I haven't had that conversation yet with Jamison and Dee – haven't wanted to think about it.

Even the master bedroom is strangely bland, as if the house is already for sale – the surface of the round-mirrored dressing table empty of Millie's many potions and perfumes and beads and bangles and rings.

It's as if the house is holding its breath, or I've caught it asleep.

The grand dining room is neat, the symmetrical old table dusty. The sun comes out from behind the clouds, and dust motes swirl in its rays, through the glass, an echo of the grand windows of the sitting room.

The fireplace is empty. Do rose clippings burn? It's icy in here. I continue to the kitchen, apprehensive. Millie's life-long dance with duty to her home always ended here, here where I wasn't welcome, but every kitchen holds memories. It was here after my long days I'd sneak chunks of chocolate or instant coffee as Millie slept in our bed, here where I'd grab a bowl of cereal before I headed out early again each morning. I search in vain for a kettle. The electricity is off anyway. I turn a tap for a sign of movement, for evidence the place is more than an empty film set – for a sign that I actually passed the best years of my life under its old roof.

Yellow water gushes out. Another pipe needs replacing. I let it run clear, then find two glasses, and take them out, one for me and one for Lucy. She's going strong. She wasn't wrong about her love of roses.

Millie loved roses in vases. She loved the romance of them, but never the hard work.

Lucy turns to me, grabs the glass with gratitude and downs it with gusto.

"Perfect," Lucy says, a word Millie never uttered once. It's not fair to compare them. I was a young man when I fell under Millie's spell. I'm wiser now. Or am I?

A thorn has nicked Lucy's cheek, the blood a red ruby. I pull out a tissue and hold it out.

"Oh?"

"One of them fought back," I say, as I lean down and dab at her cheek. Her breath is warm on my hand. I've patched a thousand cheeks or more; stitched them, disinfected them, removed skin cancers and splinters, even a fishhook. There is nothing to this small gesture of kindness, nothing more than common sense. Any friend would dab at the cut on Lucy's cheek, especially if she was doing them a favor.

But those eyes.

Chapter 30

Lucy

Dirk's face is all kindness, his lips thin in a smile of concentration. He must have been an excellent doctor. Considerate. I've had some doctors treat me no better than meat.

My cheek doesn't hurt at all. Perhaps it's the cold, but with Dirk's hand so close, I sense the warmth of it, of him.

Being in this winter garden is so different to being with him at the ball, when we were surrounded by strangers and I kissed him, to prove to Bart I was still attractive, despite his treachery, and Dirk was the closest thing. That kiss was a tactic, self-defence – essential, and selfish of me.

This kiss is different, so slow yet inevitable I don't even see it coming, don't even know if it's Dirk's idea or mine.

In the quiet garden, surrounded by thorns and overgrown branches, we are alone in the dead of winter.

My lips brush his fingers in a kiss of gratitude, for his company, his kindness, for this gift of a garden to borrow, for the feel of the clippers in my hand again and the promise of spring, hidden deep in the roots of the roses, so thick and old they are like giants' fists, stubbornly alive against the winter cold.

His other hand rises, and with the back of his fingers, he brushes my cheek, and then, with both hands, tilts my head to his, and bends and samples my lips, once, twice and then again in a kiss so deep it takes away my breath and leaves me speechless.

"Doc O'Connell! Is that you?"

He breaks away, straightens and steps away from me.

"Mrs Munze," he says.

"Did I disturb you?"

"Mrs Munze. Ms Beston. Ms Beston is teaching me about roses."

Mrs Munze is not convinced.

"Haven't seen you here much, Doc. When you coming back? We miss you. Doc Tappy is good, but he's not like you."

"Thank you, Mrs Munze. It's too soon for me to make any big decisions, you understand."

"Whatever you need, Doc. How's the house?"

"House is fine, thank you, Mrs Munze. How's your family?"

Mrs Munze clearly has a large family. I bite down on my smile and head back to the roses, snip, snip, snip, as Dirk listens to Mrs Munze and nods patiently, beside me.

I love this part of keeping roses. I snip at an angle near the base of a leaf, careful to choose a bud that will open the plant to more light as it grows, never back into the tangled centre.

I'm down on my knees as Mrs Munze moves away. I give her a wave and grab at Dirk's leg to catch his attention, and it's there again, acute awareness of the man. I snatch back my hand as if his body scalds me. It does.

"Where do you want the clippings, Dirk?"

The clouds come over again.

"Can we burn them?"

"Some of them, sure. The dry and dead ones." I show him the oldest ones, shrivelled almost black.

"Want me to sort them? I can make different piles from now on. You'll need gloves if you're going to help. The thorns stay savage year round."

As I keep working, he enters the house and returns with his coat and hat and gloves, and works silently beside me. It's lovely to have his company. Bart never showed an interest, beyond checking the garden as a backdrop for interviews or footage.

From a back shed, Dirk finds a big old bucket. He ferries the dry wood inside the house, and then heads out somewhere in the car.

"That's enough," he says on his return, just as I'm tiring and the last of the roses nears completion.

He grabs the crook of my arm, hauls me up and I lean against his strength, my bones less supple than I remember. I've been working away quietly at the garden at Brighton Court, along the edges Professor No can't see properly from his apartment, and making progress, but that work is varied. Millie's rose garden is vast. Pruning it has been a joy, but my muscles and joints protest. Dirk leads me inside.

The interior is beautiful, if strangely empty and impersonal.

He takes me into a formal dining room. On the table is a bottle of wine, two tumblers, a loaf of bread on a chopping board with an old knife, and some cheeses and olives on a plate.

He turns two chairs around to face the fireplace, then holds a match beneath a stack of advertising brochures nestled beneath the dry rose clippings.

"I should have taken you into town with me, but we'd never get away. Even buying these few things I ended up in eight long conversations."

"Must be nice to be so popular, so needed."

"I hate it."

He opens the wine and offers me a glass as fire leaps in the grate and the clouds darken again outside. Sitting is heaven. I'm suddenly ravenous. There's nowhere else I want to be.

As we eat, we talk about his childhood and touch on his life with Millie. His words rush out as if he hasn't spoken in years, in a lifetime. His words tumble like a waterfall and then it's my turn, and the sky is dark and the bottle empty.

"I can't thank you enough, Lucy."

"It's mutual. It's good to talk."

"I can't talk to Jamison or Dee like this. They loved their mother, of course. I'd never take her memory away from them."

His face is all angles in the firelight.

"You're a good man, Doc O'Connell."

He shrugs.

"Not good enough to make a plan. I've drunk too much to drive. I've kidnapped you, Lucy, for totally selfish reasons. There's no heating, but there are quilts. You could pick a bed, any bed. And it's bread and water for breakfast."

"Luxury," I say. "I love this simplicity." I break into a song from *My Fair Lady* – All I want is a room somewhere.

We sing it together, arm in arm up the hallway and then he tucks me into one of the single beds and my eyes close.

Later in the night, I wake, shivering. I pile all the quilts I can find onto the single bed but still can't get warm. Is it midnight? Moonlight flows in through the dining room window as I tiptoe down the corridor to the main bedroom and creep in beside Dirk. We're both fully clothed.

This is nothing but a way to prevent myself from freezing to death, I tell myself as I push my back against his slumbering warmth, but when his arm comes around me and he nestles me closer, I know it's a lie.

Doctor Dirk O'Connor is more than a helpful neighbor, a friend with roses, or a dance partner. He is more than a generous and thoughtful; more than clever and kind. Doctor Dirk O'Connell is a total catch.

Chapter 31

Dirk

I wake in the freezing old bedroom, the only warmth the slumbering form beside me. Millie never let me cuddle this close, not for long, and never all night. Lucy sleeps heavily. Her breath makes soft mist in the semidarkness.

Around me, the old house creaks as wind whistles and roars outside. I go to leap up, to rush to the clinic to sort out the never-ending paperwork, but my heart slows and I realize I'm free of it. That was the past.

Lucy wakes slowly, gives a languorous smile, then yawns hugely, turns to me, closes her eyes and snuggles back down for more sleep. I am so tempted to surround her form with my own, to nestle her more closely and discover her, to run my hands across her curves, and wake her gently, with caresses, with kisses. It would be so easy. Too easy.

Suddenly, I'm wary. Drifts of our conversation beside the fire last night come back to haunt me.

Lucy told me she loved pruning the roses, loved this house. She told me all about her shabby chic furniture, and suddenly I can see it all ahead of me like a trap, like a spider's web. Before I know it, Lucy Beston will not only have another diamond ring. She'll force me back into this old maddening, demanding house; back into my old routine, into the routine I hated.

I am not doing it. I am never coming back to this house, to be its slave. I don't care how alluring Lucy Beston might be, and I like her, I do. I'm a little bewitched by her, I'll admit, but I am no college boy. I'm a grown man and I will not be trapped again.

Walt was right. I am free; freer than I'll ever be. Jamison keeps telling me I was a sportsman, and sportsmen need sports cars. He says a man with a sports car can date anyone, any time. Not that I want to. But I know what I don't want, and that is to be trapped back in a house like this beside any woman with her eyes on a rose garden and a house as pretty as a picture. Never needed it and don't want it now. Not ever.

Chapter 32

Lucy

Dirk is quiet this morning. Did I disgrace myself somehow? We're both still fully clothed when I wake.

He paces back and forth rubbing his arms, clearly in a hurry to leave. I'm slightly hung over. We drink water, upend the cups on the counter to dry themselves, and he rushes to the car to get the heater working. As I approach, he lowers the roof, and we speed through the countryside. When it starts to sleet, Dirk pushes a little button and the roof appears out of an invisible partition in the back. It slots itself into place. Magic.

"Amazing," I say.

He stays silent.

"This car just does what it's told and doesn't even talk back," I say.

He slings me a look, as if maybe there was more to my comment than the obvious, which is true, then goes back to studying the road as the scenery glides by. There's a lot of emptiness around us. I shiver.

He cranks up the heating and I thank him. We're polite as strangers.

As we pull up near the apartment and he kills the engine, he turns to me, all serious.

"We can't take this anywhere, Lucy," he says, and I'm stunned. "I'm sorry."

"So you admit there's a 'this' between us."

"There's nothing between us." He holds himself at a distance. Did I do something wrong? I need to know.

"And why can't we take this 'nothing' anywhere, Dirk? I know you like me. Are you afraid of what your children will think? Would you really give them that much power over your life? They're adults. They might understand that their father enjoys some company now and then, or even more often – some companionship in life. You wouldn't want them to be perpetually lonely, would you? Set them a good example, Dirk."

"There are so many things wrong with your argument."

"Explain."

"You miss the important one, Lucy; the practical one."

"What's that?"

"We're neighbors, Lucy."

"So?"

"If it goes wrong, we have to see each other every day."

"And you couldn't cope with that, Dirk, a grown man like you?"

"Could you?"

"If you're saying you couldn't bear to see me with anyone else, then I'm flattered. You really like to win, don't you? "

"It's not like that…"

"We were honest with each other in the garden before Mrs Munze turned up. We were honest with each other as we talked by the fire. We like each other. We're great together. Great company. We could be more. I don't have that instant rapport with everyone, Dirk. Tell me you feel it too."

"I like you, too, very much, but I'm an old-fashioned man, Lucy. I talk about cars and engines and tools and diseases. I don't know how to talk about feelings."

"Do you know what, Dirk? My daughter and her friends would call you 'commitment-phobic.'"

"Your daughter. How's that going?"

"You're shirking the subject, Dirk."

"Me? Commitment-phobic? I know all about commitment, Lucy – commitment to family, commitment to my father's dreams, commitment to my 'educational opportunities,' commitment to the team, and then decades more of it – to my patients, to minimize their suffering and maximize their healing, whatever else was or wasn't going on in their lives, not to mention commitment to Millie and her dreamhouse … so don't you dare accuse me of commitment phobia, Lucy."

"But …"

"And you don't know the half of it."

In the plush leather bucket seat, my phone dings and I check it. It's Donna, pressing me to commit to that fresh assignment.

Freya really needs a favor, Donna text reads.

Freya's her sister. She runs the cleaning and housekeeping side of the family business. Norths, or something.

She's short staffed. Needs someone to housekeep for a week. Three clients. Can you do it? They'll be local jobs for you. Not much travel in it.

Sure, I text back. It's a no brainer. I'm so lucky to know Donna and her family, with their jobs coming out of the woodwork. The unpacking work has slowed down, with school back in. There's always a great rush of jobs during school holidays. Cleaning's not my favorite, but I can wear headphones and zone out while my body does the work.

She texts me a booking link. I fill it in without too much thought, then turn my mind to Phoebe, crossing my fingers that this time, she will respond to my message.

Chapter 33

Dirk

Lucy's busy texting in the car. Good. I'm still fuming. "Commitment-phobic?" I am made of commitments, so propped up with good intentions I can barely sit down, let alone relax, and then there are all the invisible commitments I'd almost forgotten. They pounce on me when I'm not on guard, like responsibility for little sister Jill and my demanding nephews; like Jamison's never-ending needs. They land on me with the fragrance of orange blossom at dusk in spring; and the sound of a violin after dark.

When I find a parking space near Brighton Court, Lucy is out of her side in a flash. She meets me on the sidewalk.

"Have I offended you, Dirk? What did I say?"

Lucy's hands reach out to mine, cover them gently and squeeze.

Those high cheekbones, and her eyes – so sincere. I've never told anyone the whole of it, not even Millie. What could it hurt to share my sorrows? But Lucy and I are neighbors, and if this fragile thing between us, whatever it is – if it breaks, how will it be to pass her in the stairwell every day and have to stare her down, forget what we've shared? How could I ever bring someone else to Brighton Court? Or see her here with somebody new?

Lucy is right. As long as I hold her at bay, our relationship has no name. Nothing is ventured, and nothing gained. But nor is anything lost.

"Let's play ten questions again," Lucy says as we walk companionably down the hill towards the apartments.

"This is not a game," I say.

"Then what is it, if it's not a game?" she says, as she stops and pins me with her eyes. "Is it war? Is it peace? Am I suddenly the enemy? Dirk, you must have played a hundred games of soccer and saved even more goals, your efforts and triumphs on show for hundreds of thousands of fans. So what 'game' is it you can't play with me? Friends share, Dirk."

"Leave me alone, please, Lucy," I say, and I turn away from her. Already I'm hurting her, I know it, and I can't bear it, not any of it. I need my own space, my apartment.

But when I get there, and my breath settles from all the steps, it's all too perfect. The housekeeper has sprayed the place with something. I throw open the windows and lean out, and it's then that I see her; Lucy Beston, running up the hill like a wild thing, my words behind her.

It was a mistake to take her to that house. I can't wait to sell the place, but I won't be forced to sell this one, too. It's convenient. It's comfortable. It's a fresh start. What more could I possibly want? I force the image of Lucy's lithe body as far away as possible from my mind – her warmth, her vivacity, her subtle sense of humor, her bright eyes, the set of her chin – and that calculated kiss on the dancefloor, in front of hundreds of people, including Jill and Jamison and Dee.

My phone rings.

"So, who is she, Dad, the mystery woman?" says Dee.

"Lucy, my neighbor. I went to introduce you at the ball, but she was already leaving."

"Is she that drug addict who was on tv?"

Chapter 34

Lucy

As Dirk heads into the building, I lean down and check my letterbox. Just then, my phone dings. Is it Dirk, having second thoughts about brushing me off?

But it's Phoebe. I fist pump the air. She still wants to see me. She agrees to meet at Esther's and gives me a date and time, three days away.

My heart sings at Phoebe's overture. Maybe she'll agree to visit me at Brighton Court. Maybe it can be like old times, and she can stay with me from time to time.

There's an envelope in my letterbox. From Phoebe? I dive on it, but it's from a realty company. I'm just about to crumple it up and put it in the recycling when I realized it's addressed to me – unlike most junk mail. I tear it open, glance at it, then read every word carefully again.

No. Oh no.

I can't get to the real estate office soon enough. I run up the hill again, puffing, and thrust the letter at the secretary, the same one who took all the papers when I signed the lease. The paper shakes with my fury and dismay.

"Is this true?" I say. "It says here my apartment is going to be sold, but I've only just settled in. Can they really do this? I signed a whole bunch of papers promising I'd stay for a year. Didn't they have to do the same?"

"I'm sorry Mrs Beston. There's nothing I can do about it." She sounds bored. I am anything but. I'm horrified.

"But I love my place. I do. Will I have to move?"

"It depends on who buys it. The new owner might want to keep it as an investment property, and selling a place already rented to a reliable, stable tenant is an asset."

"But I'm not just some kind of pet; a paying pet; available to the highest bidder."

"I don't have any power over the realty industry, Mrs Beston, I just work here."

"Ms Beston. Ms, please. I'm divorced."

"I'm sorry, Ms Beston."

She turns her eyes back to her computer, dismissing me. I want to rail against it, rail against her, but it's nothing to do with her, really.

"Well, I'm sorry to interrupt you again, but do you have any idea how much money they want for it?" I may be in luck. My heart soars. The timing could be perfect. If the settlement money comes through in time, I'll buy the place myself – then nobody will ever force me to move again. Maybe once I own the apartment I really will be able to install that pizza oven in the garden. We can have parties. All the dread is replaced by a great rush of hope. I may be able to stay at Brighton Court. Forever.

"There's a price expectation on the back of the flyer, Mrs … Ms Beston."

I flip it over and try to absorb the amount. I swallow my shock. It's exorbitant, of course, but my old house was huge, perfectly kept, and decorated with impeccable style, if I say so myself. Hope and despair battle inside me, but I choose hope. I will give this opportunity everything I have.

"Well, thank you," I say. "See you at an open house, I guess."

"Oh no. I have to stay here and look after the rentals all day."

"Of course. Thank you."

"My pleasure, Ms Beston. Oh, and there will be open houses every Wednesday and Saturday until it's sold, and at other times if we phone you in advance. You'll need to keep the place clean."

"I always keep the place clean. I love it. So are you saying I'll have strangers traipsing in and out, poking inside my cupboards?"

"I'm afraid so, Mrs … Ms … But only between noon and one o'clock on Wednesdays and Saturdays. An agent will be on site the whole time. Your things are safe."

"Yes. Right."

As soon as I step outside, I phone Felicia Tonkersen, my attorney. I don't care if she charges by the minute. I explain my plan and she says she'll try and speed up the final agreements, including the deposits from the sale of our old place.

"Thank you so much."

"My pleasure, Ms Beston. Keep me informed."

I phone Donna and tell her all the good news, about Phoebe, and the bad news – my predicament and my plan to secure my own future, here at Brighton Court.

"I hate the whole buy and sell thing, Lucy," Donna says. "So many disappointments. So many dreams trashed. You know there can only be one successful buyer."

"I know, but why shouldn't it be me?"

"Optimistic Lucy. That's my gal. Well, I can't lend you any money, but I'll send you a list of buyers' agents my family uses. You'd better find one straight away. Do you have savings? Will you need a loan officer? I can get you some documentation showing you've had regular work with us, but it might not be enough. Do you have a credit history?"

"No. Bart did everything. But I can ask my divorce lawyer to show proof of my expected settlement. With any luck I should be able to buy it outright."

"Lucy! I wish I could help."

"You already have, Donna. You know you have. You couldn't have done any more for me and I'm so, so grateful. Thank you."

"Sorry I can't stay on the phone. I have an appointment with a new international moving company interested in using our services. At least there could be more work for you if you're paying off an enormous mortgage, girlfriend. I'll put in a good word for you if it all comes off."

"Thanks, Donna. Good luck!"

She pings me through her list of buyers' agents immediately, and I check them out. It's not encouraging. Yes, they all have the best reviews, but when I phone them, one by one, they say they're flat out representing other buyers. Then I find a new one online. No reviews, but her face is sweet. Hilary Cheng. She answers straight away.

"Hilary Cheng, buyers' agent. May I help you?"

"Oh, Hilary. Thanks so much for answering. It's Lucy Beston and I want to buy the apartment I'm renting. Near downtown. West side of the river. Full brick. Big old thing. Solid."

"I know the area. I'll need the exact address. What's the asking price? Do you need a loan officer? Do you have savings?"

I tell her my situation and she reassures me she knows what she's doing.

"Thanks for this chance, Lucy," she says. "It's so hard to establish a reputation in this industry when you're new, but I won't let you down."

She tells me she'll contact the seller's agent for me. "Do you have an offer in mind?"

I tell her about my old place, and we toss values back and forth, and halve them.

"There'll be closing costs and my percentage to cover as well, Lucy. You won't have to pay moving costs, as you're already there, but have you costed insurance? Do you have a downpayment ready to go? Twenty per cent is the general rule."

The sign goes up outside Brighton Court the next day, and my apartment is featured in the local paper.

Brighton Court is described as "tightly held" and all its features lovingly described. It makes me more determined than ever to make it mine. Already I'm repainting the bedroom in my mind, and replacing the scratched old bath with something more elegant. It's unsettling to know I might be outbid for it, but at least I have a plan.

I knock on Dirk's door several times, but the only time he's there, he tells me he's just leaving, off to babysit his grandchildren. I smile. I'd love to go with him and make out on the sofa when they're all asleep, like in the olden days, when I was in high school and a boyfriend was allowed to sit with me.

On Wednesday, I'm torn between tidying my place up for the open houses, or making it as messy as I can. I hang around near the front door, and when an older couple comes in the front gate, I phone Donna.

"The place looks alright, but the plumbing's atrocious," I say loudly, and I see the couple turn to each other. "And my neighbors are crazy. I can't wait to move out. Hip hop blasts day and night. I think they compete, or maybe they teach it, right below my bedroom."

"Lucy?"

"Shhh, Donna. Just pretend for me, will you?"

Like a good friend, she throws herself into it, and I put her on speakerphone, up loud.

"And the motorcycle gang?" she says.

"Oh, you're right," I say. "Awful! The motorcycle drives me crazy. Davey revs up before dawn every day. I think he's some kind of chef."

"Does he specialize in cooking sauerkraut?"

I keep her on speaker phone as the next prospective buyers come up the front stairs."

"Yes. Sauerkraut. And kimchee. The place smells like old cooked cabbages and garlic for days and days."

We keep it up for an hour. Dear Donna. She says she's unpacking a huge kitchen and glad to chat as she fills the cupboards. I owe her.

"All gone now. We're safe until Saturday morning."

We discuss painting the place a vile color, but I can't really do that without the landlord's permission. She suggests I tack up some death metal posters, but I know I can't live with them. I've only just arranged the furniture the exact way I like it, with pale pink throw rugs and pale green scatter cushions toning in with my favorite shabby chic pieces. Now that my whole haven is under threat, I need my peace and quiet more than ever.

I throw myself into creating more lamps, and if I don't clean up as well after myself as usual, I forgive myself. The second bedroom is a mess of fabrics and half-finished projects by the following Saturday, and I don't care.

On Sunday, children's laughter summons me to the window. Down in the garden, there are two of them, jumping up and down, all energy. There's a red ball. My heart jumps when I see Dirk with the children, holding the ball above their heads and to the side, teasing them as they reach and miss and laugh and squeal. They need more space to play. Too bad Professor No disapproves.

I pull on a warm jacket, grab a bunch of grapes and some bananas, my gardening gloves and clippers, and rush down all the stairs and out into the cold.

The kids squawk and Dirk holds a finger to his lips to quieten them. "Focus on the ball," he says. "Don't waste your breath."

Caught up in their game, they barely notice me, or Dirk chooses to ignore me. The Doc's still got it, a lynx-like way with the ball, as if it's an extension of his will, one moment airborne, and the next, tucked up under his arm as if it grew there. Liam jumps to retrieve it and Dirk teases him and then relents. The boy's fumbles are a sweet contrast to Dirk's control. Dirk laughs and ruffles his grandson's hair, then it's Lexie's turn.

I've tried to push Dirk out of my mind, but it's impossible. Yes, I want my apartment – but I also want to be the red ball, Dirk's focus, in play and vital, as close to him as possible in the centre of his beloved family.

Chapter 35

Dirk

"A good big brother shares, Theo," I tell my grandson as he hogs the ball for himself and holds it just above Lexie's reach. He's two years older than Lexie, faster and more nimble.

"It's no fun at all if you don't share it, Theo," I say. "The trick is to play the game."

Lexie stands, hands on hips, defiant but defeated, bottom lip trembling.

"Time for a tackle," I tell her, and swoop in. I pick Theo up, turn him upside down and shake him, but he holds on to the ball as if his life depends on it.

Suddenly, Lexie's missing. The gate is closed. She can't escape. Has she climbed a tree, fallen down a hole?

There she is, in the far corner, with someone else. It's Lucy, down on her haunches, showing my granddaughter something.

"You let us know when you're ready to share, Theo," I tell my grandson, and stride towards Lucy. She meets my gaze full on.

"You're still avoiding me," she says. "Okay if I give your grandkids a snack? Phoebe was always angriest when she was hungry. Hangry."

Lexie stares up at me as if she's found a fairy at the bottom of the garden.

"Okay," I say.

Theo spots the fruit, drops the red ball and runs across to us, hands outstretched.

"What we really need in this corner is a pizza oven," says Lucy. "We had so much fun with ours, at my old house, and here, everyone could enjoy it. Do you like pizza?" she asks the children.

They nod, their mouths full of grapes. My own mouth waters.

Lucy holds them out to me and I take a few. They're sweet and juicy and perfect. I've been taking care of Theo and Lexie for three hours. The garden was a diversion that worked well for a while, but was going stale. Lucy's arrival is helpful. She's more than welcome. My gut twists.

Lucy whispers in Lexie's ear and she shoots around the edge of the fence and grabs the red ball while Theo's eyes are on Lucy. Lexie's joy is absolute.

Fruit fest over, Lucy coaxes Lexie to throw her the ball. It's an excellent throw for a four-year-old, if I say so myself – maybe she's inherited my ball skills. Lucy's catch is even better. She lobs it back to Lexie.

"Okay, Theo," says Lucy. "You and me against Grandpa and Lexie, okay?"

He nods solemnly and the game is on. We run until we're all laughing and puffed. I'm amazed that half an hour has passed. Lucy has a natural way with the children, and they love it. She continues to surprise me, this lithe neighbor with her ready laugh. She has self-respect without taking herself too seriously.

Lexie stumbles on a piece of old concrete, and when Lucy and I both reach out to steady her, we collapse into each other, arms and legs tangling, an awkward starfish of awareness. She's soft and strong in all the right places, deliciously alive and full of joy. I hold Lucy long enough that Lexie peers up at us and gives a wide smile of wonder, her grazed knee temporarily forgotten. It's only for a moment, this awkward embrace, but it replays in my mind, over and over, the feel of her. I don't want to let Lucy go.

It's time to take the children back upstairs for pick up.

"Thank you, Lucy," I say as I step away from her with the curt nod I used to dismiss patients, regretting my formality.

"See you around."

Lucy and I haven't spoken properly since I took her to my old house, and then her apartment came up for sale.

Avoiding her has been uncomfortable. I've actually missed her.

Dee tried to set me up with Bettina – some kind of fake discussion about fund management for the dementia charity, but Bettina was as uncomfortable about it as I was. I've never been attracted to her.

Then Dee found me a "friend" from one of her classes, a lovely person but I'm not interested. She sat us next to each other at a family dinner, but we had nothing to say to one another. Talk about awkward. It's made me realize how special Lucy is – that we can discuss anything and laugh and cry and enjoy each other's company. I've missed her.

"Come up with us," I say. "Dee's collecting the children. She can meet you and see for herself you're no drug addict."

But it's Matt who collects the children. After the polite hellos and farewells, Lexie running back to grab my leg and give Lucy another smile, I offer my neighbor a glass of water.

"Okay," she says, and I gesture at my lounge while I head into the kitchen.

When I return with the two glasses and place them on the coffee table, Lucy's shoulders are so slumped I want to lean forwards and squeeze one of them, and before I know it, my hand is there, on the creamy soft, curve of her shoulder.

When she turns her face up towards mine, there are tears in her eyes, but it's not about the network, she says.

"Did I offend you, back at your house, that night, Dirk?"

"No. Nothing happened."

"Should something have happened? Is that what I did wrong?"

"No. I'm an old fashioned man. I wouldn't …"

"Then why have you been avoiding me?"

"Lucy, we live so close to each other that if we become an item, and then have to break it off, it will be awkward for both of us."

"More awkward than this?"

But it's not awkward. Being with Lucy feels natural. She's as elegant as ever in my apartment; at ease with me in an extraordinary way, not in the obsequious way that so annoyed me from so many other single

women, back in Franklin. Lucy is my equal in so many ways. She's in
fine health; she can look after herself. Exactly why am I afraid?

A ray of sunlight strikes glints off her rings, shooting sparks across my
ceiling, and I lean away.

"Is it my diamonds, Dirk?"

"As a matter of fact, Lucy, my friend Walt, the divorce attorney, does
say that a lot of diamonds on a single older woman sends warning
signals."

"You're kidding me. Is that all?" She slips one of her rings off a finger
and holds it out to me. "Here. Would you like it?"

"Lucy ..."

"I'm serious, Dirk. If that's the issue, have them all." She begins to pull
them all off her fingers, to pile them in her lap. She gathers them up in a
jangle and holds them out to me on her palm.

"Lucy, that's not necessary."

"Apparently it is. You make such a big deal of my diamonds, as if only
a man could have bought them for me, or a string of men, as if I would
only love you for your money. Are you trying to suggest that the way we
can converse and what our bodies tell us whenever we're close to each
other means nothing at all? Are you accusing me of offering my love for
sale, to the highest bidder?"

"Well ..."

"Traditionally, Dirk, women may have been men's property and
women depended on their support and largesse, and sure, there's a long
way to go in reaching equality of the sexes, but we're not living in Jane
Austen's England any more. Besides, you have no idea how much
money I have, and it's not relevant; not to me. For all you know, I could
buy you out ten times over, buy you five more red convertibles. Would
that make a difference?"

"The car is Jamison's."

"You're ignoring my point."

She goes to stand, to close the door on me, but stops herself.

"But I'm not leaving until I tell you how I see this. This is our second
chance, Dirk, and I don't want us to miss it. You have no idea what I
love most about you – from the slim shock of white hair near your scar

that proves both your vulnerability and your resilience, to your faithfulness to your wife's memory."

I blink.

"I'm being honest about my attraction to you, Dirk, to your kindness – though you've shown precious little of that to me lately, but I know it still lurks there in your good heart, and that you're fighting it."

I clear my throat.

"I haven't finished," she says. "I love the way your grandchildren run to you. I see it from my kitchen window – their little faces all smiles and eagerness. So you can pretend to be cold and hard and distant, but Millie knew it and those children know it – you're a great big softie, and they love you for it, and so do I."

I go to speak, but she stands and shows me the palm of her hand, upright, as if she's a traffic cop.

"But don't you worry, Dirk. I'm not waiting around for you to propose to me."

She drops to one knee, right there in front of me, her rings like fire on the gray carpet.

"Because I'm proposing to you. Will you marry me, Doctor Dirk O'Connell MD? I dare you. Let's put an end to this cat and mouse game once and for all. I'm serious about my diamonds. Have one. Have two. I have plenty, as you've already noted. Actually all but Bart's came to me from my mother and grandmother. Tell your attorney friend that, if he's so interested. Or do you really want us to have a never-ending standoff?"

She holds them all out to me in the palm of one hand.

"Lucy?"

"I'm serious, Dirk. Come on. Take one. Take them all. For centuries women have swapped their devotion, independence and entire futures for a sparkler. I'm not asking you to do the same. If being together is just about diamonds, have some of mine."

I hold up both hands. What can I say?

"Oh, and I have a spare ticket for a post-Christmas cruise, in the Caribbean, warm and far away from Brighton Court and your lawyer friend and family expectations, Dirk, if they're the problem." she says. "I won the silent auction item at the ball. I couldn't bear the thought of setting up for Christmas and Phoebe cancelling on me at the very last minute, so I might go early and enjoy a fancy hotel to myself before I board the ship, if I have to. Though things seem to be thawing with Phoebe, thank goodness. I'm meeting her later today.

"Actually, Dirk, we probably won't even be neighbors by then, so there'll be no more embarrassing moments for you in the stairwell, trying to avoid me. My apartment's for sale, as you no doubt know. I hope to buy it for myself, but I might not be successful. I might have to move out soon. So you could just come along on the cruise and have some fun. I promise I won't make you join the deck exercises." She's sparkling again, as if she's forgiven me, as if the future could only be rosy. Her optimism is infectious.

"Thanks for the invitation, Lucy," I say. "I'll think about it." There's no way I can go on a cruise with Lucy. I can't trust myself to see her every day and every night, and not lead her on, much as I might enjoy it. I'm not interested in having affairs. Marriage? Is she serious?

"Good," she says. "Do that. You think about it." And she gives me the kind of smile that lifts my heart. I like making this woman happy; can't actually remember whose idea it was that we stop seeing each other.

"We could make it a honeymoon cruise, Dirk. The captain can marry people. I'll send you the link."

She lets herself out of my apartment and runs back down the stairs, dust motes spiraling and a trace of tropical perfume in her wake – plumeria?

Chapter 36

Lucy

So much for Dirk. Let him play hard to get. At least he knows where I stand. It's his turn to make a move, and frankly, I have more things on my mind than romance right now, like my public reputation, like reconnecting with my daughter, and, especially, securing my apartment for good.

It's Phoebe on my mind as I wait for her at Esther's teahouse.

To protect myself, I hold zero hopes our meeting will go well. Life with Phoebe hasn't been easy since she was in high school.

As exotic tea fragrances waft around us, Sabrina the waitress hovers again, ready for my order.

"I'm waiting for my daughter," I say.

"Oh, how lovely!"

I know my smile is saccharine. It matches my hands, folded too neatly on top of the table. They hide my dread.

Of course I'm way too early. I didn't want to be late.

I check Donna's message for Freya's assignment details – the addresses and times I'm expected to clean and cook for her clients.

The iced water stops in my throat, and I cough till my eyes are running.

I phone Donna on the spot.

"Donna, it's Lucy," I say. "Look, I said I'd help Freya out and I'd be glad to, really, but there's one client on her list I really can't work for. Hope that's okay."

"You can't pull out now, girlfriend," Donna says. "What's the problem? Is it who I think it is? You unpacked his place so you already know it, and talk about convenient. Easy money. Exactly what you need. Exactly what Freya needs. Exactly what he needs."

I try to tell Donna it doesn't seem right, sneaking in and out of my neighbor's apartment. Dirk's no ordinary client. He's somebody I know. A person I value.

"I really don't think I can do this, Donna. I actually care for him. A lot." The right words won't come.

"'Care for him,' Lucy? Great. Even better, my friend. You can 'care for him' literally. Give him the works. Give him your apple pie."

Maybe Donna is right. Am I being silly? She's never asked much of me, and she's been my lifeline all these past months. Still, I worry.

"You couldn't step in, Donna? Do it for me?"

"No, I can't, Lucy. You know how busy I am with all the unpacking clients. Business is great. Look, we wouldn't have asked you if there was any other option. Freya's in a pickle. I shouldn't tell you this, but a couple of her employees were caught stealing and she had no choice but to fire them. She's got new people joining, but they can't start for at least a week. I still don't see why it's a problem for you."

"I just …" What? Am I ashamed to be caught cleaning? No. I'm not too proud to clean for a wage. It's just … should I tell him I'll be in his personal space? Handling his things?

"So are you going to help us out? Please, Lucy?"

"Okay," I say. Donna's help for me was instant and endless. And I don't really know where I stand with Dirk on a personal level any more. It's not like he ran after me to accept my proposal.

Now I can go back to wondering whether Phoebe will turn up, not to mention worrying about whether I'll even have a roof over my head soon. There's no question I need the work. I'll need the money, whether or not Hilary and I can make a successful offer.

I hang up the phone just as Phoebe rounds the corner with a new haircut and a face like marble – beautiful but distant. Gone are the days she would run to my arms – warm bundle of soft bones – and bury her face against me. She'd peep up at me and give me the smiles of her heart. How quickly heaven passed.

I go to stand but she's already pulled out her own chair. She perches across the table from me, her body at an angle, a butterfly, ready to flee.

I reach my hands across the table, palms up.

"Phoebe."

Her eyes flick to mine, then hide again. She keeps her fingers clenched around her chair, not yet bringing it forwards.

I could prattle. I could fill this silence with so many truths – how I've longed to see her; how I hope she's well. I want to know how I can help her, but I've said all that before, in letters, in text messages, in voice-to-text. Until recently, into pure silence.

A strand of her hair is caught behind her right ear. I want to brush it back.

"Thanks for coming," she says, and my heart turns over once, twice. I bite my tongue on the great gush of words and thoughts I want to share.

"It's my boyfriend who thought I should meet you."

I nod again. I smile, gently, a thousand questions pounding in my chest, unvoiced. I swallow to let another second or two pass in silence, to let her open up.

"He's studying psych too; thinks seeing you is healthy."

The waitress bustles back with an ornate menu, and Phoebe turns to it. She studies the great list of exotic teas from all over the world, and subcategories – chais and fruit teas, white and black teas, ones with caffeine and ones without, teas for wellness, for weight loss and calm.

I don't care about tea. I care about Phoebe.

When she selects a hibiscus tea after much deliberation, I choose the same.

This is worse than a first date, but it's another tiny step into a better future for us. I'll do whatever it takes.

Phoebe chews at some skin on the side of her thumb, an old habit; picks up her phone, then puts it down again. She frowns at the cafe, almost empty, then stares at me, openly, her gaze a spotlight, a canon. Here it comes.

"You moved out and you didn't even tell me," she says.

I swallow. It's true. I'd wanted to spare Phoebe all of that – the depth of her father's betrayal, my wild flight, so out of control. I was lucky I didn't crash the car. My whole world had dropped away without a warning.

"It happened so fast, Phoebe, my darling," I say. "I'm sorry. I just …" I can't tell her I found her father in bed with his personal assistant. "I just couldn't go back there. I knew you were safe; busy in college. If I went back, I'd be living a lie."

"But you took forever to let me know."

"I wanted to spare you the truth as long as I could, and I guess I wondered if Bart would have a change of heart."

"You're the one who left, Mom."

"I left because your father fell out of love with me. He fell in love with the Minx …"

"Her name's Mishelle. Mom. Dad's happy. He said you didn't love him anymore."

He would say that. As his star kept rising, I was beside him with my make-up kit, all the way. I can't tell Phoebe how vain he became, how in love with his own image, how he began to believe his own PR. Over time, I realized Phoebe and I came a big fat second to Bart's ego. Bart stared at himself in mirrors more than he ever looked at us. In time, our only intimacy was when I touched up his makeup. No wonder I turned to restoring furniture. It was ultimately more rewarding. She doesn't need to hear any of that.

"Dad told me you had an affair."

My mouth drops open. Do I have to tell Phoebe her father is a liar? At least it explains why she's been keeping her distance.

"I did not have an affair, darling. And I never wanted your home to be ripped from under you; from either of us," I say.

"That's not what Dad says."

I close my eyes. I don't need to hear more of Bart's lies. Bart is my past.

"On a practical note, darling, I need to know your bank account details. A settlement will come through, maybe soon. I want you to benefit."

Phoebe stares at me; stares at my rings. I pull one off and try to give it to her, but she waves me away.

"Why not? My mother gave them to me; and her mother gave them to her."

"I know, but you can't buy love, Mom. There are so many more important things going on in the world than this. Global warming. Climate change. Refugees with nowhere to go."

"You're absolutely right, but we all need security, darling."

I haven't convinced her.

"You always cared more for the house than for us," Phoebe announces.

I can't nod at this, but I want her to keep talking. Maybe once she's said it all to my face, we can move on.

"Your whole 'shabby chic trash to treasure' business? Those photos with me in frilly, old-fashioned little girl clothes … I was just another accessory, another prop for your Instagram photos. You never asked me if I wanted my picture all over the web; never got my permission."

"I closed down that side of the business, Phoebe – it's all gone to ReUse – and I deleted all the posts with you in them. I only run Lucy's Lamps now – and no photos of you, I promise."

"Good."

"Phoebe, I don't know what the best way to tell you would have been." I can't get the pleading out of my voice. It cracks as I try to explain. I stare at a spot on the side of the sugar bowl; twist the lid on and off and on again as my words rush out.

"I know the phone was grossly inadequate; but I managed to find work, and I needed that work whenever I could get it," I say. "I had to make a fresh start. Perhaps I should have driven up to see you, but I couldn't risk losing my job; not in those first few months."

She nods slowly. It occurs to me she's not deliberately trying to hurt me. She genuinely wants to know how her own world turned upside down.

"Let's talk about you, darling," I say, chancing a smile. "How is your course? Where did you and your boyfriend meet? What's his name? Where's he from?" They gush out after all; some of my questions; like the tea from the pot as Sabrina returns and pours it, fragrant steam rising around us.

Phoebe wraps her fingers around her cup and shrugs.

"You look great," I say.

"Really?"

Well, maybe it's not quite true. There are dark smudges under Phoebe's beautiful eyes. I want to hug her close, but she's chosen a very public place for our conversation, rather than to come to my new apartment, and she's keeping her distance.

"Why can't you just tell the truth, Mom?" She chances a glance at my eyes, then ducks her own eyes away from mine again, hiding her thoughts. At least she picks up the menu.

The waiter approaches as she scans the options. It's Sabrina again, sunny in a white t-shirt with yellow daisies. She's from Malaysia, always cheerful, despite working all hours and studying English in between. I'd sit Sabrina down for a chat with us in an instant if I didn't think she'd lose her job. She could tell Phoebe about her own barefoot childhood, so far away, her own troubles making ends meet in a new city. Maybe they could be friends.

Phoebe stares at the menu and begins to speak.

"I'm okay. It's okay. Jaxon's from Oregon. We met at a party. Nothing like how you and Dad met."

What am I supposed to say?

Phoebe replaces her cup in the saucer and turns it around and around. She spotlights me again, her gaze unfiltered, vulnerable.

"How do I know if he's the one?"

"Oh. Well." I'd love to have an answer, but I'd thought Bart was the one, and now look at me. She's waiting, eyes on mine. "I don't know, Phoebe."

"But …"

"You're different to me, and I have no doubt Jaxon is very different from your father."

"Did you think you'd be together forever?"

I nod.

"That's what marriage is, Phoebe. It's a public promise – a commitment to be together forever, and I wanted that. But you're right about the house. I did love it. Maybe too much. Maybe it became a distraction. And then, in a way, a kind of … consolation. I loved your father, but we saw each other less and less. He was in demand day and night, on screen and off it. I worked alongside him in the early years, but then I was busy raising you."

"So now it's my fault?"

"No. Not at all! We couldn't love you more. Phoebe. I tried to keep our family together. And I failed. But I wasn't alone in failing. It takes two to honor a commitment."

"Dad says you lost interest in him."

Did I? I loved being a stay-at-home mum – meeting Phoebe at the gates after lessons each day, walking her home, hearing the news, laughing at her stories, offering her comfort through the bullying years, helping with her school assignments, doing the makeup for all her school plays.

And as she became more independent, I turned my attention to the garden, to my shabby chic business, then starting Lucy's Lamps.

"Maybe we lost interest in each other, Phoebe. Your father had a very interesting career. I don't really know why he stopped loving me. It scares me, that love can be so transient."

"So you don't trust love?"

Suddenly I understand why Phoebe has agreed to see me. And I lean across the table and take her hands again as she waits for my words.

"Love is the best, Phoebe. Don't ever let what happened to me and your father stand between you and your own boyfriend, or any future boyfriends for that matter. You are two completely different people. And you do know the old saying, that 'it's better to have loved and lost than never to have loved at all,' don't you?"

"Platitudes."

"Sometimes platitudes are all we've got, Phoebe. Besides, love has a way of sneaking up on us, whether or not we're looking for it."

"Have you moved on already?" Phoebe's gaze is hard as a brick fence.

"Yes. No. Well, things happen, Phoebe. You meet people."

"You've met someone?"

"I didn't say that. But your father has clearly moved on." I'm not yet ready to tell her about Dirk. There's nothing to say about him, anyway. He's a neighbor, a friend, an acquaintance – a mere distraction. That's not true.

Dirk is a force. Compelling. Impressive. Okay. I have more than a crush on my silver fox neighbor. But I have no idea how he feels about me.

"I won't rule out marrying again, Phoebe. Not at all. The break-up with your father made me question everything in my life and it hasn't been easy. But that's no reason not to love again."

She listens, lets me speak.

"I'm so, so sorry you've been hurt, Phoebe. It hasn't been great for me either, you know, but I've thought about this carefully. It's over. So now I don't want to waste a moment being bitter. Life is beautiful. It's an adventure. It will never be the same as it was, but it might even be better."

There's the hint of a smile from her, sunlight between clouds, and my heart lifts, but then she turns away.

"I've had to move on and fill my life with new ideas and new people," I say. "Most of my friends were part of Bart's crowd of admirers." I don't want to go there. It's not for her to hear how shallow those friendships proved to be; how most of them simply shifted allegiances and stuck with Bart and the Minx.

I have to be careful what I say. Donna has told me Phoebe likes the Minx. They're not that dissimilar in age – they know the same bands; are both on TikTok. The Minx invites Phoebe to concerts when she gets free tickets. I've turned my back on her, but Phoebe can't. Not if she wants to see her father. I don't want her to have to choose between us, to demonstrate loyalty to me. That's irrelevant now. I've voted with my feet.

I tell her about my apartment, how I'm hoping to buy it.

"It's in an old block, solid, comforting, with lovely light, and district views, and there's even a bit of a garden I'm working on. I'd love you to visit. Maybe next time?"

She doesn't agree; nor does she disagree. She pours more tea for herself, hesitates, then fills my cup, too.

"Thank you," I say. "And thank you so much for coming to this café. Did you see all the beautiful boutiques and bakeries and wine bars? There's room for you in my apartment. You're welcome any time. You have my address. Bring Jaxon. I'd love to meet him. When you're ready."

She's silent, but she's taking it in. I'm grateful. Baby steps. My baby, all grown up.

"I'm proud of you, Phoebe," I say. She's been brave, to move on by herself. I want to kidnap her and take her shopping, to buy her new shoes, take her to a movie, make pancakes for breakfast with her, and laugh at the voices and music on the crazy cartoons. I want to pick her up and twirl her around as I did when she was four, until she's so thrilled and laughing and full of joy she knows nothing but love.

"Keep in touch," I say. Already her eyes have edged away from me, towards the distance. Our precious time together is almost over.

"See you," she says, as she stands, but it's just an expression, habitual, not a promise, and she waves one hand and turns away. I fight the impulse to run after her and tackle her to the ground and cover her with kisses until she giggles – my beloved child.

She turns back to me for a moment, as if she can read my mind.

"I have to go, Mom. I have class. See you next time."

I want to ask when we'll see each other again, but she's already gone, the rest of her tea slowly going cold on our table.

Chapter 37

Lucy

At home again, I sit for a moment on my sofa, as Phoebe's words roll over and over in my mind – "see you next time."

I love it that there'll be a next time, even if it's so unspecified.

I sit up with a jolt.

It's Thursday. I'm supposed to service Dirk's apartment today. I check my watch and it's dire. I have just fifty minutes to get in there and get out before he returns from his weekly lunch with Jamison.

It's possible, except for the pie. There's no way I can bake it in that amount of time – or can I?

I flick on my oven, race to my fruit bowl and peel and chop the apples in record time, nicking my thumb with the knife in my haste. Ouch. Retrieving the bandaid wastes precious moments. Usually I make the pastry from scratch, but this time I use frozen pastry – usually reserved for my easy party cheese scrolls. I partially cook the pie in the microwave first, and then it's in my oven, hotter than usual for faster results, and I'm out my door and into Dirk's place in under five minutes – a personal best in anyone's books.

It's not as if Dirk is a messy man, but I rush to create those lovely suction lines on his carpet in the obvious spots, use the hand towel to wipe over the bathroom sink, cabinet top and mirror and squirt some cleaning fluid at the shower. At least the place smells clean.

I change the sheets and throw the old linen in the washing machine, then have second thoughts and leave them in a lump by the door. There's no way I can cycle it all through the washer and dryer in ten minutes. I'll do it at my place and sneak it in later. Tonight is his choir rehearsal night.

I'm back in my place before four, front door shut, and pant with relief – only to realize I left the damp towels in the bathroom. I peer out the front window. No red car, though he might have parked further up the street if there wasn't space…

I'll have to risk it. My nose tells me the pie is done. It's a clincher. I'll drop the fresh pie onto his stove, snatch up the towels and disappear pronto.

I'm almost back to my place when I hear him coming up the stairs. I rush towards my door with my key out and drop it, his towels clutched against my chest.

"Smells great in here," Dirk says as he passes me. He's handsome in his exercise clothes, tall, an attractive combination of energetic and relaxed. I'm so glad I managed to place fresh towels in his bathroom. My mind shouldn't go there. Especially not now, so I focus on his words.

"Like apple pie," I say. "Cinnamon. Nutmeg. Nice."

"Mmm," he says. "Oh. Can I help you?" Why does he have to be such a gentleman?

"I'm fine," I say, as I bend to retrieve my key.

"Allow me," he says, and he beats me to it, goes to hand it to me with a flourish, then spots my armful of towels, does a double take and inserts the key into my lock.

I flush as he inspects my expression, frantically morphing from alarm to faux gratitude. His eyes drop back to his towels just as I twist my key and push myself and the bundle inside. Maybe he didn't notice.

"Everything okay, Lucy?" he asks.

"Fine. Great. Thanks. See you." I close the door and lean on it from the inside, still clutching the towels. Did I get away with it?

Chapter 38

Dirk

Jamison's lost weight. His smile is hearty enough – he's pleased to see me, but whatever's on his mind has not gone away.

This time, I insist we lunch at a place I know; less of a fish tank than his club. I'm determined to find out what's on his mind, and if it takes a private booth in Baxter's to get him to talk, so be it.

Walt took me here when he started his own campaign to get me to move back to the city. The beer's cold if forgettable, and the ribs and hamburgers hot. Not a place for Dee. Nothing vegan here.

"Out with it," I say, once our orders are placed and the drinks delivered. "And don't you dare say 'out with what.' For starters, why don't you want your car back?"

"Okay. I thought you might like to buy it."

"But why?"

"Turns out I overspent on it, or at least the repayments are killing me."

"A money man makes a mistake like that?"

"I'm not proud of it, Dad. I was expecting a raise, but Brent's holding out on me."

My boy's lips are thin. He's miserable.

"And?" I say.

"He says he wants more from me – 'skin in the game.' But I don't have that kind of money. When I came in and set up all the IT, he said I'd make partner in six months – laid it all out for me on an invisible platter – the salary, the perks, the shares. But he reneged, Dad. Big time."

"How can he do that?"

"My mistake. Nothing in writing. Plenty of fine print in our heads. All that candy was predicated on quotas, and nobody's made quota this quarter, least of all me. I thought all I had to do was make the IT sing. Turns out I need to bring in capital, too."

"Mighty expensive overheads in a set-up like that," I say, and Jamison nods.

"Brent was great when we were at college, Dad. He had the vision, the examples of companies that did what we were about to do and made it big time. All I had to do, he said, was set up the systems."

"But you've done that, haven't you?"

"I have. Worked day and night on it for the first two years out of college, back when we worked out of a garage. But Brent wanted to go too big too fast, and I had no choice but to stick with him. I'd already invested so much time and come up with so many customized systems that will only work for his set up."

Our food appears, but Jamison has no interest in food. Now he's talked, he wants my input.

"What are your choices, son?"

"Take him to court for breach of promise, with money I don't have."

"Or?"

"Stick with him and hope we can turn the business around."

"Or?"

"Convince you to invest in the business."

"In a business with someone you no longer trust?"

"There's that."

"Come on, Jamison. Or …"

"Leave him and set up my own business?"

"Or get a job. Or teach. Plenty of people lead good lives passing on their skills. Your degree is in IT, not wealth management, isn't it? You have vast amounts of freedom, Jamison. To your credit, you've been single minded about Capital Plus Investments, and you've made it work. I've seen you pour every spare minute into creating those systems, and then some more. What that tells me is that you could do that with another new idea, and another, and another."

Jamison sighs, head in his hands, his food still untouched.

"Nobody's saying it's going to be easy, but I can tell you, son – you keep going in this direction and you'll make yourself sick. I saw it all the time. Trapped people, with big families and farms they couldn't make pay enough to service their debts. I could be wrong, and I say this with love – but my guess is the only thing trapping you is your pride."

Jamison snaps his head up and stares into my eyes.

"You wouldn't be ashamed of me, Dad? Giving up on CPI? You said you were proud of me."

"I was. I am. Always will be. Sure the place is impressive. Too impressive, in fact. No place for an old doc like me. But you might choose to stay and fight and take your place at the top. All I'm saying is it's not compulsory. You can make a different choice any time you like, and you'll have my moral support, but not my financial support. Otherwise what might look like kindness, will just be trapping you somewhere you don't want to be."

He sighs again.

"So no, Jamison. I don't want to buy your car. I don't want to join CPI, and I don't want to give or lend you money. It wouldn't be doing you any favors. You can come stay with me in my new place, but only for a short while if you need a roof over your head; only while you work out what you're going to do."

I know my boy, his face still serious, his stomach in knots. He nibbles at a fry, then eats two at once, and another. He asks me about myself and barely listens to my answers.

But by the time we leave, he's eaten half the hamburger and there's a new spring in his step.

Back at Brighton Court, I run into Lucy in the hallway. She's behaving strangely. For the first time, she rushes to get away from me. It hurts. I know I have to sort out my feelings for her, to give her some kind of answer to her proposal. I don't like this awkwardness between us.

Chapter 39

Lucy

The next time I run into Dirk in the hallway, he's all dressed up, on his way out.

He stands there, my great big man, tall in his tailored suit, his legs and arms a tiny bit long for anything off the shelf. He searches my face, those dark eyes everywhere, alert to any trick.

I won't move. I won't let him pass, not without touching me.

Oh, he might turn around and go hide in his big, perfect apartment, or he can advance, and leave that cold, lonely old jail and agree to live another life, with me.

There's that faint fragrance of mothballs on his suit again. It's such a lonely smell. I want to reach up and touch his shoulder, run my hands along to meet behind his neck, and gently pull him close again, this warrior of a man with lines on his handsome face. It's as ruined as mine. We're a perfect pair. I don't budge.

No one can accuse me of throwing myself at Dirk O'Connell. Well, there was that time at the ball, but that was a matter of self-preservation, with Bart and the Minx right there in the middle of the dance floor, flaunting their love for all to see. And Dirk stepped up. Even after that hideous interview, he helped me keep my dignity. He was generous then.

I suspect Dee disapproves of me, but she has no right to run Dirk's life, especially not his love life. Nor does Jill. I'm cross with Jill. We could be friends. I gave her one of my lamps. She's ignoring me. If only she'd warm up, I'd offer to organise a fundraising fashion parade for her. I've run them before, in my old garden. There's no one more qualified. I could give her a break, learn to use the till. I'm good with people. Or I could give her a good cut on sales of my lamps. We could sit them along the tops of the shelves, with one standing lamp in her change rooms. Soft lighting is flattering. She'd have more sales.

Besides, whatever Dee and Jill and Jamison might think, Dirk and I are sovereign beings. We are the captains of our own destinies. We can make our own mistakes. Seize the day, I say. Seize each other.

After our last conversation, it's Dirk who needs to make the next move, here and now, a genuine one. I know I'm a flirt, but I'm alive, and I know how fleeting life can be.

I've fallen for Dirk, but when, if ever, will he reach for me? As himself. Not as the famous soccer goalie, or the physician; not as Millie's dutiful, devoted widower, not as Jill's generous brother, nor as the aging father of two independent children, each as complicated and beloved as my Phoebe. As himself.

He goes to walk past me, to my left or right, but I will stand here and be seen. I am no ordinary passerby or temporary neighbor, not some stranger to smile politely at and then ignore. I am Lucy, a woman who knows how to live and how to love, and I am ready to love Dirk with all my heart and mind and body. I lift my chin. I might be shorter than him, but I'm just as real.

I'm done with chasing Dirk. But I am not invisible. Now it's up to him.

Chapter 40

Dirk

It's choir night. Dress rehearsal. I'm running late. Someone's in my way. It's Lucy. What does she think she's doing, blocking my exit?

We stare at each other.

This woman does things to me. So much trouble. She's the one to watch, the kind of kid who gets behind your guard on the field, and before you know it, you regret everything.

I knew women like that, before I met Millie, and afterwards, a few times, while my guard was down, before I made friends with loneliness and got my life in order again, safe and stable, here at Brighton Court.

"What's so wrong with change?" Lucy asks me, as if she knows what I'm thinking.

"What change?" I ask. There's no smile from her this time, no guile, no charm beyond her almost feline beauty – just her question, hanging in the hallway, hovering above the gray landing that needs recarpeting.

"Always so suspicious, Dirk. I guess that's why you're still on your own."

"Is that such a bad thing?"

"I know what you're doing," she says.

"What am I doing?"

"You're blocking me."

"Blocking you."

"I'm not a ball, Dirk. I'm a person. A woman. A woman who loves you."

"What are you talking about?"

"Once a goalie, always a goalie, but this is no ball game. You can let me in, you know, into your goal, into your life. But actually, the ball's still in your court, Doc O'Connell."

I still don't know what to say. I fold my arms. Unfold them. My hands swing, too big, beside me. My fingers flex and relax. I raise one hand to my chin, a habit, and stroke my cheeks with my fingers on one side and thumb on the other, feel my bristles.

Her voice is a whisper, so quiet I have to lean down to hear her.

"What if we were on the same team, Dirk? Think about it." She holds my gaze for a few seconds – more – not smiling, not frowning. She lifts her head, then steps aside to let me pass.

I try to chuckle as I descend and get into Jamison's car, but my heart's not in it. My heart's confused.

That night, after rehearsal, I'm aware of every sound from Lucy's apartment below mine. I wonder where she is – in the kitchen, in her living room, feet curled beneath her on the couch, in her bedroom. I remember how she felt in the big bed in Franklin, so warm beside me as she slept.

I lasso my imagination, force it to the ground and straddle it. Lucy is just a neighbor.

Instead, I turn my mind to Jamison's latest request, that I help him set up his own company, harnessing AI to come up with wealth management options faster than Capital Plus Investments, faster than anyone else.

Next day, I'm in my exercise gear, pulling on my new walking shoes when I get a call from Jamison, right in the middle of his working week, in the middle of the day. I pick up, thinking someone's cancelled on him for lunch at the club. I'm watching my weight but I have all the time in the world, more time than I know what to do with.

I'm not prepared for his tone of voice - strained. Is my son crying? He can barely get out words.

"Jamison? Son?"

"Dad …"

"Are you okay? Where are you? Has there been an accident?"

"Not exactly. Yes. But not like that. Dad?"

"What is it?"

"Dad, I need your help."

"Can I call the police?"

"No. No. Where are you?"

"Brighton Court." I say, mind spinning through possibilities. He can't have crashed the car. I still have it. "Where are you?"

"Downtown."

"You busy?"

"No. Need me to come pick you up?"

"Yeah. Be great, Dad. I'm sorry. I'm a mess."

It's not the first time Jamison's asked directly for help. That's what I'm for. We never stop loving our children. But it's the first time in a decade, maybe. A memory of an incident back when he was in school flashes back at me, of rescuing Jamison and his friends from a party when they drank alcohol underage. I took them to a back room of the clinic to sober up – kept their secrets quiet under patient confidentiality. They were sick enough to have learned their lesson.

He's drooping when I collect him, shoulders hunched, tie hanging off, suit coat crooked, one half of the collar turned up. He's dejected, unshaven. Haunted. I wonder if he's been drinking.

"It's all over," he says, the minute he's in the passenger seat.

It's on the tip of my tongue to tell him it can't possibly be over for anyone aged under fifty, especially someone in good health like Jamison. He's a puppy, the whole world at his feet. But I hold it, get him home to Brighton Court, let him sink onto my sofa.

"Out with it," I say.

"I'm ruined." He pushes his fingers through his hair; won't meet my eyes.

"Tell me."

"Can I move in with you? I've been evicted."

"Why's that, son?"

"Didn't pay my rent."

"Why not? You've got a job."

"That's gone too, Dad. They cheated me. They promised me so much. I trusted them. I'm a fool. I'm so ashamed. You'll take me in, won't you?"

"It's not drugs, is it, Jamison? Or gambling? We'll get you help."

He shakes his head and groans, head in his hands. His shoulders are
shaking. My son is sobbing. I'm at his side in a heartbeat, my arms
around him. I cradle his big head against my chest until he calms.

"Whisky or water?" I ask.

He chooses water.

The truth comes out – the swindlers, the way they extorted my son's
money, promised him wages that never came; demanded he pay "hurt
money" into their business; wrote him out of the documents, then locked
him out of the office.

"Do you need to see a lawyer? Walt would help you."

He shakes his head.

"It's my own stupid fault, Dad. I'm ruined."

"You're not ruined. Nobody's ruined until their dying day, and you're
in good health, so you can stop that self-pity talk."

"But …"

"You know how I thought my own life would end with that head
injury. I was younger than you – all my dreams in smithereens. I got on
with it. I dreamed up something new and made it work. Wasn't the same,
but it worked well enough. I've lived a life. Since when did you become
a quitter?"

"I owe half a million dollars."

"Then get a job and pay it back."

"It's not that simple. I signed non-disclosure documents. They've
trapped me."

"What do I know about the world of money and finance, Jamison? I'm
a simple country boy. Maybe you just can't work in that industry
anymore, but you're able bodied. I know about work. It's blood, sweat
and tears, but it pays the bills."

"Can I move in with you?"

"Not much room here, Jamison, but you're welcome while you get
your act together. Make a plan. I'll help you, of course I will, but I'm not
made of money and I'm not earning any more. I've let my registration
go. You have an education. Get another job. Take it easy here for a few
days; of course you can. But then get on with it. Do you need food?"

"Not hungry."

"Then sleep. You look like you've sleepwalked all night."

"I did. Two nights."

"Jamison. Take a shower. I'll leave you some pyjamas on the end of the sofa. Take it easy now, son. You're safe here and I love you."

He's sleeping like a baby fifteen minutes later; like a baby with a three-day growth, snoring like a man, but his body the same shape beneath the throw rug, curled up.

Were we too soft on him? Or too tough? Did he reach too high with Capital Plus Investments? Any job would do, to live a good life.

Millie's not here to discuss it with. I head to the whisky myself, just for one, as the sun sets, and I wonder for a moment what Lucy is doing. She's mentioned troubles with her own daughter, Phoebe. Until now I haven't truly appreciated her concerns.

Jamison asleep is no longer a grown man. He's still curled on his side, shrunken, like his softened form as a boy and baby – often all I ever saw of him after my own long days of labor, with patients, at all hours. Did I not spend enough time with him?

Then a memory comes back to me; of not so long ago. I'm on the settee in Franklin, after Millie died. I'm staring at the wall, and Jamison comes in, alarmed to find me so still, so quiet. It must be midnight. It's cold. I don't care about anything anymore.

It's Jamison who brings a rug to me. He wraps it around me and sits close by. He phones Dee. In hushed voices they talk about me as if I'm not there – decide to move me closer to them. I go along with it. When they find the Brighton Court penthouse for me, I don't argue. I'm done with Franklin. Gradually I find my feet again. I'm still finding them, still working out how to live without Millie, without my crazy job, without quite enough to do – but at least I'm my own free agent again, no longer in limbo.

One thing I know. I will do anything for Jamison, as I would for Dee and my grandchildren. I will never stop loving him, no matter what.

So next morning, when he wakes, when he's showered and shaven and dressed, and we're eating a decent breakfast of bacon and eggs and cinnamon toast – his favorite – I know exactly what to say.

"Jamison. I'm neither ignorant nor indifferent, and I know I might project confidence, because I'm an old white male, but I'll be the first to tell you that most people – me included – we make it up as we go along.

You're not alone in feeling lost sometimes. My patients got better by themselves, apart from the obvious things, like needing stitches or settings for broken bones, or antibiotics. And as for your mother – nothing in my power could save her, so how do you think that made me feel ...

"But know this, son. You can't stop trying. You can't stop doing your best. And if you don't believe in yourself, who will?"

"But ..."

"No buts. You're safe and you're welcome here, but not indefinitely. I have my own life." I'm not yet ready to tell him about Lucy, about how I'll want my own space, my own privacy, to see where time with Lucy might lead.

"Lick your wounds, Jamison. Rest and recover. Then you get back out there. You've got a brain. You've got a top education. Use them. Do your research. Retrain if you have to."

I don't tell him what else I'm planning. This is no time to go soft on him.

Chapter 41

Lucy

I've cleaned and restocked the other two places. One's two streets away and the other is up the hill. I can't put off going into Dirk's apartment any longer. I have just two hours to vacuum, dust and tidy his place, clean the bathrooms and kitchen and prepare him a meal – all without him knowing it's me. Pretty sure he's out. Hope so.

I take a deep breath for courage as I knock on his door. There's no answer. Good.

"Mrs West's housekeeping service," I call, then let myself in.

I get the shock of my life. Dirk's not there, but a young man is. Jamison? Last time we met, he was in a tux, schmick and fit. This time he's dishevelled, but it's definitely him. He has the same build as Dirk, lean and tall and strong.

He's at the dining table, papers spread all over it, a laptop open in front of him. He stares long and hard at me, then frowns.

"Don't mind me," I say. "Housekeeping services. I can work around you. Just ignore me."

And he does. Phew. I can't pretend total indifference. Dirk's not untidy, but he does live here, unlike when I unpacked his things with Donna a while ago.

I strip his bed and change the sheets; hang his suit coat back in the cupboard; gather up his dirty clothes and sheets and towels and run them through the closet washing machine as I vacuum and dust.

I wipe the surfaces in the bathroom, straighten his aftershave. The scent is alluring. I miss the man, wonder if he'll accept my proposal, hope he will, wonder what will become of us, wonder about the young man at the dining table, worry about the sale of my apartment, then head to the kitchen.

The apples in Dirk's fruit bowl are going soft. I duck down to my place and retrieve flour and lard to make a proper pie crust. His kitchen is as beautifully equipped as I remember. There's even a fluted pie dish; the chopping board is clean and new; and the knives are sharp.

The pie is on the lower shelf of the spacious oven in a flash, a chicken casserole baking above it. I smile at the irony of it. Dirk hated all the free casseroles in Franklin, but in town, he pays for them. And I'm his biggest suitor yet. I don't woo him with sympathy and baked items, like the good widows of Franklin.

I've offered him diamonds, with casserole and apple pie on the side.

Chapter 42

Dirk

I head for Franklin, hoping the open road will clear my mind about Lucy's proposal. I would have liked to see Lucy again before setting out, to offer her my support. But she made it clear to me she wants to buy the apartment herself.

And with Jamison under my feet, I need to act now to get my own unfinished business over and done with. No point delaying it.

In Jamison's red car, I step on the gas, up the highway. Farms and fences and forests blur as the city disappears in the rear vision mirror. There's so much space out here. Too much space.

I park at the Franklin realty company, Eric Nettleford and sons. He and Millie were at school together. Everyone was at school with Millie. As we shake hands, I try to forget his wife's obsession with her bunions, and ignore Eric's growing girth and family history of heart disease. I can't move on fast enough. But there's the talk of the families, the weather, the price of cattle, the way Franklin has been discovered by citysiders wanting weekenders, by the tree changers.

He rubs his hands together when he hears what I want.

"I want out," I say.

"No! We want you back, Doc. Find a little bride and bring her back with you. Hey. Find one in Franklin. No shortage of spinsters and widows pining for ya, Doc."

"You don't want me back, Eric. You want my old house on your books, before the spring sales."

"I won't argue with you, Doc. Be a fine property for us to shift for ya. The finest. In fact, I've got hot buyers on my books for a classic like that right now. We can move this pretty quick for ya if it's what ya really want."

He names a price I never would have dreamed. There'll be plenty here for me, and for Jamison, and for Dee if he's talking truth. You never can tell with estate agents. Might drag on for years, the place needing repairs. Cracked winter pipes, new fire reg compliance, new roofing, Millie's white picket fence needing repaints. I know the place. The repairs never let up.

"Let me get back to you in an hour, Eric. I just want to revisit it one last time."

"Of course, Doc."

I told Jamison I wouldn't help him financially, but I can't say no to my boy. To give him breathing space, I've bought his crazy red car from him after all. I need wheels of some sort, and the array of choices is bewildering. Given I've finally learned how to use this one and it gets me around town okay, and to Franklin, I might as well stick with it.

It's twilight. Franklin was never at its best in winter. The town is asleep, apart from the bar. All the action is inside, behind glowing windows, as snow drifts down and smoke spirals up from a few chimneys.

It's pretty as a picture, but I know most of the people and their diagnoses, their neuroses, their preoccupations and fears. I could never solve all their problems, hard as I tried. Roger Tappy cares for them now. I am free.

The Christmas lights are up on the community tree. Near the top, a yellow one blinks on and off, on and off.

I pull up at my old house. I've done it thousands of times. This time, there is no cheery company in the passenger seat of Jamison's jaunty sportscar, and nobody at all inside the place. Strange. It is Lucy who springs to mind this time, not Millie; Lucy with her bright smile and energy. Lucy with her beautiful warm body snuggled up to mine all that night after she'd trimmed the roses.

Lucy. Am I wrong to be holding a distance from her? I miss her. When I'm done with this business with the old house, I'll reach out to her. I'd love to see more of Lucy in my life.

My footsteps resound in the old hallway. I was curious to see if anything would pull me back here, to this place where I slept every night for decades. But there are just my own echoes and memories of a life of toil.

The best memories are of my children as they ran to the door to greet me. As they still do, in my new life in the city. They are the future. This house was Millie's dream, and with Millie gone, it has become irrelevant. Nobody needs me here now.

Millie cared deeply about this house. It's like saying goodbye all over again.

I wanted to check, but I am resolved.

Back at Eric Nettleford's we shake hands, I sign a few bits of paper, and I'm out the door and back in the car pointing west again. Farewell, Franklin.

Chapter 43

Lucy

It's Wednesday again, and the number of potential buyers milling around about to inspect the place has doubled. The good news is that Davey actually agreed to cook sauerkraut and kimchee on Saturday morning, and even darling Amaryllis is in cahoots. She visited Mrs B and got her to promise to give extra-long piano lessons at the exact time of the open houses. She's going to open all Mrs B's windows, and ask that students play their scales as loud as possible.

The bad news is I've left four messages with my lawyer and she's failed to get back to me. Time is running out.

When she finally calls, I drop the lamp I've been working on. Glue and cloth splat all over the floor as the lamp frame bends and bounces down my hall. The Open House is in five minutes. I plan to leave them there, in the hallway. It's a magnificent mess. I should have thought of it earlier.

"Yes, yes, yes?" I stab at the phone and she's there, my lawyer, charging me by the second.

"We have a settlement offer from your former husband, Lucy," says Tonkerson. "Bart wants to keep the house and buy you out."

"Is it a fair price?"

She names it and I nod. It's more than I thought; enough to give Phoebe a head start in life, and secure my apartment.

"Tell Bart's lawyers 'yes' but that I'll only accept it if the money clears by the end of this week," I say. "If it's not in my account by Friday, tell him I'll see him in court and take him for everything he's got, and more." I have no idea how to do that, and whether I can afford it, but it sounds tough. Bart understands tough. "Thank you, Felicia."

I call Hilary immediately and tell her the good news. I ask her to make my formal offer to the seller's agent.

When Donna phones me for our usual loud and fake discussion about the downsides of Brighton Court. I whisper to her the good news about the imminent settlement.

And then I phone Phoebe. It goes to voicemail, as usual.

"Phone me, darling. Please. I have good news."

For once, she phones straight back, but is unimpressed when she asks me if Bart and I are getting back together, and I have to tell her the truth.

"But don't hang up on me, my darling. We're close to a settlement, and there'll be enough for you to have a good share of it. You won't be starting out in life with nothing."

"I already told you, you don't have to buy my love. I have to go, Mom."

"Of course I can't buy your love, darling. I accept that. I just want to make sure you'll be okay. I love you."

Chapter 44

Dirk

As I drive back to the city, I phone Jamison to share the news and see if he's okay.

"I didn't know Lucy Beston was your housekeeper, Dad."

"What?"

"Pretty sure it was her. Agile. Sparky. She had an apron on, but that was her alright, the woman you were with at the ball."

"Are you saying Mrs West is Lucy Beston, son?"

"Saw it with my own eyes, Dad. What's the problem?"

I'm silent as I digest Jamison's words.

I force my fury about Lucy's deception to one side as I explain to Jamison I'm selling the house. I'll split the money equally between him and Dee.

"I won't ever bail you out again, son," I tell him. "This is it. Take my advice and buy property with it if you can. It generally holds its value. It's real estate, something real, not promises from a swindler."

"I hear you, Dad. I'll do it. Thank you."

I phone Dee to tell her the same. She's sad. Sentimental about the old place. Thought she could have brought the kids back in summer, but I tell her she can afford farm stays anywhere with the funds. I tell her how much the upkeep is costing if we don't sell, and she finally agrees.

Now to confront my two-faced neighbor.

As I drive, I remember that time recently when there was something different about my apartment. Usually there's the hum of the dryer. That day it was silent. There was hot apple pie on the stove-top, in a different pie dish, but the oven was cold.

And there were no towels in the bathroom.

We even spoke about the strong smell of apple pie at her door, that time she dropped her key. It comes to me in an instant. She dropped it because she had a pile of towels in her arms – my towels.

The minute I get back to Brighton Court, I rush to Lucy's door, and knock.

I knock again.

"Lucy?" And knock again.

When she opens it, slowly, her smile is fake. She won't meet my eyes.

"Yes?" she says. It's the first time she hasn't invited me in.

"We need to talk," I say.

"Mmm," she says. But she hesitates; doesn't stand back to let me in as she usually does.

I stand firm, on her threshold, expectant. She yields.

"Give me a couple of minutes, please, Doc."

She'll be hiding the evidence.

Chapter 45

Lucy

Dirk wants to see me. He's angry, though he holds it in check. Jamison must have recognized me. That interview …

I am too hot, then too cold. It could be about anything.

I ditch my cleaning clothes, pull on a fresh blouse and slim skirt.

My best navy heels always give me confidence. I fasten my "big girl" pearls around my neck, with matching earrings, and carefully dab perfume behind my ears.

There's no time to do my hair, so I brush it and push at it with my fingers until it's acceptably neat, if not chic, apply fresh lipstick and check my appearance. I'm defensive, but I've actually done nothing wrong. Or have I? I have to make a living. I'm doing Donna's sister a favor. Dirk doesn't have to understand.

Dirk is sombre when I open the door. He's behaving like a school principal, as if I'm an errant child. I invite him into my living room, my head held high.

"Jamison tells me you're Mrs West, Lucy," he says.

"Not exactly."

"What's that supposed to mean?"

"There are a lot of Mrs Wests. It's a business name."

"Don't play games with me. When were you going to tell me?"

"Tell you what, Dirk?" I say. "Please take a seat."

He sits directly opposite, facing me, arms folded. The inquisition…

"That you're Mrs West."

"I'm not usually … I just stepped in to help out. My friend's sister runs the service. They were desperate."

"How often have you been in my place without my knowledge?"

"Just a few times."

"'Just a few times.'"

"Well, for the rest of this week. And I unpacked your boxes when you first arrived. It's what I do. With Donna. All over the city."

"And when were you going to tell me that you've been in my apartment, moving my personal items?" His tone is flat, accusatory. I'd hate to have been his opponent on the soccer field. He won't give an inch. Well, two can play that game.

"It's just been for a week or two."

"But why didn't you tell me?" He's more hurt than angry. This is not going well.

"I didn't …"

"I thought we were friends, Lucy. I thought I could trust you."

"You can, Dirk. Nothing has changed." But he shakes his head. His eyes are closed.

"Dirk. I couldn't let Donna down, after all she's …

"But why didn't you just tell me?"

"Mrs West is a business. We're meant to be invisible. I would have thought you'd understand about confidentiality."

"But this is fundamental, Lucy. A matter of trust."

"There wasn't time." I snap.

"How long does it take to send a text message? You could have done it while you were in my apartment."

"But what if you'd said 'no'? It would have been a conflict of interest for me. Anyway, what's so wrong with me cleaning up after you?"

"You've been in my space, without telling me. It's about trust."

"Really, Dirk?" I stand, hands on my hips. "But of course. How could I expect you to understand? I simply needed to work. My work is casual. I have to take what's on offer. Am I not allowed to make a living? Can you not even understand that some people don't have oodles of cash on hand? I suppose as a retired doctor…"

I bite on my words as he stands. My pulse pounds. But really. Bart's betrayal. Dirk's principles. And now I'm going to really blow it. I just know it. I am far too furious to keep it all in any longer.

"And why exactly is it that you even need a Mrs West, Dr Dirk O'Connell, a smart man like you? Why don't you learn to bake your own apple pies? It's not that hard. I put that first one together in five minutes flat, a personal record, by the way, not that such feats are considered interesting enough to mention in normal conversation. And vacuuming is not rocket science."

When he refuses to comment, I continue.

"Dirk, I need this work. You know I want to buy this place. You know my Ex stole my other future and gave it to someone else, someone younger, more beautiful and less difficult, at least for now. When she starts speaking up, no doubt he'll replace her." I stop to catch my breath.

This is not about Bart. Dirk is completely different. He's not vain. Maddeningly, he's not even angry. He's dismayed. Hurt. I want to go to him, to place my palms on his arms and comfort him, offer him a kiss. Not an apology, though, because I've done nothing wrong. He's the one who's being unreasonable.

We stand and stare at one another. My heartbeat settles. His stare softens. I wait for his own apology, but he just stares at me, as if I've let him down. Well, I haven't. In fact I've been doing a great job except for that day when I put the clean towels back in there slightly late.

"It's a job, Dirk. You might not understand – a well-paid doctor like you."

"How dare you tell me I don't understand about money."

"Well, it's true. There's nothing personal about cleaning … It's just a job."

"You've touched all of my things. My correspondence. My underwear. This is a fundamental matter of trust, Lucy."

"So you want me to apologize? Is that it?"

"Walt and Jill and Dee told me I couldn't trust you, but I ignored them. I was falling in love with you, so help me, Lucy Beston."

"I don't see how this changes things."

"I expect transparency in a relationship."

He hasn't raised his voice, but he is angry. I've never seen him lose his temper. With his grandchildren Dirk is infinitely patient, but now he presses his point.

"Did you rent your apartment before or after you'd moved my stuff into my place?" His voice is precise, chilling. He is condemning me, not interested in my defence. "And in Jill's shop? Was that a set up? Did you stalk me? Did you chase me all along? Did you bump into me on purpose, to make me spill that coffee on the dress? If so, you're a piece of work, Lucy Beston."

"No, Dirk. It wasn't like that."

His phone rings, and he takes it.

"Jamison?" He holds up his hand to me. "I have to take this, Lucy."

He turns and lets himself out of my apartment, shoulders squared. If this was a fight, I don't know who won.

My own shoulders slump. I haul them up again, but my mouth turns down.

I try to go about life as normal. I worked today and there's another open house tomorrow. I have to eat. Forget romance. Forget Dirk the doubter.

My phone rings as I'm draining the pasta for dinner. When I see it's Phoebe, I drop the spoon on the floor as I lurch towards the bright phone screen and answer.

"Phoebe?"

"Mom, hi."

"Hi, darling."

"Can I come stay with you?"

"Sure. Of course."

"I got an internship just up the road from you."

"Congratulations. This is wonderful news."

"It's just for a couple of months."

"Perfect. When do you start? You can bring your things whenever you like. Need me to come with the car?"

We chat logistics as if there was never an issue between us. Was it all in my head, or does rent-free accommodation or avoiding an hour-long commute appeal? Either way, I don't care. It's my Phoebe. Of course I'll make her welcome.

It's only when she's hung up that I realize I might not even be living here if my offer is unsuccessful. I don't know where I'll be. Back at Donna's while I lick my wounds? I hate this uncertainty. I must buy this apartment, no matter what. Phoebe's request is the clincher. I simply can't afford to ruin this chance to reconcile with my only daughter.

I finally get some food into my bowl and grab a spoon and fork when the phone rings again. This time it's Hilary. Thank goodness. Maybe my offer for the apartment was high enough.

"Hilary, tell me, tell me! Can I buy it?"

"I'm sorry, Lucy," she says. "The seller's agent says the seller doesn't want to accept your offer. They say they already have a better offer, and there's another open house tomorrow, so they're not ready to accept. They want to see ..."

"But ... then I'll raise my offer. By ..." I pluck a number out of the air. It's just numbers; numbers that need to impress.

"Be careful, Lucy. I have to tell you. You need to be ready with the good faith bond. Ten per cent. And if you can't come up with all the money in good time, you may be sued."

"Yes, yes. But do make the larger offer."

"I will, Lucy. I have to wait until business hours tomorrow."

Hope fizzes in my veins, and then despair takes over. I don't ever want to fight with Dirk. But I can't back down. Even Hilary said it. I need all the money I can earn.

I pace the apartment. Can't sleep. I go down to the garden and stand in the cold moonlight. Am I as bad as Dirk says? Should I have told him I unpacked his place? I didn't know it was actually his until he brought up my groceries and I saw he lived above me. My fingers itch to grab my phone and call him back and explain. But what's the point? Dirk the Doc O'Connell is not the man I thought he was. Lucky escape, huh?

So why do I feel so empty?

Chapter 46

Lucy

I barely slept last night, dreaming of other potential buyers making offers on my apartment – e-signatures flying thick and fast, furniture going up in flames and floating away in tsunamis. My favorite sofa – in a soft blue velvet with gold piping and gilded feet – became my lifeboat.

When I wake to reality there's a lump of lead in my stomach that's about far more than real estate. Dirk O'Connell. He hates me. It's not fair.

I swing my legs out of bed and take a deep breath. This is a big day and Dirk O'Connell is a fool to reject me like that.

I reflect on how cruel it is that I have to be living right here, in my apartment, in the heart of the new life I've tried to build, while more potential buyers crawl all over it again and buyers' agents all over the city make offers on it. Is Hilary doing her bit?

I phone her again.

"Please trust me, Ms Beston. I can't do more than I'm doing."

Nor can I. Beyond sabotaging the sale while potential buyers visit, with fake phone chats about imperfect neighbors, and making a mess, today, I'm overcome with the realization this might be the beginning of the end; that I am just as likely to be forced out, to have to start afresh again.

Despite my intention to make it as unappealing as possible for those who'll come, I love this place so much I clean up the fake messes and polish it until it gleams. If I must depart, I will do so with my head high and beautiful memories. I will enjoy it until I'm thrown out.

Not for the first time, I wonder exactly who it is who decided to sell my haven. It could be anyone; even one of my actual neighbors; even

Dirk. Dirk. Would he sell this place to get rid of me? I make a cup of tea and try to laugh at myself. Sleeplessness brings out the worst in me, and paranoia is simply silly.

As I dust and vacuum, polish and preen the place, I arrange the books and vases with great care. I'm aware that the better it looks, the greater the price it might fetch, but I have my pride, and even if I must move on, I want to remember it at its best.

As I open my front door, a hideous odor of boiling cabbage and garlic greets me, and I knock on Davey's door to give him a high five. He's such an agreeable young man, apart from his motorbike revving before dawn every morning – the one detraction of living at Brighton Court I didn't make up for the other prospective buyers. I wonder why Davey lives alone.

I walk up the street and buy white roses. I polish my silver vases until they gleam. I temper my sense of doom with hope. If I'm successful and buy this place, I'll paint the living room brilliant white. I'll find an oval-shaped rug in just the right texture, in soft, gelato colors, for this tiny haven of peace in a chaotic world.

When the apartment is spotless, I turn my attention to myself. I will go down fighting, with dignity. I clean my diamonds until they're like fireworks, twist my hair into a chignon, and dress in my best peach silk blouse – the one that Dirk approved at Jill's. I team it with my navy pencil skirt.

I select my highest heels and am just finding my balance when the seller's agent and loan officer arrive, both in brown suits. They are respectful. They place extra brochures on my dining table, and ask to move some furniture so other potential buyers will have a better view of the room.

"I don't suppose you can tell me whether there have been any serious offers," I ask. "I need to know, so I can make plans to move."

The agent tells me there are at least five serious potential purchasers. Hilary calls me, and I rush to my bedroom to speak in private.

"I'm sorry, Lucy. Other offers are higher than yours. There's a lot of interest in your neighborhood. Do you want to raise your offer?"

"Of course I do, Hilary. I really want to stay."

"I'm obliged to remind you that you have to be able to follow through with the funds. If you don't, you will destroy your credit rating, you will lose my commission, and lose another percentage to the seller. Please email me your new offer if you're sure."

I take a few moments to sign into my bank account and double check my savings. Maybe there's even more in there than I realize – maybe Bart got generous. I blink, and check the statement again. I go fetch my glasses, zoom in and expand the size of the text. There must be some mistake. I sign out, and sign in again. Same result. There's been no deposit. Not at all. My savings are puny as ever. I forget to breathe, sink down onto a chair, and try to think.

I go to phone the bank, then realize it's Saturday. Nobody will answer. What can I do?

There's knocking at my door. Neighbors and prospective buyers and their friends and families arrive to inspect the place – more than ever. Surely Bart's money will come through soon. Maybe on Monday. I go to phone Felicia, but my call goes to voice mail.

More and more people turn up, crowding into my small apartment. I have to stop this torture.

And then there's Donna, who puts her arms around me. I feel a little calmer. I can do this. The apartment will be mine. I just have to make the best offer.

My heart jolts when Phoebe walks in, a young man beside her, with brown hair and a kind face.

"This is Jaxon, Mom, with an 'x,'" says Phoebe. "It was Jaxon's idea to come and give you moral support."

"Oh that's lovely, Phoebe. Jaxon, I'm so pleased to meet you. I'm Lucy. Thank you so much. I'm sorry I can't offer you tea or coffee or lunch right now."

"Don't be silly, Mom," says Phoebe. "As if. So, what are your chances? Donna told me everything. I know you really love this place. And now I can see why."

Phoebe runs her hand along the windowsill and stares down at the garden.

I glance at Donna and she nods.

"I'm not your Godmother for nothing, Phoebe."

They exchange a smile.

"I do love this place," I say. "You see how there's room for you, Phoebe? In there. I've moved most of the lamp stuff into the window seat. So, yes. I'm hopeful, but so are all these people, no doubt. I'll speak with my lawyer again on Monday. My first two offers weren't high enough, but I'm about to make another offer. Whatever it takes."

"Good luck, Ms Beston."

"Thank you, Jaxon. Please. Call me Lucy. It means so much to me that you're here, Phoebe, both of you." I long to grab her and hug her tight, but she is here as an adult, at a very public event. Instead, I reach for her hand and squeeze it. "Whatever happens, I am rich because you're my daughter, Phoebe. That's not a platitude. It's just the truth."

Her face lights up. I pull her to me after all, and she lets me, here in front of all these strangers, and I start to cry.

I let her escape and she and Jaxon continue exploring my place. He holds her hand, and I swallow – my Phoebe, all grown up and partnered. I'm pleased for them. I snatch a tissue from the hall stand and dab at my eyes.

It's crowded. People line my corridor. I scan the crowd, searching in vain for my tall neighbor, the elusive Dirk. The living room is full. Voices buzz from the kitchen and the bedroom – more and more strangers squeeze into my home. I have to act now to protect it, to save it for myself.

I slip past everyone and into my favorite part of the apartment. A sliver of sunlight filters through the bay windows and explodes off my diamonds, and I pluck a new figure out of the air. I email and text the number to Hilary and she questions it.

"You're sure?" she texts. I send a green check emoji.

"Hurry," I text. "Tell the agent."

His phone rings straight away, and I see his eyebrows shoot up. But the minute he hangs up, it rings again and he names another price, a higher one.

The view of the neighborhood through the bay windows beckons to me, tempts me to offer even more. I calculate the value of my diamonds and text Hilary I will raise my offer by another ten thousand, and another few thousand after that.

Buyers hover around the seller's agent naming figures. I am almost out of the race when Phoebe is by my side. "I can lend you another ten, Mom. You've been far too generous with me."

My eyes widen.

"Do it," she says. "I'm okay. Dad's given me some to help with the internship."

I text Hilary again, and she phones me.

"I need this in writing, Lucy. I'm sending you a fresh agreement. Use DocuShare. It has to be official."

The agent keeps turning to the corner, taking offers on his phone and checking his own documents. Surely I'm still in the game. Surely I can make an offer high enough to secure it today – to put an end to these open houses once and for all and get on with my life.

Through our agents, the invisible competition and I fight it out a thousand dollars at a time. I hold my breath and raise my offer by another five hundred dollars – not sure how I'll pay my next electricity bill; maybe I can sell the green gown on eBay – but Hilary texts back to me it won't be enough.

"The seller's agent has accepted a higher offer, Lucy. I'm sorry."

A moment later the agent makes an announcement and my blood runs cold. My apartment is off the market – sold. He names the price. Higher than my latest offer.

I feel like a total fool. I am totally trumped, and out, and spent, exhausted, bleak, utterly without hope, done.

I crumple to the couch, and Phoebe goes down with me, her arm across my shoulders, comforting me as a sob escapes.

People trail out. Donna offers me a coffee and I shake my head. The agent packs up and heads out to the next life-changing battle. He says he'll be in touch.

"About my lease?"

He nods. What a way to make a living.

"Who bought it?" I ask. "Who was the other bidder?"

"I'm not at liberty to say, ma'am."

"Of course not," I say.

Donna throws her arms around me and hugs me until my ribs hurt.

"Sorry, Lucy," she says. "Gotta run. Call me."

"I'm sorry, Mom," says Phoebe. It breaks my heart for her to see me so defeated.

"Don't worry, Ms Beston," says Jaxon, so young, so earnest. "Something will work out."

I almost laugh. Now who's using platitudes? Jaxon clearly hasn't graduated yet.

Chapter 47

Lucy

When everyone is gone; when my beautiful apartment is empty and quiet, I grab my apartment key with its jaunty diamante heart on a chain. It should be a broken heart, cut into zigzags.

I drift down my hallway and out into the stairwell.

I am empty, barely breathing. Spent. I failed. I lost. Again.

I descend the stairs, down and down and down, and lean on the door which leads to the garden. I push it open and sleepwalk out, out into the quiet chaos, cold sky above me and jagged branches all around.

I cry out once. Great snivelling sobs follow as I find my way to the old stone bench and table and bury my face in my arms.

So much for offering Phoebe her own room "at my place." By the time her internship rolls around, who knows where I'll be. Somewhere else too temporary.

My paltry efforts in this garden are pathetic. What a waste of time. And I can't even begin to think about Dirk, about my stupid hopes I could throw a ball with his grandchildren here as I cleared out more undergrowth. I liked Theo and Lexie. They were growing to trust me. Guess I'll just disappear on them.

When I raise my head there are panda eyes on my forearms. Mascara. I wipe away my tears with the back of my hand. Now I can be a raccoon. I frown and laugh at myself.

I'm just fumbling in my handbag for a tissue when a window opens, high above me. It's Amaryllis.

"Tea?"

She's a lifeline. Tea. I need herbal tea. I'd forgotten my Celtic neighbor Amaryllis asked me to drop in after the latest open house. Amaryllis always lowers my blood pressure, in a good way. She's from another world and that's exactly where I need to escape.

She opens her door wider and ushers me in as subtle incense wafts – lavender and ginger. There's soft music playing, something medieval, choral, deeply peaceful. Her green glass beaded curtain tinkles and clicks as she pushes it aside.

In the corner, her large tabby cat on a big pink velvet cushion nestles between high towers of books. He lifts his large head to size me up with green eyes, then yawns – his pink mouth wide behind sharp teeth. He rests its head back on the cushion and resettles himself with a flick of his tail.

"Thank you," I say.

Amaryllis shrugs and smiles.

"Tea?"

"I'd love some. Thank you."

"Peppermint? Dandelion? Liquorice?"

"You choose, Amaryllis. Something calming, please. Very, very calming or I will explode."

She opens a cupboard and rustles around. The teacup she gives me is pink and ornate and delicate, with a gold rim, something from the 1940s. Steam rises as she makes the tea.

We sit either side of her round table, her simple bentwood chair slightly rocky.

"My grandmother's," she says. "I've kept most of her things."

"I adore shabby chic, as you know," I say, then wonder if I'd offended her. "Not that your place is at all shabby."

She waves a hand and smiles at me, resting both hands around her mug.

"How are you?"

"Oh." I consider pretending. "Devastated. The place is sold. My offers weren't high enough. The agent just announced it's off the market, so at least I won't have to endure any more open houses."

"Forgive me, but why should the sale make any difference to you, Lucy?"

"I just wanted to settle somewhere. Settle here actually. Right here, at Brighton Court. I love it here."

She nods and blows across the top of her tea.

"So who bought the place?"

"No idea. Does it matter?"

She shrugs. Behind her thick glasses, her eyes are deep blue pools.

Steam rises from my cup in a great, fragrant cloud as she tops up my tea. I really don't want to lose this friend. Who knows where I'll be living in a few weeks. Panic grips me and I close my eyes, let tears seep out. When I've dabbed at them with a tissue and blown my nose, I notice her 1930s light fitting on three chains.

The cat yawns and stretches in a great furry arch and jumps down and twists himself around the legs of the table and chairs, and then Amaryllis's ankles and then my own. I reach down and pat the soft fur between his ears and he lifts his chin and lets me scratch beneath it. The purrs are solid rumbles. I'd forgotten the soothing presence of a cat. If I'd been able to buy the apartment, I'd have invited Merlin to visit me up there, perhaps even found a rescue cat and invited it to move in with me.

Merlin looks up at me, then jumps up and sits on my lap. He stares at me until I stroke his ears and scratch him under the chin again. I'm rewarded with a louder purr.

"Style and sheer hard work are not enough, are they?" I say.

"For what?" Amaryllis says.

"For respect. For power. It's always a losing battle. The person with the most money gets to buy the best property."

"There'll be somewhere for you, Lucy."

"But I want to stay here."

She nods.

"But make no mistake, Lucy, dear," she says. "You are anything but invisible, with or without the makeup and the fancy clothes. You are warm and generous and friendly and creative, and a wonderful addition to Brighton Court. You know I don't gossip, but I will mention that Dr Dirk O'Connell barely smiled before you arrived." It's the most I've ever heard her say.

Her words hang in the bright kitchen between us like a rainbow as Merlin purrs on my lap, eyes closed, claws gently kneading my leg. I hate to disturb him, but will have to hand him over. We've drunk all the tea, and there's an open book on the settee and three books beside it on the coffee table. I clearly disturbed Amaryllis's reading.

I've imposed on her long enough, my quiet neighbor. Behind the thick glasses, she shutters her great big eyes behind her lashes. There's no guile there. Amaryllis rarely talks, but when she does, it's straight. Maybe that's what she means about my relationship with Dirk. Maybe I try too hard. Maybe I scare people. Is there such a thing as being too friendly; too carefully groomed?

I stand. Merlin is heavy in my arms, and floppy. I hand him over, thank Amaryllis and make a vow to visit her again in future, wherever I might be living.

Back inside my perfect apartment, I know I should start packing. I wander through it, pick up the glue gun and put it down again. I just can't do it like last time – pack all my bags in a rage and find shelter. And, much as I love my best friend, I don't want to go back to Donna's, my tail between my legs. It's too much of an imposition. We're grownups. I'm past all that flat-sharing and couch surfing, surely.

Rebellion lodges in my throat – an unvoiced protest. It spreads like red-hot lava and occupies my whole body. Maybe I'll just stay here forever – be one of those difficult tenants. Let the next landlord have to deal with it. Let him or her carry me out.

I'm just heading down the stairs and up to the estate agent to see what else they have for rent in this area, when I get a call from Donna.

"What did you say your neighbor's name was; the hottie; the doc; the widower?" Donna says, voice low, her tone urgent.

"Dirk O'Connell. Why?"

There's silence on the other end.

"Donna? What's wrong? What is this?"

"I hate to break it to you, girlfriend, but you're gonna find out sooner or later."

"Find out what? Spill, Donna."

"The other buyer, with the winning offer."

"Okay, tell me. Just tell me, will you?"

"I asked my contacts through the relocation head office."

"And."

"Last name's O'Connell."

It knocks the wind out of me.

"Dirk wouldn't do that to me. Would he? He couldn't. Could he?" I remember our last conversation, his quiet fury that I'd been in his apartment without him.

"You tell me. What do I know about guys, Lucy? I'm just sharing the facts here. Unless he actually bought it for you, maybe? To surprise you?"

"No. He'd break my heart. Right down the middle. Bang in two. We spoke about that; how I want to be responsible for my own future – for my own security. Even if he had the means. If I let a man buy me something like that, I'll only worry I'll lose it again if our relationship fails. If Bart taught me anything, he taught me that my house was never actually my own. It was always half his. My place in the sun was only ever as good as our marriage. I never want to risk that again."

And then I see him out the window in the stairwell – Dirk, sauntering down the street towards Brighton Court, the red car bright as ever, parked further up the street. Despite the fact he's been avoiding me, from the deepest doldrums, my traitorous heart lifts at the sight of him.

Did he really buy my apartment from under me? How dare he! Talk about a betrayal of trust. If I were a dragon, I'd breathe fire and roar.

Chapter 48

Dirk

It's Lucy – my impressive, duplicitous, "Mrs West" neighbor.
"What's up?"
"Do you really hate me this much?" she says, hands on hips at the front gate.
"I don't hate you."
"You just bought my apartment from under me – my home, my haven. I will have to move out. Don't worry – Dirk. I won't be back. You'll never have to see me again."
"You're angry," I say.
"Rocket scientist. Properties go to the highest bidder, I know, but do you know how hard I fought to keep this place? Did you hear nothing I said? Did you not even notice how much I wanted it?"
I am silent in the force of her hatred.
Her stare shrivels me. Those eyes. She's in pain.
I swallow, try to move closer, hold out both hands, but she backs away.
"I thought you were a friend, Dirk. For a while there, I thought we might even be something more. And you knew it too, Dirk O'Connell. Tell me you didn't feel it too; what we had between us. We always had something. We still have something. That's why you want me gone. You are a very nice man, I won't deny it. But you. Are. An. Utter. Coward."
"No, Lucy. You've …"
Is this an act? She clutches at her left arm and pats at her beautiful chin, showing off her diamonds, and then she shoves me away. There in the street, her hands are against my chest, her whole body's force behind them.

Lucy stares daggers at me, then suddenly sways, right in front of me. I ask her straight.

"Is this a trick, Lucy? I'm not falling for it."

But Lucy's the one who falls.

Right in front of me – a fake faint if ever I've seen one, a swoon from the best of the old bodice rippers my late wife used to read – regency romance, she called those books. Swoons were employed at least as often as the dropped kerchief or reticule, if not as often as the fluttered eyelashes – a clear play for attention.

But no. I'm wrong.

So wrong. I've seen this before, in my surgery, and at an airport when a man who'd rushed to catch his flight dropped dead in front of me. Lucy is not pretending. Time slows.

I grab at her, to stop her head cracking on the sidewalk. One leg buckles beneath her, the other at an angle the elegant Lucy would never choose. Gently I release the leg from under her. I place it beside the other, but it lolls out. Her shoe dislodges, revealing one shapely foot. I'm distracted by her legs. They are irrelevant. I know this. There's no time to waste.

"Lucy? Lucy?" I search in every direction. A nursing student lives in our building. Where is she when we need her? Anyone? Another doctor. I need an ambulance. Nobody. Nothing but Lucy in complete disarray, motionless in her distress, helpless in this fight for her life.

"Help; help us!"

I scrabble and snatch at my phone. I stab in the emergency numbers, bark out the road names, scan the street for anyone who can help. Did the message get through?

"Help us!" I bellow, again and again. Time stalls, then stops.

Lucy's lips begin to turn blue beneath that too-bright lipstick, twinned so carefully with her nail polish. My stylish Lucy. Her eyes are closed, every darting challenge, gone. This can't be. This lively mind, stilled. If only it were just a trick.

There's one silver eyelash at the edge of each eyelid, the closed lids delicate, translucent. Lucy. My Lucy. Will I lose another love? I can't bear it. The kiss of life… I learned it so long ago, at medical college, back when my only job was to learn as much and run as fast as I could. I spur myself to action.

Lucy knows how to kiss. Our first kiss, so surprisingly sweet, hovers between our bodies, but I yank my mind to the present.

These lips are too still, helpless, devoid of all pretense, of all manipulation, of all passion; her musical voice, silenced. There's no time to lose, but at least I know how to do this.

I drop on my knees to the sidewalk and bend to her. I tilt her head, feel her neck for a pulse, without success, and clamp my right hand around her chin – the pistol grip. I inhale deeply, open her mouth, and place my lips on hers, still warm, thank goodness. I count as I exhale. I've only had to do this a couple of times in my surgery. I can't remember the counting.

I breathe into her mouth, two three. I turn my head to the right to feel my own breath exhaled from her body back at my cheek, and watch her chest fall. At the edge of my vision, her diamonds sparkle and dance in the sunlight, grotesquely lively against the stillness of her fingers.

I must breathe for Lucy – give her my own life's breath, and do this right.

I feel for her pulse at her neck with the fingertips of my left hand, but again, there's nothing.

I breathe for her again, knowing I must do more.

I unbutton her blouse, of softest silk. She loves this blouse; told me with pride it cost a small fortune. Normally the color brings out the rosiness of her cheeks. Now? They're gray.

Gently, quickly, I reach behind to unclip her bra, her skin still warm and soft as velvet. Why didn't I linger with her longer, as she asked me to do? We could have done this together, explored each other's bodies at leisure, in gratitude, not like this, frantic, desperate. Is it all too late?

I breathe my own oxygen through her body again, to keep that sharp mind alive. I am her lifeline. Lucy's never needed me more and I know it now, in my heart and mind and body and soul – I will give her everything I have.

My knees scream in pain as I rise a little to gain purchase. I find the space below her decolletage where her heart lives, her treacherous heart. I must press the heels of my hands on her sternum and pump, force her blood around her veins. This is no time for modesty. I can't waste a second. To push too gently will fail her, yet I'm loath to break her ribs, perhaps to pierce her lungs.

Lucy's face turns grayer before my eyes and urgency propels me forwards. With one hand flat across the hollow between her breasts and the heel of the other on top, I straighten my right arm and let it take my weight. Push, two, three; push, two, three; push, two three.

I turn back to her lips again, her lipstick smeared and grotesque from my efforts. She'd hate this, all of it, yet I can't stop. I breathe for her and count again and feel for her pulse and pump at her heart again and again. I am a machine. I am her heart and her breath. I am her life, and she is mine, my one reason for being, my chance to get this right. She is the meaning of my life, this helpless, lifeless, beautiful woman, my Lucy.

I hear the siren, but do not stop; do not look up.

Boots and uniformed legs surround me. Strong arms grab my shoulders and pull me away as they tear more of her blouse and apply a machine. The shocks make her whole beautiful body kick and shudder as I rise to my feet.

She's onto a stretcher and into the ambulance before someone approaches me.

"Sir, your wife ..."

"Lucy's not ..." I can't even say it.

At a shout from a colleague in the driver's seat the paramedic drops my arm and springs into the passenger seat and the ambulance screams away, lights flashing, siren blaring.

I don't even know where they've taken her.

I sink onto the front fence, my head in my hands. I've lost her before we could truly find each other.

Chapter 49

Lucy

I wake in a gray room, the sheet slippery and rumpled beneath me. My hand hurts. My arm hurts. My chest hurts. A lot. My mouth is dry.

I'm hooked up to a machine. The last thing I remember is Dirk, the white hot heat of my fury with him, and then, strangely, a sense of peace.

I'm in a hospital bed. A nurse bustles in and types something into a mobile computer.

"Hello?" I try, my voice croaky.

"You're under observation," he says and makes some notes.

I'm in a gray gown; not my color, and there's a horrendous space behind it. The thing has no seam at the back!

"What's happening?" I say.

"Close call. Heart attack. You're lucky. A neighbor saved you, from what I hear. He's been enquiring about you. Bit of a hero. Speaking of whom …"

Chapter 50

Dirk

I'm awkward with the yellow roses. There weren't enough at the first florist, so I visited a couple more and bought them out. The bunch is huge and it's a mess. The final florist offered to rewrap them all for me, but I was in a rush.

On the passenger seat, I untie the first yellow ribbon and retie it around the lot. Their stems are different lengths. The thorns prick my fingers. Is this a suitable gift for someone in intensive care? Too late, I remember the hospital won't have a vase big enough. This bunch will take up the whole bed tray.

It's late; way past visiting hours, but Enrico on night reception recognizes me and lets me in.

"Doc O'Connell," he says and salutes me.

"Enrico. How's your family?"

"Three more grandkids, Doc."

"Congratulations."

"Know where you're going?"

"Unless the wards have all changed."

"No big changes, Doc."

I sprint up the fire stairs, the ones I used when I needed to get through rounds in a hurry, or on the odd occasion when I had famous patients, and the media tried to grab me for comments.

I'm puffing by the time I reach the seventh floor. Lucy was right. We should walk together in the evenings. So what if I cry at the scent of orange blossom. So what if she sees my tears? More than anything, I want to share my memories with Lucy, and make more – many more – together.

The light's still on in her room; just the lamp behind the bed. She leans back against the pillows in a hospital gown. Her eyes are closed as I reach the door, but they flutter open, their lenses dark, then brighter as she recognizes me.

I try to hide the blooms behind my back, suddenly shy, wondering if I've made a mistake. She was furious just before she had the attack. Will I be welcome?

"Dirk?" Her voice is croaky. She clears her throat and speaks again. "Doc O'Connell? You're the last person I expected to see."

"I need to apologize to you, Lucy."

She has the grace to stay silent. I wouldn't blame her for lashing out. Is it wrong for me to be here? I don't want to trigger another heart attack, but I've spoken to my colleagues. As I suspected – Myocardial Infarction, the gradual narrowing of her arteries, and a heart attack brought on by intense stress. She mentioned her mother died early, perhaps of this. These days, patients are stabilized and given stents. Lucy's likely to be fine now.

"May I come in?"

She nods.

"I'm so glad you're okay, Lucy."

Her silence punishes me. Where is her easy smile? But I deserve this. I lapped up her attention for weeks, for months. I batted her away, repelled her advances, used her when it suited me, then gave her a hard time about her job.

The chair is full of spare pillows and an extra blanket. I don't want to lord it over her, so I drop to my knees beside the bed. An old injury sparks pain up my thigh and I close my eyes for a moment.

When I open them, her eyes are on mine, and I close mine again in relief. She hasn't forced me out, not yet.

I hold up the roses.

"This is a ridiculous amount of roses, Dirk. What is this? Are you going into floristry?"

"I wanted to say sorry about the apartment – that you missed out – and to ask for a second chance."

"A second chance?"

"What if we were on the same team, Lucy?"

Lucy shakes her head and closes her eyes. Her voice is faint. There's no smile.

"You knew I wanted to buy that apartment, and you went ahead and bought it anyway," she says.

"No, I didn't."

"Don't lie to me, Dirk. Donna told me you did. She has inside knowledge and she never lies to me."

"Nor do I."

"But …"

"O'Connell is a very common name, Lucy. Oh. Wait a minute." My phone vibrates. "I'll take this. Back soon."

"Dad?" It's Jamison, his voice thick with excitement, with enthusiasm, with something I haven't detected in him for far too long – with hope.

"Yes, son?"

"Where are you? I've got news. I did what you said, Dad. I made a decision about the Franklin house money, a sensible one. I did it straight up, before property prices rose again."

"You did?"

"It was a no brainer. I'd already done the research – for you, when Dee and I recommended Brighton Court to you. It's a solid building in an up and coming area. It's all about urban renewal. For people wanting proximity to downtown or the buzz of theatre and restaurants, you can't beat your location. It's already rented out, or I can live there myself for a while. Can't go wrong."

"Wait. You bought in Brighton Court?"

"Yeah. That place below yours. Made the winning offer this morning. All the paperwork's come through now. It's mine."

"Ah."

"Aren't you going to congratulate me? I followed your advice, Dad."

"Yes. In general, it's good, son. Specifically … Jamison. Can I call you back?"

"Sure, Dad."

Lucy has sat up more in the hospital bed. She's managed to comb her hair, and I breathe again, grateful she might still think I'm worth impressing.

Lucy Beston has always demanded my attention. My hand abandons my raspy chin and drifts through space to alight on her arm, smooth as alabaster, warm as the sun on my windowsill. I run my thumb back and forth against her creamy skin.

"You're uncomfortable, Dirk. Pull up a chair. Or can't you stay? Is this a passing effort, to appease your conscience?"

I'm not accustomed to Lucy being so still. Lucy's a darter, a dodger – quick of mind and quick on her feet, always two steps ahead of everyone else. Lucy's the element of surprise, the plotter and planner I never saw coming, the striker.

Even prostrate, Lucy's striking. All five feet three of her. She wouldn't take up much space but oh, how much color she has brought into my world.

Lucy's earlobes are bare. No glitter today. Even without makeup, she's eye-catching – those high cheekbones, and a strength behind the set of her head, even as it is, on a hospital pillow – a kind of pride. Lucy Beston is a survivor, a warrior. If I met her on the soccer field, I'd be wary, on my guard.

And something settles. I walked all afternoon. I haven't been home. A new realization dawned that my visit has only confirmed. Lucy is awesome. She fills me with awe. With deep certainty, I know. If Lucy's a player – and she is – I want her on my team. Always.

I go back down on my knee, but she blinks. For the first time, I fear she will turn her head away, dismiss me without a backward glance.

Lucy inhales and I am sucked forwards a quarter of an inch in the space between us. Her eyes are mesmerizing, liquid intelligence, full of soul. I can't look away. It's a standoff, even though she's pretty much lying down. Her hair is fragrant – lime and coconut, a Hawaiian holiday.

I want more of that, more holiday, more Lucy, more Hawaii. We could go there, away from Dee and Jamison and Jill, and be on our own – together.

I see us on her cruise or at a beach or bar, beside the sea, relaxed, and Lucy laughing – not like this, serious and so still I wonder what's wrong with her, besides her medical condition, which has stabilized. I checked her chart on the way in. Is this an ultimatum?

My heart ticks up a notch or two, though neither of us has moved. She's right. It's like 1993; US versus Brazil, with one minute to the end of the game, and only Dirk the Doc O'Connell between national shame and victory. The save. My head. The goalpost.

"Lucy, I have to explain about the apartment. I'm sorry I haven't been more available to you, as your apartment went up for sale."

"You knew I wanted it, Dirk. I gave it everything. But you went ahead and trumped me. You are so competitive … I just want somewhere to live; my own place to call home. For people like you, it's just an investment. You already have a place to live. Two, in fact. As if you need more investments."

"What? No. You still think I bought it? Why would I do that?"

"To punish me? For cleaning your place and not telling you? I don't know. Not nice, Dirk. I'm in no position to stand up for myself. I don't even know exactly what happened. What am I even doing here? Apparently you were there. Do you want to tell me?"

"You were furious with me – well, now I can understand why – but then you blacked out and fell. I tried to cushion your fall, but worse, your heart stopped. I gave you CPR and the kiss of life until the ambulance crew got you going again."

"In the street?"

I nod, and she shakes her head, closes her eyes and opens them again, pinning me with her stare. Her laugh rings out.

"What is it?"

"Hard to be mad at you if you saved my life."

"I'm a doctor, Lucy. It's what doctors do."

"I know. You'd 'do it for anyone' same as you'd bring up their groceries." She turns her head away.

"Doesn't mean I wasn't glad to save you."

"Oh. So you were 'glad to save me?'"

"Yes." If she's fishing for compliments, I'm ready to oblige. "Brighton Court is far too quiet without you."

"I'll be gone for good as soon as I recover."

"You don't have to be."

"Oh? You'll take pity on me? Let me stay with you, or pay you rent? If I move in with you, I'll only be able to stay until you tire of me and throw me out for a younger version; like Bart did." She closes her eyes again, as if she's disgusted with me.

"I'm not Bart. Hear me out, Lucy. I bungled things. I was wrong to attack you about the Mrs West thing, but I didn't buy the apartment."

"You didn't?"

"Jamison did."

Chapter 51

Lucy

"Jamison? Your son?"

Dirk nods. I hold out one hand and he takes it, gently but firmly. His is warm. I squeeze it and he squeezes mine back. My stomach flutters.

"Independently," Dirk said. "I had nothing to do with his decision. Well, I gave him the finance – the Franklin house sold straight away – but I had no idea he'd buy your apartment with it. Only just found out. That was him on the phone. I'm sorry you missed out. Lucy, I don't care how many diamonds you have."

"You're making no sense, Doc."

"I've only ever done this once before."

"Done what?"

"Fallen in love. Lucy, will you marry me?"

"Do you want me to have another heart attack?"

"No, no! Think about it. We're good together. Remember when we danced? And at the house in Franklin? I want to wake up next to you every day."

"Funny way to show it. I know we're good together, but you gave me the brush off big time. I want my own security. I don't want to rely on a man's loyalty again. No offence, but you are a man."

Chapter 52

Dirk

I swallow. Lucy doesn't want me to provide her with a home, like Millie did. I guess if she wants independence, but still agrees to see me, it's a draw; a win, of a kind.

"I didn't expect to fall in love again so soon, but you're irresistible, Lucy Beston. I want to make you happy. Lucy?"

"Mmm?"

"Can we wind back the clock, right back to decades ago, before Brighton Court?"

"Why?"

"Remember when you did my make-up after my injury? You said you had a crush on me. Back then, I asked you out and you turned me down. Now I want to ask you again."

"Okay."

"When you're out of hospital, will you go out with me?"

She reaches for my arm and pulls me close.

"Only if you let me give you a haircut."

Chapter 53

Lucy

Back from hospital, I pack slowly. It's good exercise. I study the properties for rent in the local paper, but none is as nice as the ones in Brighton Court.

In my letterbox there's a flyer for a Christmas concert – carols by candlelight – up at the old church on the corner. I message Phoebe and invite her, with or without Jaxon.

Christmas was always the network – the shows, the parties. Sometimes the network was at our home. We had at least three photo shoots around our huge tree in the living room. I'd love helping make our place into the set, decorating the tree and loading it up with gifts.

Phoebe and Jaxon are coming for drinks with me on Christmas Eve. I try not to dwell on the thought of them joining Bart and Mishelle on Christmas Day. I'm practicing using their real names, for Phoebe's sake.

At night, the neighborhood around Brighton Court sparkles with Christmas lights. Donna and I have been busier than ever unpacking ahead of the holiday. Seems everyone wants to be home for Christmas, even if their home is brand new.

Donna will join her large family for the day, and I won't tag along. She invited me – what a friend – but this is their time. Donna and I are practically welded together every working day in these busy weeks. We'll take a break.

I'll just be glad of a rest – glad for a break from scanning the internet for apartments to rent.

I go for a walk. There's a frenzy of pre-Christmas interest at Jill's and the other boutiques and I'm happy for them. I pick up a small plum pudding at the deli, and some smoked turkey – a feast for one.

As I round the corner, I see the little church. A Christmas banner advertises the choir. The concert is this evening; Carols by Candlelight. The church is so pretty, I rush home and dress, excited as a girl. I'll carry the candle for my mother.

Darkness takes away my shyness with this crowd of friendly strangers. There's a smell of cinnamon and spice.

"Stay for drinks," says the older lady in a red velvet hat as I give my donation. "Mulled wine!" She winks.

"Thank you." I wink back. Perhaps I will.

Another volunteer hands me a battery-operated candle. I suppose it's safer than the ones that dripped hot wax.

The pews are hard but I barely notice as the church fills. Organ music fills the darkness, an odd note or two making it all the more special. An extended family sits alongside, the youngest daughter swinging her booted feet beside me, like something off the cover of a Christmas card. We exchange smiles.

The pastor welcomes us and invites us to switch on our candles. The lights dim and the choir emerges from behind us, and I startle to see Dirk file past and take his place up there among the baritones, serious, shoulder to shoulder in his black robes, eyes on the conductor. He stares at me and smiles, and I beam and sparkle my diamonds at him. He turns his attention back to the conductor as the music begins.

I love this man. He's more handsome than ever with his hair cut short. I make out his voice occasionally, the same one I overheard at the art gallery on my first night in the neighborhood.

The children beside me keep switching their candles on and off as we sing along when invited, but mostly I let myself disappear in the mellow darkness and let this Christmas blend with the best memories of all the others. With my voice, I send my thanks out and up, beyond the stained glass windows, out into the universe.

Later, as drinks are handed around, I see Dee and Matt and Lexie and Theo at the edge of the crowd. When Dirk appears he grabs my hand and

leads me across to them. When Lexie sees us, she runs to Dirk, and he
lifts her in his arms.

"You remember Lucy, Dee?"

Dee hesitates; sees the way Dirk and Lexie smile at me.

It's Matt who steps forward and shakes my hand. Dee follows suit, and
then surprises me.

"Would you like to join us for Christmas lunch, Lucy?" Dee says.

"I'd love that," I say. "Thank you."

Theo claps his hands.

"More presents!" he says, and Matt shakes his finger at him..

"Would you like me to cook something?" I say. "And I'm really good
at cleaning up."

"In our family, everyone brings something for the table, and we share
the clean-up," Matt says.

"Thank you, Dee. Thank you, Matt. You must tell me what to bring.
Maybe some of Davey's sauerkraut?"

"Davey's sauerkraut?" Dee asks.

"Long story," says Dirk. "Tell you later."

Dirk walks me home, his arm around me, as if he owns me. I love it.

Chapter 54

Lucy

Dirk and I fall into an easy rhythm of visits. Sometimes we'll share a simple dinner at his place or mine, or walk together to a local restaurant. He never says "no" to a walk and talk, and we chat non-stop about all the years we missed, between our first meeting and our engagement, about our children's milestones and the world events we saw from our own corners of the everyday world.

Always, Dirk makes me welcome with his smiles, or a touch on my arm or wrist.

I would almost be content, but every day is bittersweet. I'm still packing. I really don't want to move away.

One night, I remember the teaspoons under the window seat. I sit up, heart galloping. They remind me that someone else lived here before I did. Maybe the original owner had more than one Brighton Court apartment. I can barely wait for morning.

Next day, when I drop in on Mrs B, she has just baked a date loaf. She sits me at her bright kitchen counter and hands me a slice, warm and dripping with butter.

"I love my lamps, Lucy," she says as she pours me a coffee. "You sure know how to decorate. Really brightens up the orange around here. I've been telling everyone about you."

"So glad you like them."

"I'd leave them on all day if I didn't have to pay the power bill. First time in my life I've longed for night-time, that's for sure."

I smile and munch and sip as she chats about her friends, and then I hold up a hand.

"Oh, am I prattling?"

"Mrs B, I just want to know who owns these apartments. I was thinking that even if I missed out on buying my apartment, if I could approach an owner directly, I might be able to buy another one, especially as my alimony will come through soon."

"Ooh. Yes. Good thinking, Lucy. Let me think… Well, we know who's in the penthouse, don't we?" Her special smile makes me blush, and she pats my hand.

"In your place, an older lady lived there for a very long time before you moved in. I might be wrong, but I thought she was related to Professor No. Helga? Hedda? Kept to herself. She was friendly enough, but very formal. Very proper, always beautifully dressed; old fashioned."

Should I tell her about the spoons? Telling Mrs B about anything might be a bit like broadcasting. Soon everyone would know.

"We saw less and less of her over the years, and then the removalists arrived. She had beautiful furniture. Very old fashioned, like something out of a museum, just like Professor No's furniture – that's what made me think they might even be related – not that I ever asked – and next thing I knew, the place came up for rent, and you moved in.

"Say, when are you going to finish fixing up our garden, Lucy? Still planning on a pizza oven? Great idea. Take my word for it. Don't you ask Professor No. Just do it."

I go to the realty company, but the receptionist tells me there are privacy laws and she can't give out any information. Then I remember who might be able to find out. I call Hilary.

"Sure, Ms Beston. I'll do some searches for you."

I tackle the garden with renewed enthusiasm. The exercise warms me up through the last of winter. It's easier to see the form of the original garden with so many plants dormant, and wet days make the weeds easier to pull out. Dirk helps me trim back some of the taller plants. It's another way of being with him and I love it.

Late next day, my phone lights up.

"Hilary?"

"Lucy. Good. Sorry to call so late, but I thought you'd want to know. I've had a call from the seller's agent. Another apartment in your building is coming up for sale, and they're open to offers. They say this one's in worse condition than yours, but it's on the same floor, on the south side, so you'll get winter sun. Can I make an offer for you?"

"Yes. Please. Oh, Hilary! Start with my original offer, but then, you know how far I can go. Well no. Not that far. It was unrealistic. I really want to give my diamonds to Phoebe, and not have to sell them. Try my original offer and then add up to twelve thousand max. Fourteen thousand. Make it sixteen. No more. Please. Quickly. I'm so excited!"

I barely sleep awaiting Hilary's response.

Next morning, there's a knock on my door. It's Amaryllis, with rare spots of color on her cheeks.

"Sorry about all the boxes," I say.

"Lucy, can you come down?" she says. "Professor Raynor wants to see you."

I smooth my hands over my outfit – jeans and a soft old sweatshirt, smeared with glue gun stains. My elderly neighbor is a formal man. Even when I garden I look better than this.

"Don't worry, Lucy. His mind might be twenty twenty but his eyesight is … Just come. Now." She strums at the air as if it's her harp, hurrying me up.

I snatch my keys on the way out. At the foot of the stairs, she raps on his old door and it creaks as he opens it. He stares at us, then steps back, allowing us in.

He shuffles into a formal room. It's dark in here, with heavy drapes across the windows, bookshelves – smells like old books – an ornate dining table, French polished, stacked at one end with documents, and eight ornate dining chairs lined in velvet around it, their seats slumped with age and wear. My fingers itch to re-web and reupholster them. There'll be horsehair inside, for sure.

Our host gestures at the seats with a papery hand, and Amaryllis and I sit.

Amaryllis keeps lacing and unlacing her fingers, sitting straight as the teacher's pet. Her smile is close-lipped but insistent.

"Ms Beston," says Professor Raynor, formal as ever.

"Yes, sir," I say, astonished he should address me correctly. I thought older people resisted the "Ms" tag, even though it's official. Perhaps "correct" is more important to him than "preferred."

"It has come to my attention that you wished to buy the apartment you were renting."

"Yes! Yes. I did! I do! That is, there's another one for sale. I've made an offer."

"Ms Beston, I do not wish it to be widely known, so I'd appreciate your confidentiality."

"Of course," I say.

"Media folk are not known for their discretion," he says.

"That was decades ago. My former husband is still on air, but we are divorced, which is why I want to buy …"

"Yes, yes," he says. "Amaryllis assures me you are of good character."

I glance at Amaryllis.

"As I say," he says, "it is not widely known that my late sister and I inherited Brighton Court from our father, a most industrious shipbuilder whose services were paramount during World War II."

I nod.

"My sister, Hildegarde, did not marry. She owned the penultimate floor of Brighton Court, all eight apartments, including the one you rent – she always felt she should have inherited half of the building; never let me forget it; but all that's in the past. When she died, those apartments came to me.

"I am a simple man. I live frugally, as you can see, especially now that I am largely incapacitated. I had always planned to live at the top of Brighton Court, Ms Beston, to enjoy those views, but it is too late now. I can no longer climb stairs safely.

"I have sold several apartments over the decades to meet my living expenses. I sold the penthouse recently, and then your apartment. I was going to sell another in six months, but given Amaryllis's pleas on your behalf, and given that I was formally contacted by the real estate office about your buyer's agent's approach, and given what I have seen of your character – including your sensitive improvements to the garden – I am willing to sell you another, provided, of course, I receive the usual assurances and documentation from your representative, and provided we can complete the transaction within seven days. I understand the tenant is moving out of Number Forty Five. This is on the southern side. It is an unimproved apartment, not dissimilar to your own, but with an older bathroom and kitchen. And I am willing to sell it to you for slightly less than I received for Number Forty Nine, due to its … tired … condition. Work will be needed.”

I stand. I float. I do. My eyes snap from his eyes – almost hidden behind thick glasses, to those of Amaryllis, also bespectacled. Are they related? Is this real?

“Sir. I … of course. I … How can I thank you? I …”

He holds up a hand to silence me. Mr No is definitely not a hugger.

“It is to my benefit to have good neighbors, Ms Beston. This is a selfish act on my own part.”

“No. You need to know how grateful I am.”

If I lurch at him and hug him I might break his bones. The deal may be off.

“I can’t thank you enough, sir,” I say.” You need to know I’ll forever be grateful. You can’t know what this means to me – Amaryllis, Professor.”

Tears blur my vision. Gratitude wells up as if it will engulf me and float me, high above the table. I reach out to Amaryllis, ready to gush, but she grabs my hand and pulls me to the door.

“Seven days, Lucy,” she says. “And it’s almost Christmas. You have calls to make. Keep your eye on the prize.”

Epilogue

Dirk insists I meet him in the garden.

I love the big cushions I made for the concrete garden benches, in tropical fabric. I haul them out from under the stairs. Professor Raynor turns a blind eye to them. He sat and talked to me for ages last time I was down here, as I hacked away at the weeds – about Brighton Court, about his father's ship-building business during the war, about the changing city.

Tiny red leaves unfurl from the clipped roses as the spring sunshine warms my face and shoulders. Behind them, thanks to all the pruning, the two orange trees are responding to more sunlight, new leaves emerging. Another couple of months and there'll be fragrant blossoms.

I'm still in my old apartment, paying rent to Jamison while I plan renovations of my own. There's talk of elevators for the entire building.

Dirk appears, bearing a tray.

"It's a special low-cholesterol crust," he says, "but I can't get that same crispy crunch effect for the apples."

I laugh.

"You liked my special pie? You have to create that version in no time flat. Usually you pre-cook the apples. Not when you're rushing to hide your identity."

He smiles, but his mind's on something else. He places the tray on the old table, reaches into his pocket with determination and clears his throat. Oh.

"A while ago, you proposed to me, Lucy," he says. "I accept. But just to make extra certain …"

Right there, on the rough ground, on the bright green tendrils of new grass, he goes down on one knee, focussed, deliberate.

"Yes," I say. "Yes, I'll marry you, Dirk O'Connell. Yes."

"I'm an old-fashioned man, Lucy. Let me do this right. Just as well you have ten fingers."

He takes a ring out of a green velvet box and holds it up. It soaks in all the pale green garden light of the spring afternoon and shoots it out again in every direction. Better still is his smile, so determined, so sincere, so pleased with his surprise for me.

Dirk's hands are warm and firm as he reaches for my own left hand.

"Yes," I say again and I laugh and cry and press my lips against his clever fingers. I drag him up and he pulls me in, enfolds me in an embrace so strong that I am held there, caught, safe against him, warm and cherished and treasured, as if Dirk and I belonged together always, and always will.

A curtain twitches. For an instant, I glimpse Professor Raynor. He actually smiles at us before the curtain drops.

Acknowledgements

I am deeply grateful to so many individuals, without whom my books would not exist.

While my Brighton Court series was inspired by some of my own experiences of apartment living, it also reflects the reality that many people do live in medium and high density circumstances, with all the inevitability of companionship and conflict – fertile grounds for fiction.

It is always risky to name individuals, as there is such a danger I will omit you, but here goes: Thank you, Bruce, and the other interested members of my family, and thank you, friends and fellow creatives, readers and reviewers who enjoy my work. I treasure each of you!

I thank industry professionals Bernadette Foley and Pamela Hart, and all of you who have so generously offered me refuge as I write, including Bruce and MaryAnne Terry, Robyn Herklots, Virginia Handmer and Lighthouse Arts, Newcastle. To my Yaegl "sister" Reverend Lenore Parker, from further north, on the Clarence, thank you always for your gracious acceptance. I write with gratitude on the lands of the Gai-mariagal, Darkinjung and Awabakal people.

I gladly acknowledge the generosity and brilliance of all of my writing buddies, beta readers, proof readers, generous reviewers and VIPs, including Gail Franks, Cindy L Spear, Marilyn and Tim Cartmill, Pauline Reid, Trudi Lo Preto, Jan McIntosh, Heather Kirk, Annette and Brian Billingham, Jo Jukes, Kris Revson, Ella Sweetland, Ella McLaughlin, Jan MacNally, Alex Jones, Jordan Harcourt-Hughes, Terry Collins, Carolyn Lancaster, Dr Sally Preston, Dr Marg Rainbird and my dream boss Shauna Colnan, who encouraged me to pursue my own dream of writing fiction.

I thank treasured friends the late Karen May Mitchell, the late Narelle Jones and the late Libby Jones OAM – always in my heart.

Thank you Athena Raftopulos for so carefully listening to the first outline of each story and offering valuable feedback. Warmest thanks to so many others, including Gai Cottee, Ruth Tremont, Prue Weaver, David Ginty, Trevor, Marion and Sharon Hall, Sara Acton, Karen Tinker, George Raftopulos, Bryn Loftus, Tessa Loftus, Edith and Stephen Connelly, Jane Kenny, Mrs Lim and Vanessa Gorman.

To Debbie Phillips and her Australian Romance Readers Association members, to Jackie and her Facebook Global Girls Online Book Club followers and to countless Romance Writers of Australia members, thank you. Thanks too, to the gracious Julia Quinn and the unforgettable Elana Johnson.

Thank you to Cecilia Wong and to all librarians including Judy Park and Marisa Bottaro, and to book haven heroes the world over, including Allison Reynolds at Galaxy and Abbeys opposite the QVB in Sydney's CBD, Better Read Than Dead in Newtown, Scarlett Hopper at Romancing the Novel in Paddington, the Book Nest in Mudgee, Betty Loves Books in Newcastle, and Sarah at Tea at Elevenses in Cessnock.

To my husband, whose feedback is essential and who is the inspiration for all my heroes, thank you.

And to the readers who share with me the joy my books have brought into their lives, thank you all – from my heart. I write feel-good fiction because your heart matters.

Don't miss out!

Visit www.amberjakeman.com to find out how to order other novels by Amber Jakeman. Sign up to receive occasional email updates.

Escape to the Coast novels

Buy *Summer Beach*

Buy *Midnight Beach*

Buy *Sunset Beach*

House of Jewels novels

Buy *House of Diamonds*

Buy *House of Hearts*

Buy *House of Spades*

Buy *House of Clubs*

Buy *Full House*

Escape to the Coast series

Remember the feel of sand between the toes, sunshine on your shoulders and the frisson of a holiday romance? For thought-provoking and heartwarming contemporary fiction, welcome to Burradeer Bay! The books may be read in any order.

Summer Beach

Summer Beach is a love song.

How can you find your way home – past a tripwire?

Sam's an LA computer-coding workaholic.

Jake's a reluctant rockstar who denies his songwriting talent.

When Sam returns to an Australian backwater to sell her family's beach house, gruff neighbor Jake stymies her plans – then steals her heart.

Beneath Sam's house lies the tragic time bomb that will blow her world apart.

With help from best friend Fliss and Jake, can Sam embrace her future – before it's too late?

<u>Buy *Summer Beach*</u>

"I could not put it down. Amber delves into the layers of a person's heart and peels away the facades. This novel oozes love, kindness, friendship, neighbourly care, courage and emotional healing. I highly recommend this heart-warming and uplifting story, no matter the season. 5 Stars." Cindy L Spear

"I was totally invested in this book… 5 star review/rating." Pauline

"Absolutely loved this wonderful book. This is one of those cosy feel good reads we all like to curl up with now & again. 5 stars." Sandra

Midnight Beach

How long will true love wait?

In scenic Burradeer Bay, the midnight beach keeps secrets.

When a plan to sail away with her forbidden love goes awry, Nola waits faithfully for Kento's return.

Decades later, after one too many clashes with Bronte, her high school dropout niece, Nola questions her own life choices, and flees.

A distinguished man arrives, and an antique coral ring links the past with the future. But remorseful Bronte and frenemy Jasper can't find Nola.

Will Nola miss her second chance at love?

Midnight Beach is a dual timeline double romance, the second heartwarmer in Amber Jakeman's *Escape to the Coast* series. The books may be read in any order.

<u>Buy *Midnight Beach*</u>.

"This is a must read but be prepared to stay up late and not get all the chores done because it is impossible to put Midnight Beach down. 5 stars." US reader

"Romantic. I smiled at the ending. Five stars." Pauline

"A glittering ending filled with hope. Heart-warming. 5 stars." Cindy L Spear

Sunset Beach

A rom-com about a rom-com!

An ambitious would-be author, a jaded publisher, and a fabulous (unfinished) rom-com ...

'Meet cute' becomes 'meet hate' when Sarah goes all out to pitch her book to a famous publisher at a remote beachside writers' conference.

Earnest Oscar is a mere stand-in, questioning the industry and his life path. Disappointed, Sarah's not so furious she can't seek his help.

With his PhD about bestsellers, Oscar can spot a fangirl a mile away, but the unforgettable Sarah actually has talent.

When all Sarah's hopes are dashed, on the sunset beach, Oscar must rescue Sarah's story - and her belief in love.

Can Sarah and Oscar follow their dreams by rewriting their future - together?

<u>Buy *Sunset Beach*</u>.

This heart-warming and uplifting read about new beginnings, fresh awakenings, golden business opportunities and unexpected romance— glitters with endless possibilities. 5 Stars" Cindy L Spear.

"Sunset Beach took me away to a place of beauty, romance and love. I thoroughly enjoyed the quirky characters and beachside setting. It was an opportunity to escape while opening up a world of possibility and hope for us all." Carolyn

House of Jewels series

Fall in love with the Huntley family of jewelers! The heart-warming *House of Jewels* series follows their romantic fortunes in Australia, France and the US. The books may be read in any order.

House of Diamonds

Handsome James Huntley the Third faces a challenge or two at his Bondi Junction jewelry business.

Sparkles fly when newbie jeweller Stella Rhys sets up her home-made jewellery stall outside his shop.

She steals the limelight at his expensive PR stunt, and then she steals his heart.

Instant enemies, and fighting their attraction to each other, Stella and James become entangled in a social media war.

In this "enemies to lovers" romance, will this dazzling couple ever work out what to do with an engagement ring?

Buy *House of Diamonds*

"Easy to read, feel-good book. I enjoyed it." Kris Revson

"It's the perfect 'bedtime read'. I really enjoyed it." Annette

House of Hearts

What does it take to be lucky in love?

Opposites attract in House of Hearts, set on the edge of Las Vegas.

Gambling addiction therapist Dr Lisa Bakker never breaks rules, but her bad boy client Will Huntley, good-looking youngest heir to an Australian jewelry business, breaks them all.

The one rule neither can ignore is the two-year dating ban between clients and therapists. Will calls Lisa his "Queen of Hearts" but her hard-won career hangs in the balance.

What will it take to win her hand?

Buy *House of Hearts*

"... a wonderful love story with a number of twists in the plot... I really enjoyed it."

"Was amazed at your extensive knowledge on counselling procedures and rules, a myriad of psychological conditions, and gambling addiction (and the triggers). Great research!" Jen

"Many congratulations on another bestseller." Annette

"I really liked it." Robyn

House of Spades

Can love call again later in life? He calls her a trespasser. She calls him a hermit and thief.

Free spirit and serial single Flame Rhys has sworn off love, but try convincing her reclusive neighbor Ross Archer.

Fiery redhead Flame accidentally rekindles the widower's passion for life, for his land and a wife.

But is there more to Flame than meets the eye, as Ross's daughters suspect?

Flame is a runaway bride in this heartwarming enemies-to-lovers rural romance.

<u>Buy House of Spades</u>

"Your book inspired me to rewild parts of my property."

" ... some delightful insight into the subtropical climate and people of northern New South Wales."

"Flame is awesome."

House of Clubs

Who holds the key to her heart?

When stylish Australian widow Cynthia Huntley moves to France and begins to renovate a centuries-old property, she and handsome handyman Émile tussle over a "perfect" chandelier.

Cynthia lets the mysterious yet gallant Émile into her house, but will she let him into her heart?

What is Émile fleeing? And what is worth seeking in life?

As winter closes in, will Cynthia abandon her French adventure? Or can she and Émile claim love again later in life — together?

Buy *House of Clubs*

"Love this romance. Love the ending. And I love how I seem to learn about a certain topic in each of the stories." Gail

"This book took me to the south of France. There's more to it than meets the eye."

"From the opening paragraph I was hooked and never once during the reading was I disappointed. Well, except maybe when I came to the last page but that was because I did not want the story to end!" Cindy L Spear

Full House

What can you do when you've friend-zoned the one you love?

Nicole Huntley, marketing manager for her family's international jewelry business, froze out family friend Scottie back when they were teenagers.

Now he's the Huntleys' financial advisor. Newly divorced, the affable Scottie needs somewhere to stay. Nicole offers him space, never expecting to fall for him — hard.

But when fate deals the Huntleys a high-stakes fresh hand, "conflict of interest" threatens to shatter her family, destroy their retail empire — and to break her heart.

Get ready for the showdown in *Full House*, a "second chance" romance.

<u>Buy *Full House*</u>

"An exceptional novel."

"Full House rounds everything out and hope springs once again from potential disaster. A well-deserved 5 Stars!"

"The best feel-good book I have read in a long time. Full House pulls all of the series together in a way that made it impossible to stop reading.

"They are all five-star winners."

Novels by Amber Jakeman

***House of Jewels* series**
House of Diamonds
House of Hearts
House of Spades
House of Clubs
Full House

***Escape to the Coast* series**
Summer Beach
Midnight Beach
Sunset Beach

***Brighton Court* series**
The Chase at Brighton Court

Visit www.amberjakeman.com to find out how to order other novels by Amber Jakeman. Sign up to receive occasional email updates.

About the Author

Amber Jakeman writes feel-good fiction because your heart matters.

With readers in more than fifty countries, feel-good fiction author Amber Jakeman writes about hearts and hope and the power of love.

Amber was a journalist, teacher, editor and professional communicator before succumbing to her addiction to uplifting endings.

Her heartwarming novels explore serious themes such as sustainability, women's empowerment, homelessness, addiction and grief, yet with a light touch, an international flavour and positive resolutions.

Amber has appeared at more than a dozen readers' events around Australia, and writes regularly on romance and women's fiction.

Writing with gratitude on the lands of the Gai-mariagal, Darkinjung and Awabakal people, Amber Jakeman warmly acknowledges Australia's first storytellers.

Visit www.amberjakeman.com to find out how to order other novels by Amber Jakeman, and sign up for occasional email updates.

About the publisher

Lorikeet Press publishes good books for readers of all ages.

Visit www.lorikeetpress.com for more information.